WHERE THE SHADOWS ARE SHOWN

A horror short story collection
by Josh Schlossberg

Josh's Worst Nightmare
JoshsWorstNightmare.com

Grudging Tolerance of
Where the Shadows Are Shown
(from more successful authors)

"Buckle up, because Josh Schlossberg runs us through a gamut of emotions in this stellar horror collection, from touching poignancy to the absurdism of high comedy. Together, these stories offer a unique vision and voice in the literature of the uncanny."

-Douglas Ford, author of *The Trick*

"*Where the Shadows Are Shown* seethes with tales of hubris, vengeance, and ill-intentions. Here, exposed for all to see, is the dark side that lurks within us all."

-Shannon Lawrence, author of *Myth Stalker: Wendigo Nights*

"Josh Schlossberg reveals some of the darkest aspects of humanity, then strips away the veil, exposing the black beating heart that lies beneath the surface. *Where The Shadows Are Shown* is a masterclass in storytelling and Mr. Schlossberg is a master shadow-shower at the top of his game."

-Daemon Manx, author of *The Ojanox Series*

"Schlossberg delivers tales that revere a natural world inhabited with characters spoiled by yearning, anger, and entitlement. *Where the Shadows are Shown* is an original collection that is witty, surprising, at times gross, and always scathing in its assessment of humankind."
-Angela Sylvaine, author of *Frost Bite* and *The Dead Spot*

"With these tales, Josh bleeds onto the pages his passion for all the wonders of the world diluted with an undertone of dread and hopelessness. As reliable as our shadows, the darker aspects of human nature are on full display here: the propensity for rage, envy, lust, and violence, tainting such sacred ground. Each tale is unique; brutal yet subtle in delivery."

-Mark Towse, author of *Nana* and *Chasing the Dragon*

Cover design by Don Noble.

PRINT ISBN: 979-8-9912403-0-7

EBOOK ISBN: 979-8-9912403-1-4

Printed in the United States of America

"Creepy Old Dude" originally published on Season 19, Episode 24 of *NoSleep Podcast*, 2023

"Happy Campers" originally published in *R is for Revenge* from Red Cape Publishing, 2023

"Long Strange R.I.P." originally published in Issue #5 of *The Rock N' Roll Horror Zine*, 2019

"Drain" originally published in Volume IX, Issue III of *Bards and Sages Quarterly*, 2017

"Levi Cures the Plague" originally published in *Witch Wizard Warlock* from Three Cousins Publishing, 2023

"Hot On the Trail" originally published in Issue 9 of *34 Orchard*, 2024

"Viremia" originally published in Book 2 of *Campfire Tales* from Deadman's Tome, 2017

"The Cat's Meow" originally published in *Disturbed Digest* from Alban Lake Publishing, 2018

"Sorry To Hear That" originally published in *Dark Town* from D&T Publishing, 2023

"The Dungwich Horror" originally published in *Aphotic Realm*, 2020

"There Is No Zombie Outbreak!" originally published in *O is for Outbreak* from Red Cape Publishing, 2022

Table of Contents

Introduction:
Where The Shadows
Are Shown

I, for better or for worse, am a "shadow-shower." No, I'm not talking about a stand-up bath in the dark, but someone burdened with the power to reveal the underside of life. It's why I call my horror writing "shadow fiction."

Of course, gloom isn't all I see. And certainly not what I seek. To the contrary, what I yearn for is wonder, beauty, and good will, and I take great joy in wild nature, eye-pleasing forms, and kind deeds. Which is exactly why I find it hard to look away when I witness the destruction of landscapes, the ravages of disease, and cruel blind bigotry.

This reflex to critique has many down sides, including the compulsion to always try to "fix" things, a tendency to forget to be grateful, and inevitably being smeared as a complainer. Except labeling a shadow-shower a negative person is like calling an architect a hole-digger; excavating the basement is just the necessary first step for building a house.

1

To be crystal clear, I don't promote bitching and moaning for the sake of spreading misery but thoughtful critique in hopes of achieving a vision of how things might be. Because let's not forget that nearly every good part of society today—freedom from slavery, banning deadly chemicals, the weekend—is the result of curmudgeons who wanted a better world, and who pushed for it no matter how tough it was for them...or how many people they pissed off in the process.

In fact, I'd argue that the most negative people are those pretending the shadows don't exist. Who, through their inaction and/or attacks on those daring to advocate for positive change, either maintain a subpar status quo or aggressively promote the Great Unraveling (my go-to term for societal breakdown and ecological collapse).

But how does writing about what's wrong with the world help anything?

If the goal is only to point out what sucks about existence, shrug one's shoulders, and sulk away, then maybe that's not so useful. Yet what about offering readers a chance to care about some intriguing characters, connect with a picturesque setting, and get swept up in a dynamic plot as a way to psychologically prepare them for the challenges of real life?

Yes, my wish for you, dark reader, is not only to relish the fun—if sometimes disturbing—ride I'm about to take you through the realms of biological and folk horror, supernatural and weird fiction. But to peel back the veil to what's *behind* the prose, acknowledging the shadows so as to navigate through them into the light.

Darkness 'neath The Pines

Narrow are the paths we tread,
and winding are the ways.
The light that guides us through the woods,
at times, will fade away.
If then you dread the sound
of muffled footsteps from behind,
lend an ear, but never fear,
the darkness 'neath the pines.

Because you loathe the shadow
and the gloom that must descend,
your torch flares to chase the dimness
hiding 'round the bend.
Though the path seems clearer now,
you all too soon will find:
To light your eyes just magnifies
the darkness 'neath the pines.

If instead you douse the torch
and let your sight adjust,
you'll find the forest, pressing close,
nothing to mistrust.
The hunching forms beside the way
vanish from your mind,
and before too long you see nothing wrong
with darkness 'neath the pines.

The winds that stream through trees,
through all the waving boughs,
whisper wordless lullabies,
and you begin to drowse.
You slumber for a while where
the branches intertwine,
and taste the peace that stirs the leaves
in darkness 'neath the pines.

On waking, fears transform
into truths for which you've yearned.
Now the path that lies ahead
can be your sole concern.
But if the lure of scented bowers
intoxicates like wine,
don't lose heart, you'll soon be part
of the darkness 'neath the pines.

Creepy Old Dude

Three days in a row. Three days in a row I took my morning walk around my new neighborhood—a kind of Rocky Mountain suburbia where tall meadow grass sprouts from the sloping yards of earth-toned homes— and he was walking up his driveway.

Three days in a row, just after seven a.m., I left my cul-de-sac, perking my ears to make sure no car was coming around the blind curve, and walked onto the road along the ridge of the hill. Cool autumn air warming in the rising sun. Breathtaking view of snowcapped mountains in the distance. Skinny old guy with the perv mustache walking his ugly little poodle on a leash.

As always, dressed in puffy winter jacket, wool hat, jeans, and boots, he waved without a smile. Not some normal greeting but insistently, almost wildly, like something was off about him. And though my hand felt like a twenty-pound plate, I waved back.

Mathematically, the chances of meeting him at the exact same spot, where the driveway from his modest ranch home met the street, two days in a row had to have been one in a thousand. But three days? More like one in a million. Especially since, a full three weeks after moving out of hot noisy Denver, these were the first times I'd laid eyes on him.

Irritated, I kept walking along the ridge and down the hill, turned around and went back up. Sure enough, he stood in the shade of the ponderosa pines where my cul-de-sac connects to the road, as if waiting for me, his dog snuffling the grass. He waved again in that same frantic way. My stomach turned even though I hadn't eaten breakfast.

You might be wondering what's the big deal about an elderly man walking his dog and saying hi to a neighbor? Why would I even notice such a thing, much less let it bother me? I'll tell you why. It was his vibe. A heaviness rising off him like heat from summer pavement that almost made me feel like puking.

And, no, I'm not that way with anyone else. I have no problem greeting the husky middle-aged jogger huffing by on his morning run. Happy to smile at the kids—boy of maybe eleven, girl of probably nine—waiting for the school bus. I even nod at the twenty-something blonde in the red Jeep who speeds past me every weekend morning on her way back from who knows what late night escapades.

Yet this guy, I couldn't help but tense up when I was around. Like he'd done me some wrong, and I was holding a grudge my conscious mind couldn't remember, though my body did, deep in my bones. Because I'm polite, I always waved back. Still, it took a ton of effort, and afterwards I felt rotten, like I'd thanked someone for spitting in my face.

That Friday before I went to bed, I set my alarm for six a.m. No way he'd be up that early on a Saturday. Yet out in the cool dawn, does and fawns nibbling the dewy grass, there he was again, walking up his damn driveway. I was so angry I crossed to the other side of the street. Still, I knew he saw me, the heaviness dropping on my shoulders like a wet coat.

I walked slowly this time, hoping he'd be gone from my cul-de-sac by the time I got back. No such luck. My stalker stood in the same place he always did at the junction of the road. Done with being nice, I marched past, ignoring his wave. And when I was most of the way to my house, turned around to give him the finger. He was already gone.

What the hell did he want from me? If he hadn't been such a frail old bag of bones, I'd have been afraid for my safety. But since I could've probably killed him with one good punch to the head, it was nothing more than creepy. Though plenty at that.

The next morning, Sunday, I waited until after breakfast to take my walk. I wasn't even surprised when he was there again, pacing up his fucking driveway like it was the most normal thing in the world. I can't even articulate how much I hated this man.

I was so mad I didn't even nod at Blondie as she whizzed by in her Jeep. Grinding my teeth, clenching my fists, I hurried back to the cul-de-sac, wanting only to get inside and lock my doors. I shook my head at the maniac as I went past. He didn't react. Just kept waving.

On Monday, I skipped my morning walk and only headed out when I got home from work. He was there at the top of his driveway, of course. Always there. I turned around and went straight home to call the cops.

Breathlessly, I told them a crazy man was following me around my neighborhood. After a few minutes of trying to explain the gravity of the situation, and them reminding me that excessive friendliness wasn't a crime, I accepted they wouldn't be any help. I hung up.

Tuesday and Wednesday I didn't go for a walk at all, just off to work at my usual time. On Thursday I ventured out a couple of hours after sundown, the night brisk and quiet. My heart pounded by the time I got to his driveway, except, wonder of wonder, he wasn't there! Then my guts turned to cement at the scuffle of footsteps, the patter of little paws.

Red hot with rage, I was done. Absolutely done. "Hey, asshole!" Not having to see his wrinkled face made it easier to confront him.

The footsteps stopped, but he didn't say anything. I could barely make out his figure, a dark stain in the night like an ink spill on a black page. "Why are you following me?"

No response.

"Well, I'm on to you," I spat, voice shaking with anger. Or was it fear? "And if I catch you anywhere near me again, I'm gonna beat the living crap out of you."

I stalked off into the night, pulse pounding in victory. One thing for sure, I got my point across. No way he'd still be out when I got back.

I turned around at the bottom of the hill and trekked up again, half hoping he was waiting for me so I could keep my promise. I imagined myself sweeping out his spidery legs and kicking him in the spine. Or shoving him hard in the chest so he fell on his bony butt. Or even just rearing back and decking him. While it's true that, outside of grade school scuffles, I've never hit anyone, this time I knew I'd deliver. And damn the consequences.

On first glance, the cul-de-sac looked empty, but it was pitch black out, so I couldn't be sure. I strode along, and, indeed, no one at the junction. I felt something inside of me that'd been tight for weeks finally unspool.

Next morning, up and at 'em at my usual time. Though raring for a fight—verbal, physical, both—I had a feeling the old guy wouldn't be there. And I was right, no sign of him on his driveway. I even waited a minute to be sure, but the door to his squat little house stayed shut.

For the first time in weeks, I enjoyed my walk. Fresh air in my lungs. Mountains glowing in the rising sun. Quiet. The whole reason I moved up from the crowded, stinking city.

Happily, my luck held the next morning, too. And the next. For a full blissful week I saw neither hide nor hair of the weirdo and his scrawny dog.

Now, Sunday morning, the old man still MIA, I start to feel a tiny bit bad. With the break I've had, I'd be okay seeing him once in a while. It was just the everyday thing that bugged me. As I stroll along the ridge road, blood singing in my veins, sky pastel blue, I wonder if maybe I was overreacting.

After all, dogs need to go out at least a few times a day. So, of course, the guy would be out there first thing in the morning when everyone gets up. And, again, in the afternoon and evening, which happened to be the other times I took my walks.

By the time I get to the bottom of the hill, it dawns on me that these strolls with his dog might be the only way the old codger breaks up his day. I don't think he's married or works, so he probably looks forward to his little trips around the neighborhood as much as I do. And what if the reason he kept bumping into me is because he's lonely and wants to talk but is too shy to say something?

What if *he's* not the monster here...and I am?

On my way back I hope I'll catch him in the cul-de-sac so I can apologize. Strike up a little conversation. Get to know him a bit. A few minutes out of my morning won't kill me.

He's not there. And my heart sinks. Still, it's not too late to fix this.

Whistling a happy tune, I amble down his driveway and knock on the front door.

I'm jolted by a deep loud barking from inside. No way that tiny poodle is making these sounds. Before I can worry if I've got the right place, a clean-shaven thirty-something man in collared shirt and slacks answers the door. Behind him, a brunette in blouse and skirt holds a snarling Boxer by its collar.

"Sorry to bother you," I say tentatively and a bit confused. "Is that older fellow around? Your dad, maybe?"

He squints. "My folks live in Phoenix."

"Oh, hers, maybe?" I nod towards the woman, who struggles to keep the growling dog from charging.

The man shakes his head, and I catch a whiff of his piney cologne. "They're in Denver. What's this about?"

I figure they're just being protective. In my kindest voice I ask, "Who's the elderly man who lives with you?"

He gives me a blank look.

I dry swallow, nervous for some reason. "With the poodle."

"Sounds like you got the wrong address." He shrugs. "Sorry, we're getting ready for work."

My armpits drip and I'm jittery as if I've had too much coffee. Surely, I haven't been hallucinating. Before he can close the door, I blurt out, "You're saying an old man with a black poodle doesn't live here?"

Before he can respond, the woman, who's finally calmed the Boxer to a low whine, chimes up, "You mean the guy who used to own the place?"

"Used to?" My tense shoulders relax. At least I'm not seeing things. "When was that?"

"We've been here almost three years," she says. "The realtor mentioned him. Guy in his late seventies?"

"That's him!" I sigh with relief, certain I've figured it out. "He still in the neighborhood? I think he's got dementia and keeps forgetting he doesn't live here anymore."

The woman furrows her brow and shakes her head. The Boxer is finally quiet. "He didn't move. He died."

"No." Dizzy, I stagger back a step.

"You can look it up online." She nods. "Winter of twenty-nineteen, I think. Someone speeding past a stopped school bus almost ran over a couple of kids. At the last second, the guy pushed them out of the way. Got creamed himself. Poor little doggie, too."

The sky spins, and I rub my eyes until I see stars. That's when the Boxer breaks free and bolts towards the door. The man slams it in my face just in time.

In a daze, I stumble up the driveway, tripping over my own feet. A ghost. I've seen a freaking *ghost*. I threatened to *beat up* a ghost! No wonder the heavy vibes coming from the old guy—he's dead! Then a chill down my back. And maybe out for revenge...

Nauseous, I pace along staring down at the cracked pavement. If ghosts are real, does that mean there's an afterlife? A cartoonish image comes to mind of my grandparents dressed in white floating on a cloud.

Does everyone become a ghost, or is it like the books and movies where they have unfinished business? How many are out there? Have I seen others before and not known it? Can everyone see them or just some of us? And what about the poodle? Dogs can be ghosts, too? Can all animals?

Brain boiling like a tea kettle, I reach the top of the hill. Why is this guy haunting *me*, of all people? It's not like we have any history—before last month I hadn't even set foot in the neighborhood!

I'm so caught up by the whirlwind of thoughts, I don't notice I'm in the middle of the street. Not until the red Jeep roars around the blind curve, headed straight for me.

The Lemon Tree

Russ lugged the three-foot leafy tree in its ceramic pot into the sunroom, flooded with afternoon light from its southern exposure. It wasn't supposed to freeze that night—the forecast was high thirties—but with mid-September in Vermont, you never know.

He wasn't even sure why he bothered. Though the tree kept growing, its oblong oval leaves a dark glossy green, it'd never flowered once in its five years of life. The experts all said you could grow lemons in Vermont, soaking up the late spring and summer sun outside and then indoors when the season changed. The trees were self-pollinating, after all. But not if there were no flowers. He poured water from the can over its roots, which tricked deep into the dark soil.

Many times, Russ had thought about giving the barren bush away and getting a Bonsai tree instead. But he never had the heart, as it'd been a first anniversary gift from Linnea. With real meaning behind it, a callback to the lemonade he'd made for their first date picnicking on the shore of Lake Champlain. Having just moved up north from sunny Georgia, she'd told him it tasted the way her Gram used to make it. Instead of store-bought lemons every anniversary they'd make a new batch from their own crop.

Sadly, half a decade later, not a single lemon. He fingered the smooth waxy leaves as if trying to rub circulation into a cold hand. A dud. Like him.

After years of trying with Linnea, he finally went to the doctor and was diagnosed with something called azoospermia. Parts all intact, hormone levels normal, his body wouldn't make any swimmers. Which meant they couldn't even artificially inseminate. And no operation to cure him. "Be fruitful and multiply" simply wasn't in the cards for Russ.

He turned on the fan, the artificial wind swaying the small tree's branches and fluttering its leaves.

By the time Russ had brought up adoption, he and Linnea had already stopped being intimate. "What's the point?" she once muttered under her breath in response to one of his bedtime advances. Though he pretended not to hear, it was like a kick in the nuts. Which shouldn't have bothered him, since it seemed he didn't have much worth protecting down there, anyway.

One day Russ came back from work and was unsurprised to find a moving van in the driveway. Linnea filed for divorce a week later, and it was all finalized in a month.

He bent over to pluck a single yellow leaf from the underside of the tree. If he was being honest with himself, it wasn't fond remembrance but spite that kept him nursing the thing. Crushing the dead leaf in his fist in a burst of citrus scent, Russ promised himself he'd make it bear fruit if it killed him.

Online, Russ learned that aside from lack of light—not an issue in the south-facing sunroom—the most common reason for lemon trees not flowering was poor fertilizer. Never a fan of chemicals, he'd stayed away from the commercial stuff. The unanimous advice was to try compost tea, a liquid brew of the organic material.

It turned out to be upwards of eighty bucks for a single bottle with who knows what inside. And he was already paying some company twenty bucks every month to take his food scraps away. Why not make the tea himself?

After calling and canceling the service, Russ drove to the home and garden store. Ended up dropping almost three hundred for one of those fancy spinning bins with separate chambers for fresh and mature compost, as well as a smaller bin to keep by the sink. Over the fall and winter, he'd make the perfect batch and in the spring brew the tea to feed the tree.

During the following weeks, composting became Russ' new after-work hobby. He bought more fruit and vegetables than before—organic only—eating lots of eggs and even picking up a coffee drinking habit because the shells and grounds were supposed to make primo compost. He, of course, kept out meat and dairy as well as avocado or peach pits, anything that wouldn't break down. Sometimes, instead of storing his leftovers in the fridge, he'd feed them straight to the pile.

To his dismay, a full six weeks later, on a brisk October autumn, the compost in the outside bin was still a goopy, rancid mess. He stuck his hand into the bin; cool, not warm the way it was supposed to be. Perplexed, he went online and learned the sliminess meant there wasn't enough dry material. The suggestion was to use tissues.

A little gross, maybe, but from that point on every time Russ blew his nose, he shoved the snotty paper in the kitchen bin. Unfortunately, almost month later, the first light snow on the ground, the compost was still slippery and cold. Clearly, he wasn't using enough tissues.

Though that wasn't exactly true. Russ did throw out a thick wad every night before falling asleep. He hadn't found the confidence to jump back into the dating pool and had to stave off the loneliness somehow. Snot was one thing, but that...that was disgusting.

Or was it? Was there really that much of a difference between bodily fluids? So, he started adding those into the compost, too, spinning the outside bin like an old-timey organ grinder on the street.

Sure enough, by midwinter, despite temperatures dipping into negative double digits, the compost started cooking to the point where he could almost warm his hands off it. Often, after making the week's deposit, he'd catch himself staring at the chunky, multi-colored future soil, the way a normal man would with a brand-new car in the driveway.

Soon, Russ left that side of the bin alone to mature and started feeding the second chamber. His life was little more than a monotonous blur of work, drinking, TV, and sleeping. But the pile gave him something to focus on. To care for. To give him hope.

By spring's first thaw, Russ reached into the mature stuff, and, to his joy, brought out a handful of moist, perfectly crumbly soil. It was ready! Grinning ear to ear, he scooped a few shovelfuls into a burlap sack, dropped it in a bucket half filled with water, and let it soak overnight.

The next day after work, he poured the compost tea—murky black as a forest swamp—into a mason jar. Almost giddy, he went into the sunroom, knelt beside the tree, and cautiously as if it were a five-hundred-dollar bottle of scotch, poured a third of it over the roots to seep into the soil. Then he went back outside to brew a new batch.

As he'd hoped, in the first few days of May, a tiny cluster of white buds sprouted from the juncture of one of the tree's top branches. And a few days later, the first delicate blossom, a snowflake that smelled like Linnea's hair after a shower. Then another bud and another, each coming to full flower a week later. And the week after that, the earliest flower morphing into a pock-marked green nubbin the size of a quarter.

He kept the compost tea flowing, the bloom stage being the most important time for the health of the fruit.

The next week brought more and more buds, flowers, and nubbins. By mid-June, ten lemons were on their way. Silly as he knew it was, Russ couldn't have been prouder.

Over the summer, to Russ' immense satisfaction, the lemons plumped. The earliest one stayed well ahead of the pack, growing larger, rounder, and yellower. But it was slow going, and by the end of August Russ worried he wouldn't be able to taste his own lemonade until after a frost. Which was like going for your first swim of the year on Halloween.

Late one night, he was caressing the fruit's smooth dimpled skin. Squeezed it. Lifted it a bit. And then—oh crap!—it broke off its stem to drop in his palm. Horrified, he stood there staring at it like a puppy's head that'd popped off.

He'd gotten greedy and picked an unripened fruit. Except when he sniffed it, it smelled sharp and sweet the way it should. Maybe it was ready, after all.

He hurried to the kitchen, set the squat little sun on the cutting board. Got a knife from the drawer and warily sliced off the very end of the nubbin.

The knife fell out of his hand to clang on the tile.

He blinked and blinked to try to form what he was seeing into something sane. Something remotely in the realm of logic and sense. But the awful vision wouldn't clear, and his veins were ice.

From each of the seven segments of lemon, two pairs of tiny stumps—threaded with slender white bones—dripping clear juice onto the cutting board. Meanwhile, the cut-off nubbin encased fourteen miniature severed feet, each with imperfectly formed flippers instead of toes. Peering closer, the bones appeared to be made of seeds, stretched out and articulated into a rudimentary form. And none of them moving.

Russ' chest felt tight, like he was wearing a shirt three sizes too small. Somehow—impossibly—two-inch creatures were trapped inside each section of the lemon. And he'd cut their frigging feet off.

His first instinct, crazy as it was, was to grab his phone to call 911. He pushed the 9 before he stopped to think. What would he even tell them? If anywhere near the truth, it wouldn't be an EMT they'd send but a psychiatrist.

Whatever those things were, the way the juice leaked, they had to be suffering. He tore a paper towel from the roll, folded it in half, and stuck it against their ankle stumps. Seconds later, the liquid stopped seeping through. And when he gently peeled the paper away a few minutes later, the area had dried.

But were they even alive? Only one way to find out.

Nimbly, he peeled the fragrant leathery rind down to the fruit's white sticky layer. Pinched apart the first two segments. And gasped in wonder and horror at the tiny humanoid fetus inside both pulpy cells. White veins ran across the bulbous foreheads, eyes skinned over, flipper hands, a smooth patch where there should be genitals, and knees drawn up with the shins ending in stumps.

And they were deathly still. He peeled the other segments apart, and all were puny statues. Russ' stomach turned over, and he felt like puking.

Were all the fruits like this? Whatever they were—he had no reference point for this—they weren't fully formed. Preemies. He'd picked it too soon.

But didn't they save preemies all the time? Warmth and oxygen. Of course, these were no normal babies, so maybe they needed to stay wet. Heart racing, he ran paper towels under the warm water and wrapped each of the segments like pigs in a blanket. And paced around the kitchen mumbling to himself.

Twenty minutes later he peeled the towel away from one of them. Still no movement. His heart sunk. Then a wild thought. What if they were trapped in the segment?

With the tip of a fingernail, he pierced the thin skin and let the juice bleed out. Then, carefully, carefully, scooped out the fetus with his pinky and held the motionless kachina doll in the center of his palm.

He hung his head. They were gone. It was possible he'd suffocated them by not freeing them sooner. But he was pretty sure they'd been stillborns. Stillfruits?

Russ had no idea what to do with the bodies. So, he covered them with a few paper towels, poured himself four fingers of whisky, and wandered into the dark den to plop down in front of the TV. Nursing his glass, he tried to enter the world of a rom-com where dead lemon fetuses didn't—couldn't—exist. But every few minutes, his mind kept wandering back to what was on that cutting board.

When the movie ended, fully drunk, Russ stumbled back into the kitchen. Tore the paper towel off like a bandage and stood a long time staring at the wee ones.

Unable to stop himself, he went into the drawer and fished out a fresh steak knife. Without preamble, he sliced a vertical line into one of their little stomachs. Juice welled up but it was just translucent pulp inside. And a little higher up, a ribcage made of seed bones. He cut all the way to a stringy spine made of the same stuff.

And then into the head through the thin skull. Just more pulp. No way the thing could've ever been alive.

Finally, he slit the layer of white skin over the eye. A blind orb stared back at him, green as summer leaves. Green like his own, in fact. Russ made a weird sound between a blubber and a whimper and fell back against the counter.

A lucid dream! It had to be. It wouldn't be the first time.

He shot to his feet. Grabbed the knife. Stuck the tip into the pad of his middle finger and pressed until it broke skin. It stung like hell—worse with lemon juice on it—and a drop of blood welled out.

This was no dream. The one ray of hope snuffed out.

Unless he was hallucinating! He'd smoked plenty of pot in college, even taken mushrooms a few times, and had seen his share of weirdness under the influence. Though it'd always been organic patterns, walls pulsing or trees swaying, dull colors made vibrant. No straight up conjuring of objects that weren't there.

He closed his eyes tight as he could, ground his fists into them until he saw stars.

Madness. Some stressor—maybe abuse he'd blacked out as a kid—had finally caught up with him and broken his mind. He was seeing things, and such would be his life from then on, wrapped in a straitjacket inside a padded room.

He opened his eyes, the kitchen coming back into focus along with the lumpy paper towels. Somehow insanity didn't feel right either. He'd always been even keel and hadn't noticed anything wrong until that moment. Which wasn't how mental illness worked, was it?

He leaned against the counter, the sharp edge biting into his skinny rear. No, the toughest answer to bear—yet the one that seemed to be the truth—was that this was really happening. And the only way to move forward was to try to make sense of it.

A quick online search for "lemon babies" only pulled up a bunch of YouTube videos of infants making funny faces after being fed the sour fruit for the first time. In the meantime, he couldn't keep looking at those things in his kitchen. He took the cutting board outside. Used the shovel to dig a small hole in the unfinished compost and dumped them in. Covered it over.

When he pulled the shovel back out, the sharp tip had speared a tissue. Thoughts a jumble, none of them making the least bit of sense, the bleeding dawn sky reeled overhead like in a planetarium.

The next month dragged by for Russ. Every morning dawning with dread, every night tossing and turning with dreams of what he'd seen—what he'd done.

Was he really entertaining the idea of his spermy tissues brewed into compost tea somehow fertilizing the flowers? His working hypothesis that he knocked up a frigging tree? It was madness. Impossible madness! But what other explanation was there? The teensy stillborns were real, and, however they came about, *he* was the one who brought them into being.

He stopped composting or even watering the tree, and always kept the sunroom door closed. Tried his damnedest to not even think about what'd happened. He knew he should get rid of the thing, dump it in the woods somewhere, but he didn't even want to go in there, much less touch the monstrosity. Eventually, it would die, and he could pay someone to haul it away.

Finally, one particularly drunken Friday night, he got a hold of himself. Remembered there wasn't any such thing as "unexplained phenomena," only science the world hadn't made sense of yet. And science was nothing more than the workings of nature. And nature certainly wasn't anything to be afraid of.

He marched over to the sunroom and threw open the door. Eight of the lemons, plump and golden, weighed down the branches. One more fallen into the pot.

Chest tight, hands shaking, he picked up the fallen lemon. Sure looked normal enough. Sniffed it, and it smelled fine, too. Maybe it'd been a random mutation, some fluke, like a two-headed snake. And every other fruit would be ordinary.

He brought the lemon into the kitchen. Rinsed it in the sink. And then started peeling the rind down to the white pith. So far, so good. Stuck his thumb between two segments and pulled them apart.

He cried out, vision swimming.

A gooey clump of organs. Slimy intestines like a ball of snakes. A glistening brown slab that might've been a liver. But worst of all was the purple heart. And it was beating.

Reeking blood slicking his fingers, Russ dropped the thing in the sink with a gooshy plop and puked on top of it.

His mind stalled, unable to make sense of the sight before him, his brain not a complex enough model to process the reality. Though one word did float through his head. Abomination.

If this fruit was ripe, what were the others like? He didn't want to know. DIDN'T WANT TO KNOW! He sluiced the mess down the drain and flicked on the garbage disposal. Faucet rushing, it clanged and grinded for over a minute with a foul stench until he turned it off. Then washed his hands.

Teeth grinding in fury, he stormed into the sunroom, yanked the tree out of its pot, roots and all, and dragged it outside into the yard like a bad dog. After dousing its base and trunk with lighter fluid he lit a match.

And held the flame until it burned down to his fingers and went out.

Whatever these things were—however horrible—he'd created them. The least he could do was give them a chance. And if they weren't meant to live, a respectful send off.

He grabbed a colander and picked the remaining eight lemons, setting each one gently inside. Then back to the kitchen to peel the next one over the cutting board.

If it was even possible, this fruit was worse, a clumpy, winding maze of pale flesh tubes. A brain.

"Nooooo," he groaned. After hacking it into four chunks, down the drain it went.

The third lemon was nothing but pink and blue twining veins and arteries. He gagged but had nothing to throw up. Another burial at sink.

The next one had the typical lemon segments. And like the preemies, still little forms inside. But these—oh my God—were all skeleton and no flesh. When he chucked them in the disposal, a loud snap and then the rattle of broken metal.

Russ didn't think he could handle much more but had to get it over with. He figured he was numb at this point, anyway. Boy, was he was wrong. Number five, a pulsing mass of black jelly that stunk of the grave. Bile or rot, he didn't know. Didn't care. Down the drain even though the disposal wasn't working anymore.

The following fruit was simply one giant seed. He got out a hammer to try to crack it, but it was seed—bone?—all the way through. He tossed that one into the outside compost with its siblings. Because that's what they were, right?

Or maybe parts of a whole, where, if put together they'd make one creature? But no. Because fruit number seven had a layer of skin, which, when peeled back revealed another brain, a shivering heart, and twin bloody crescents of pulp that had to be lungs. Into a garbage bag and into the can.

Another was all genitals, tiny foreskins, scrota, and labia, but in an M.C. Escher geometry that made Russ' eyes hurt.

Last one. And it would be over. And he could try to pick up and glue together the broken pieces of his sanity. What now? A pile of crap? He laughed out loud. Or how about a giant booger? Or, even better, a pool of semen, the culprit of the atrocities.

He peeled. To his astonishment, writhing translucent babies inside each of the eight segments. Yet, hallelujah, all normal-looking, perfect fingers clenched into fists! Ten tiny toes a piece, fully intact feet. Eyes closed. No genitals.

Carefully, holding his breath, he separated each of the sections and set them down on their own wet warm paper towels. Then, with a fingernail, carefully pierced the outer skin to drain the juice. And, with the gentlest of touches, delivered the first fetus from its citrus womb.

In a magic moment, the newborn opened its eyes. Bright green like Russ'. Then, a pang in Russ' heart, it reached for him with tiny sticky arms. Of course, no sounds because it didn't have internal organs, much less vocal cords. Indeed, the chest didn't rise or fall either, so technically it wasn't even breathing. Yet somehow it was "alive," perhaps the way a virus was.

The question was, for how long? He wrapped it in the towel with only its head poking out.

He birthed—hatched?—the other seven and swaddled them in towels. Then waited with shallow breath for them to die. But they didn't, all of them wriggling like worms, blinking and making Os with their mouths.

He wasn't going to name them—that'd make the inevitable loss that much worse—but to keep them apart he gave them numbers, One through Eight.

Gaping mouths like baby birds, he didn't think they could eat—where would the food even go?—but clearly they were hungry. Or at least some impulse inside them triggering that reflex. He stuck the tip of his pinky in Three's mouth and felt a slight suction. Which grew stronger until it stung, and Russ had to pull his finger away.

After maybe twenty minutes, mouths even wider, universal language for "Feed me!" Alright then, but what? Unless they were more like normal babies than he'd guessed.

Out to the 24-hour drug store for a jug of milk and medicine dropper. When he got back, he warmed the milk in the microwave, tested with a finger to make sure it wasn't too hot, then a single drop in One's mouth. It spat up the milk instantly, face a scowl of hate, little lips sealed tight. Same thing with Two. So much for milk.

Over the next few hours towards dawn, they got more and more mouthy, more insistent, angrier, Russ racking his brain over a possible menu. Since they had no teeth, solid food was obviously out of the question. But he was sure that if they didn't have something, they'd die. Think!

Then a chill. The way One had sucked on his finger, it should've been obvious right away. As the sun slanted through the window, Russ left a message at work, saying he wouldn't be in that day.

In the closet he found Linnea's sewing kit and got out a needle. Doused it with rubbing alcohol in the bathroom. And then pricked the pad of his finger. Sucked several drops of blood into the dropper and made himself go back into the kitchen.

He squinted at the little critters. Tiny vampires? He pictured jabbing all his fingers, track marks up and down his forearms and legs like a heroin addict. Face pale and anemic from loss of blood. Soon capturing and bleeding the neighborhood cats. And then, in time, like in *Little Shop of Horrors*, moving on to humans to feed the growing bloodlust.

Hand trembling, he dropped the blood over Three's mouth. It missed and ran down its weak chin and scrawny chest. Russ tried again. This time he got it dead center. Eyes slammed shut, Three spat out the blood like One and Two had done with the milk.

"Whew," Russ whispered to himself, the invisible belt around his chest loosening a notch. Still, he tried with Four just to be sure. Who spat it up even quicker.

Russ let out a long slow breath. Even though he'd yet to solve the mystery, at least he'd scratched the most disturbing possibility off the list.

Pacing around the kitchen, he tried to figure out what babies gestated inside a citrus fruit could possibly eat. Then it became clear. The same thing that gave them life in the first place!

He still had some leftover compost tea in the jar and sucked up a dropperful. And gave some to Five, like a parent on Christmas morning hoping he'd bought his kid the right toy. Not only did Five spit it up, the tot thrashed about in a bug-eyed hissy fit. Russ was terrified he'd poisoned it, but a minute later it settled down and resumed its open-mouthed begging.

Wait! A lightbulb flashed on in the darkness of his mind. Maybe they weren't hungry but thirsty! He rinsed the dropper and tried some cool water for Six. Six drank it down yet instantly popped its gummy mouth again, hungry as ever.

Russ hung his head, all hope gone. They were nothing but cosmic mistakes, born only to die. As are we all.

He leaned over them to say goodbye. And the first real cry in a long time, born of frustration and grief and guilt, broke through.

"I'm sorry, little ones," he blubbered.

With its teeny translucent tongue, Three licked its lips. And again, as another tear fell from Russ' eye. Tears. Could it be?

Quickly, he put the dropper to the corner of his eye and sucked up the lingering wetness. He gave it to Seven. Who lapped it up like a hungry dog, and, seconds later, closed its eyes with what could've only been a content smile.

With bated breath, Russ tried Two. Same thing, lip-smacking followed by cozy nap. By the time he was on to Three, the dropper was empty.

No other option but to keep crying. Except it wasn't like a faucet he could turn on and off. If anything, he felt joyful right then, finally cracking the case as to how to keep the little wonders alive.

But he had to. He tried to picture the saddest things that had ever happened to him. When he was eleven, the vet neutering Russ' puppy and accidentally not cauterizing the wound properly afterwards, the yellow Lab dying of internal bleeding that night. Not a sniffle.

At sixteen, his grandmother dropping dead of a heart attack in front of him and trying to do CPR on her—and failing. A pang of sorrow but still dry-eyed.

Those things were sad. Traumatic perhaps. But they'd happened decades before and even if the wounds hadn't entirely healed, they'd scarred over.

He needed something fresh. Something raw.

Closing his eyes, an image of meeting his lovely Linnea at the cocktail bar after assuming her to be a friend of his friend only to realize, after twenty minutes of chatting, that she was a complete stranger. Driving three hours through a literal blizzard to visit her at med school. Their inside joke about every time either of them said something that got a laugh, they'd put out a hand and say, "Gimme money!" It wasn't the good memories that got him crying but the mournful fact that they'd never make new ones together.

It worked so well, he sucked up enough tears in the dropper to feed the others, who all joined their siblings in peaceful slumber. A weight off his psyche, around sunrise Russ caught a few hours of sleep and roused himself in the afternoon to find them wide awake again.

When he went to change One's towel, he was shocked to find its pale body a full inch larger. Same with all eight down the line. If they grew that quickly in a few hours, how big would they get in a week? Would they max out at the size of a doll or make it to full human scale? Or were they destined to be giants?

He pulled up another memory of Linnea—the last time they played Scrabble and how he'd never play that game again—which got him another few squirts from the dropper. Fed, the babies went back to sleep.

Russ called his boss and told her he'd need Friday off, too. She wasn't happy, reminding him he was out of sick days and needed to be in on Monday even if he was hacking up a lung. He said he'd do his best.

After hanging up the phone, Russ stood there for some time watching them sleep. If someone would've told him a week earlier that he could've spent a full hour watching babies sleep, he would've laughed in their face. But he'd never felt this way before, a warm glow as if he was bursting with life. Along with a fresh vulnerability, like a soft spot that even the slightest touch could bruise.

He slept soundly. In the morning, they were bright-eyed and bushy-tailed again, clearly hungry again by their mouthing, though not as furiously as they had been. And, when he changed their dry towels, they'd each grown another inch or so.

Russ tried to come up with Linnea scenes again. But instead of making him sad, he found himself glad for the memories. Melancholy, perhaps, but not teary, as if he'd finally processed the grief of the divorce.

He tried to think of far more awful things like the latest school shooting, the devastating floods in Nigeria, the daily death toll from the current viral outbreak. To no avail. Terrible as those events were, without a direct personal connection, they couldn't affect him on an emotional level.

A movie. He needed to watch a movie.

Dependably, *Forrest Gump*, sappy and impossible as the 90s blockbuster was, got the waterworks flowing, and he was able to feed them—each grown another half inch—that morning.

On Sunday evening, he brought out the big guns and watched all of *Schindler's List* without getting up, taking care of the night feeding. They ate but didn't go back to sleep, probably because they were still hungry.

"I'm sorry, that's all I got," Russ whispered. "I'll try again in the morning, I promise."

He got up with the sun, and, before waking them, pounded some water, and went to surf YouTube for the saddest videos he could find. Finally, he remembered something that had him bawling years ago. He typed in, "Baby hears Mom," and watched the short clip of the infant with brand-new cochlear implants listening to her mother's voice for the first time. While tears shone in the eyes of the mom, the nurse, and even the baby, not a drop for Russ.

They were twice as big as the day before, a full five inches long and plump as potatoes, bawling their silent cries. No way Russ could leave them like that—he didn't even bother calling into work. Why in the world wasn't there paternal leave?

For hours he scrolled through YouTube—a dog saving a woman from drowning, a soldier surprising his family coming back from war, REM's "Everybody Hurts" music video—to try to make him cry, but he got nothing. Maybe it was like sleeping, where the more you forced it, the harder it was?

By Tuesday, Four and Seven looked almost comatose, green eyes—*his* eyes—glassy in a hundred-mile stare. They were dying. And it was Russ' fault. Sick to his stomach, he raced off to the drugstore for artificial tears.

Four and Seven didn't care for the stuff. No outrage, just dribbled it out. Maybe because it wasn't natural? So, Russ tried three different solutions of saltwater for Three, Five, and Eight. No dice. Russ was frantic.

It was clear they needed not salt water and not fake tears but real ones. But he wasn't some actor. Though, come to think of it, didn't they have some trick? He looked it up online and learned about something called a tear stick made of menthol where you dabbed a bit under the eyes, and, boom, you were Meryl Streep.

He ordered one for overnight delivery. In the meantime, all he could do was sing to them as he changed their towels.

The menthol stick came the next morning. Russ broke open the box and applied it. Holy cow, it worked! He got enough in the dropper for a couple of feedings. He'd figured it out, and from that point on, they'd be strong and healthy.

Except, even after two drops a piece, they still gaped hungrily. Another drop all down the line. They sucked it up only to beg for more.

He was mystified. He'd cried for them, fed them more than their share. How could it not be enough?

"What do you want from me?" he yelled angrily. And accidentally stubbed his toe on the kitchen island, the pain so bad he looked down to make sure he hadn't snapped the dumb thing off. And then realized he was crying. He sucked up the tears in the dropper and fed them. They lapped it up, and, one by one, dropped off to sleep.

Russ should've been relieved, but he wasn't. Because he understood. Yes, they needed tears. But not just any tears, only those of sadness and pain.

That afternoon, to Russ' chagrin, they were hungry again. He got out a hammer and smashed his pinky. And they fed.

Except they were famished again that night. Hammer poised, he aimed for his ring finger. Raised the tool. And stopped mid blow.

His heart leapt. Other people's tears! Weird as the ask would be, people would do anything for money.

Then his heart sunk again into the muck. Even if he could, he knew what would happen. The babies would reject it. Why? Because they only wanted *his* tears. Maybe it was biological, the way a mother's breast milk dished out not only the perfect nutrition but immunity.

The next morning they were ravenous, kicking and flailing their arms in eight tiny tantrums. Russ was an empty tank. Instead, he took each baby in his hands, lay down on the floor, and set them by his eyes to suck at the teats of his empty tear ducts.

Russ' breath caught. Teats. Mother. The babies needed their mother.

Linnea had wanted nothing more than to have a kid with Russ. And the fact that they didn't was why she left. But things had changed. Not only could she save the kids, the kids would save the marriage!

For the first time in months, Russ called Linnea. She didn't pick up, and he didn't leave a message. As he hoped, by the time he changed the babies' towels, she called back.

"Hey," Linnea said, neither snippy nor warm.

"I need you," was how it came out.

"Russ," her voice sympathetic but firm.

"Can you come over?"

"What? No. It's time to move on. Past time."

Russ didn't reply, trying to figure out what to say. The wheels whirring in his head, needing them to land on the jackpot.

"We gave it a try," Linnea said. "I don't have any regrets. It just didn't work out."

Not what Russ had wanted to hear, but he wasn't going to give up so easily. "Something happened. And I think it might fix everything."

"It's too late."

"Too late? For what?"

"I'm pregnant."

"Huh?" Knees weak, Russ' eyes blurred.

"I'm having a baby."

"But-but—" he could barely choke out.

"Why can't you accept that we want different things?" She was annoyed.

And so was he. He cleared his throat. "You're right."

"I'm glad you can see—"

"I wanted you for who you are. You wanted me for what I could do for you."

"Russ, that's not fair—"

Crushed, he hung up the phone. The babies feasted like a football team at an all-you-can-eat buffet after the big game.

Linnea, hair wet from her shower, was warming her hands on her mug of coffee in the kitchen, about to take the first sip of the morning, when the doorbell rang. Hoping it was the crib she'd ordered, she waddled along in her socked feet to the door.

No cardboard box on the stoop, just a small Styrofoam cooler, the type you'd buy at a convenience store for a last-minute picnic. An envelope was taped on top. Rubbing her big belly, she peered down the empty tree-lined street. No one on the sidewalks, no car driving away.

Curious, she unsealed the envelope with a thumbnail, the front of the card reading **SORRY** in fancy font. She had a hunch, and, indeed, when she opened it, recognized the crooked handwriting right away. Russ. She let out a small sigh.

It'd been a shame the way things turned out between them. He was a good man, and she'd really loved the guy. The diagnosis hadn't been his fault, and she still felt a little guilty for losing some attraction to him because of it. The truth was, she was pretty sure she'd have gotten over it if he'd been open to other options. Yet his outright refusal to even consider a donor meant he'd chosen his ego over their marriage—their future child!—and that was the real dealbreaker.

She felt herself getting sad, a tickle in her throat. Swallowing, she again reminded herself to leave the past in the past. After all, she was pregnant, and, even without a partner, it felt right.

Yes, she was finally on the right path, both for her and her little one. Still, the least she could do was read his note.

> *Linnea,*
>
> *I'm so sorry for what I said on the phone. I was upset because I still miss you. But I realize now that I've got to let you go. Knowing that, I wanted to make one last gesture, both as an apology and a thank you for all the great times we had and the love we shared.*
> *-Russ*

She nodded approvingly. That was something, at least, admitting his mistakes and trying to move on. She wouldn't respond of course, but maybe in a few months she'd send him a holiday card to let him know all was forgiven.

Kneeling down, she lifted the lid of the cooler. A tall thermos on a bed of ice. She unscrewed the lid, sniffed, and smiled. She'd recognize Russ' lemonade anywhere, which, while she'd never told him, was even better than Gram's. And he'd been kind enough to gift her one last batch.

She sat on the steps in the brisk morning air and took a sip. Mmmmm. Delicious as ever, equal parts bitter and sweet, pulpy yet refreshing. A longer swig, gulping it down. Then, oops, a seed in her mouth. Which she spat out on her palm. And screamed at the tiny green eye blindly staring back at her.

Happy Campers

Driving quickly along the dirt road through the dark, I try to keep it under forty so I don't miss one of the curves and drop off into the gulley.

The bare hilly landscape is eerily beautiful in the glow of the three-quarters moon, a high ridge bristling with broken snags like a porcupine's back. Twenty years ago, it would've all been forest. But the fire a decade before—the largest in Colorado's recorded history—made the bones of the land jut out, hunching slopes studded with boulders, downed logs strewn every which way, clumps of sagebrush and other plants I don't know the name of.

Most people don't like the burns, finding them ugly and off-putting. To me, they're comforting because, unlike dense tree cover, nothing can really creep up on you out here. Except the cottontails bounding into the sweep of my headlights, which I keep braking to avoid.

If it weren't for what happened, I'd be enjoying the drive, the way I did on the way in from Denver to camp for a couple of days. Of course, in that case, I'd still be sleeping in my tent on my air mattress by the purling creek.

But now I'm rushing back towards town, not sure where I'm going exactly, just that I've got to keep moving.

I snatch a glimpse in the rearview mirror of the little boy lying still in the backseat, half-covered by the tarp. Shuddering from a cold settled deep in my bones, I flick my eyes back to the empty road and toe the gas.

Twelve hours earlier

The afternoon sun shone down on me as I drove my hatchback from the wilderness trailhead, through the wide-open burn, back towards the campground after a nice ten-mile hike. Outside the fire area, the pinewoods had been shady, pleasantly warm but not hot. And the best part was I'd had the trail to myself, just an elderly couple in the parking lot eating sandwiches out of the back of an SUV.

I was looking forward to enjoying the few last hours of daylight to splash around in the creek, read my book, and munch some crackers and cheese. Since it was only me and a quiet family at the campground (two young parents and a well-behaved little boy in a minivan), I'd keep soaking up the silence of the forest like a sponge which I could slowly drip out back in the noisy city.

I smiled as I followed the road out of the burn back into vibrant green ponderosas, untouched for a couple of football fields to either side of a rushing creek. I turned onto the drive into the campground, threading the needle between the water and a rocky hillside.

A faded American flag hung limply from a pole stuck into a stump at the edge of the first campsite. Taking up most of the parking spot was a large pickup, cooler and fishing poles in the bed, empty gun rack in the cab.

Two men in baseball caps, flannels, and jeans sat in camp chairs by a huge fire, sucking on green bottles, a pile of dead branches beside them. They'd set up a massive cabin tent a few feet away. Not the kind of folks you typically see at National Forest campgrounds—"good old boys" was the polite term—but public lands were for everyone, so who was I to judge? I waved as I drove past, but they didn't seem to notice.

Parking at my site at the far end of the campground, I turned off the ignition. Soon as I got out, the noise hit me. A loud booming voice from what could've only been the newcomers' truck radio. A commercial for erectile dysfunction, of all things. How was there even reception this far in the woods? Unless the radio waves traveled further because of the open burn.

Then the chunking chords of an old Van Halen song, and I slammed the door hard with a groan. Now, don't get me wrong, I *like* classic rock. But every morning and night back in town I endured the couple in the adjacent condo banging, thumping, and slamming doors, yelling at each other, and worst of all—from the minute they got home from work until the middle of the night—their blaring television. And that's on top of the constant car traffic, the nonstop barking dogs, the recreational construction of rich, bored neighbors, all damned day long.

I went over to my tent under the fat spruce to see if it was any quieter. It wasn't. I kicked the dirt in frustration.

The reason normal people come out to wilderness is to savor that rare taste of peace. So, what kind of a-holes take their noise with them?

Inconsiderate ones, that's for sure, with no thought whatsoever for anyone else. Not grown past the stage of psychological development where you learn to put yourself in another's shoes...that of the average five-year-old.

But it was more than the complete and utter disregard. The real question was, why, on the rare occasion they're out in the wild, would they *want* to listen to that stuff? The only sounds *I* wanted to hear were a squirrel's chitter, a raven's croak, the hissing creek, and the whistle of the wind.

I unzipped the tent and grabbed my book from the mesh pocket on the ceiling, short stories from my favorite nature writer. I'd have to go down by the water to read it. Before I zipped back up, I checked to make sure my machete in its leather sheath was still tucked underneath my air mattress, in case some animal came sniffing around in the middle of the night.

That's when the obvious answer came to me. Fear.

Guys like them pretend to be rugged outdoorsman, but the truth is they can't go more than a few minutes without the shouts of civilization covering up the wild murmurs of nature. All to block out their own thoughts about who they are and their place in the world; thoughts that, if they paid attention to, they might not be so happy about.

Book in hand, I walked down the trail to the brushy mucky banks of the creek where I'd set up my chair. To my dismay, David Lee Roth's squeals easily cut through the rush of water, and I tossed my book on the chair. Thinking maybe I should set my tent up outside the campground, I followed the creek downstream looking for a level and not too muddy spot. Unfortunately, the woods soon petered out back into the burn. Plus, I almost stepped on a big clump of animal crap, most likely bear. Which was the only reason I needed to stay closer to the car.

Grumbling, I hiked back upstream, telling myself they'd probably turn off the radio any minute. I plopped down my chair to read, but after a few minutes of AC/DC screeching I gave up. At the car again, I dug the cheese out from the cooler and crackers from a bag and sat at the picnic bench. At least the crunching intermittently covered up Foreigner whining "Cold as Ice."

Thankfully, sundown was only a couple of hours away, and, surely, they'd knock things off at that point. Until then, I wasn't going to sit there and fume. Though my legs were sore from the hike, I grabbed my book and chair, walked along the drive past my tormentors—both getting sauced by the bonfire, "Satisfaction" droning from their truck—through the narrow way between cliff and creek, and onto the road. Climbing the hill, I walked back into the burn, ten degrees warmer than under the trees. And I could still hear the frigging radio rising up from the little patch of forest below.

It took fifteen minutes of walking up and over into another gulch until the music faded. I picked a spot with a stunning thousand-acre view—where the creek snaked out of the trees to glint along the scrubby rock—and cracked open my book with a sigh of relief. It was ridiculous the lengths I had to go to for this little bit of quiet. My simmering anger made it difficult to sink into the story—a woman in love with a man who sometimes turned into a mountain lion—but finally I did.

Only when the sun started to sink behind the higher ridges, the valley below disappearing in shadow, did I reluctantly trudge down the road to the campground, praying for silence. Despite the coming night, it was still quite toasty, rocks exhaling the heat they'd breathed in all day.

Sure enough, soon as I came around the bend, the Eagles' "Take it Easy" broke like shards of glass in my eardrums. Unbelievably, as I got closer—jaw clenching, molars grinding—it was as if the radio was even louder, the SOBs turning up the volume like a security light.

Boozing by the fire, they hadn't moved a muscle, the blaze large enough to engulf a standing man. My only hope was for the ten p.m. quiet hours. Of course, without a ranger or camp host, the regulations didn't mean didley squat. And with the closest station more than thirty miles away, there was almost no chance of one showing up that Tuesday evening. Indeed, I'd bet on exactly that when I chose not to leave the twenty-four dollar per night charge in the self-service box.

By the time I got to my site, I'd finally come to terms with the fact that the only way to escape the racket was through sleep. So, barely dark as it was—just after eight, according to my cell—I brushed my teeth, washed my face, put all stray items in the back of the car, and crawled into my tent.

Naked except for my boxers, I slithered into my sleeping bag, which I left unzipped because of the heat. Another commercial from the radio, the most obnoxious one yet from "Denver's harmonica playing finance guy."

After the crooked bankster had repeated his phone number four fucking times in a row, the dull opening guitar licks of "Layla."

I shoved the pillow over my head but couldn't smother the noise. After a few minutes, flickers of light through my closed eyelids. Could it be?

I pushed the pillow away and opened my eyes to more flashes of light. My heart leapt.

Begging for a storm that would send the rejects inside, I unzipped the flap and peeked out my head. Alas, the air was thick as stew, not a cloud in the starry sky. Heat lightning flashed somewhere deep in the mountains, of no use to me.

And I wasn't the only one suffering. How about the poor family next door? Taking their little boy camping, maybe for the first time, and having to put up with this concert of the cliches?

More than that, it was the principle of the thing. The only reason this was happening was no one had ever told those backwoods idiots what's what. I'd give them another fifteen minutes, and if they didn't shut up, I'd go over there.

Not a minute later the piano chords of another song I used to like—Journey's "Don't Stop Believing"—ruined forever by overplaying. And I couldn't stand it anymore. Kicking off the bag, I tugged on my clothes, slipped on a headlamp, and, righteous blood pumping through my veins, marched over.

Closer to the newcomers' site—the family's tent glowing, not able to sleep either, no doubt—the music booming louder, I feared for a second they'd started a forest fire. But, no, they'd just heaped on every dead branch and stick in the area to feed one of the biggest bonfires I'd ever seen. Lucky the night was calm, as even a stiff breeze could've spread the flames to burn up that last oasis of green.

I reached the edge of their mobile boom box. Not wanting to startle them, I turned off my light and called out, "Hellooo!" They didn't seem to hear, and one of them tossed a bottle into the fire.

I came around the other side of the truck and called out again. This time they turned their heads. Waving a hand and grinning like Ned Flanders from *The Simpsons*, I waltzed into the firelight. They sat up straight in their chairs, looking me up and down grimly.

"We'll pay in the morning," the older of the two, maybe late forties, face lined, grey in his beard, grunted.

"Oh, I'm not the camp host," I said, and they immediately relaxed into their seats.

"Well, shit," the older one said.

"Wanna beer?" The younger, clean shaven one, probably early thirties, offered. Age aside, from facial features to husky build they looked a lot alike. Maybe cousins or even brothers.

I hesitated, as if reaching a fork in the trail while hiking in the woods.

My first option was that of the weakling, to turn around and scamper back to my site, tail between my legs, and hope they ran out of steam.

Or I could take the right fork—the chill guy path—by drinking that beer, trying to make friends, and then, once we'd found some rapport, ask if they'd consider turning the music down.

The leftmost trail was that of the hardass, where I'd refuse their bottom shelf swill, cut through the bull, and demand quiet.

Of course, standing there by the heat of the enormous bonfire, it was too late to say nothing. The chill path was obviously the best option, since showing them respect would be the most likely way to soften them up. But the last thing I wanted was to waste the few remaining hours of my retreat with those lowlifes. Besides, respect isn't something that's given, it's earned. And desecrating one of the last unspoiled places didn't make the grade.

No, my decision had been made soon as I got out of my sleeping bag. I reminded myself I wasn't doing this just for me but for the family and all those unfortunate enough to cross those jackasses' path in the future.

"I don't want your beer," I said sternly, "I want quiet."

Younger man's smile dripped off his face like I'd slapped him.

"It's been hours," I added, trying to soften the blow.

"We're not telling you how to spend *your* night." Older Brother shot me a poison glare. "So, how about you don't worry about what we do with ours."

"I'm not the one ruining anyone's night," my voice shook as I tried to hold in the anger.

"You are now," Younger Brother drawled.

"I'm not even telling you to turn off the music, just to lower it so I can go to sleep."

"Ever hear of a little something called private property?" Older Brother slurred, sliding his beer into the chair's cup holder.

It was a ridiculous way to frame things in a federally owned campground.

"But that's the thing," I said patiently as I could, an edge creeping into my voice. "The noise you're making isn't staying here, it's coming over to me."

Their eyes were dull in the firelight, and I realized I'd be as likely to change their minds as get back a stolen piece of meat from a pack of wild animals. These two dimbulbs didn't have the cognitive capacity—certainly not the moral and ethical development—to process my argument. Much less agree with it.

Clenching my fists, I cycled through all the things I wanted to say—*You should be at some dive bar not a campground. You have no respect for anyone but yourselves and belong in prison. Scumbags like you are everything that's wrong with the world*—but I left it at a pathetic, "Quiet hours are ten o'clock" and stamped off in a huff.

I'd barely passed the family's glowing tent when the radio—now a commercial for "O-O-O-O'Reilly!" auto parts I'd already heard five times that night—turned up even louder. I had the impulse to pack up and drive somewhere else, but I simply didn't have the energy to break down camp, find a new site, and set back up again. I thought about sleeping in my car, but I was too long to fit in the hatchback without curling myself into a tiny ball.

Out of options, I stormed back to the tent, crammed pieces of tissue in my ears, and tried to sleep. But it was so damned warm I was sweating. And my mind raced with the injustice of it all. How troglodytes like those not only had the run of every town but insisted on bringing their degeneracy out to the wilderness.

After stewing in venomous thoughts for some time, I finally accepted that while I couldn't stop them from shattering the stillness, I *could* punish them for their transgressions. Once again, it wasn't about me, it was the principle of the thing.

The sixties/seventies marathon went on for maybe another forty minutes—the shallowest cuts from Steve Miller Band, Bad Company, and Aerosmith—as I plotted my revenge.

Obviously, the drunk dipshits would crash out sooner or later. And, of course, they'd sleep in. So, the plan I chose was simple: Get up before the sun. Pack my stuff. Deflate their tires.

Okay, I admit it wasn't the grand scheme of a criminal mastermind. More a childish prank than full on karma. But it would inconvenience them (quite a bit if they didn't have an air compressor). It would make them angry. And, most important, they'd never forget it, so maybe next time they'd think twice.

I set my phone alarm for five a.m. And lay there as "Feel Like Makin' Love" floated over through the night, no longer resisting the well-worn power ballad, trying to hear it the way I had the first time when I was a teenager and thought it a pretty rad song.

Sharp beeping woke me, and I swiped off the alarm. Full dark and other than the hissing creek, dead silence. A bit cooler though still balmy. I'd finally drifted off to sleep, dreaming of a tall thin silhouette scattering ashes in the creek.

My eyes were scratchy, head heavy, body wanting nothing more than to sink back into slumber. But my brain was already chugging along, telling me I needed to follow through with my promise to teach the rednecks—probably deep in a drunken stupor—their lesson.

More or less awake, I deflated my mattress, packed my sleeping bag, and broke down my tent. Over to my car, opened the back, tossed in my stuff, and shut it again quietly. Then, holding my breath, I listened...Blissful quiet. A part of me wondered if it was too late to just curl up under a tree. But I shook the cowardly thought away.

After a quick sweep of my headlamp to make sure I'd gotten everything, I flicked it off and padded along the dirt drive. Not a light nor sound from the family's tent. On to the brothers. I stopped short.

Older Brother sat in his chair, sleeping bag over his legs, orange embers pulsing in the fire's grey ash. But from the way he slumped over, I could tell he was asleep. And snoring from the tent told me Younger Brother was, too.

The only sound that of my cracking knees, I squatted on the far side of the truck next to the right front tire, unscrewed the valve cap, and pocketed it. Then, with the tip of my house key—careful not to jangle it against the others—I started letting the air out.

A hiss as if from a monstrous snake, and I pulled my hand away. Inch by inch, I rose up and peeked over the hood. Older Brother, drunk as a skunk, hadn't moved a muscle. And the sawing from the tent hadn't let up one bit.

Grinning like an idiot, I deflated the first tire most of the way, then did the same with the other three until the pickup sunk low on its suspension. All the while, the caveman brothers off in la-la land.

I was most of the way back to my campsite, snickering with glee, when I remembered I'd forgotten to put the caps back on. I don't know why it mattered to me, other than the satisfaction of a job well done. Or maybe how taking the time to do so right in front of them was the cherry on top of the revenge sundae.

I hurried back to the truck and reached in my pocket. Not a minute later I had three caps on, one to go. But that last one slipped from between my sweaty fingers onto the dirt and under the truck. Blindly, in a half-panic, I felt around but couldn't find the stupid thing. I was about to give up when my fingertips brushed the little piece of plastic, and I screwed it on with a few quick turns.

I'd gotten to my feet and was about to take my victory lap when something in the fire shattered—one of the beer bottles, no doubt.

Older Brother started up from his chair, looking all around him. I froze like a rabbit, pretty sure he hadn't seen me. But he was staring at the truck and even in the dim glow of the firelight had to have noticed how low it was sitting.

Indeed, with a "What the fuck!" he threw off the sleeping bag and launched to his feet.

Nothing to do but run. I sprinted into the dark, figuring he'd take off right behind me. A few seconds later, I risked a glance behind. No one there.

Almost at my car when I heard the shot. Probably just a warning into the air, but it was my cue to skedaddle.

I threw open the door, dove in, slammed and locked it behind me, and hunched below the windshield. I was about to start the ignition when headlights split the night. The brothers were moving the pickup, flat tires and all. Were they going to ram me?

It only took a second to clear up the mystery. They were parking across the narrow drive between the creek and steep hillside, cutting off my escape.

It finally dawning that I was a sitting duck, I got out of the car, opened the trunk, grabbed my machete in its leather sheath, and fled into the safety of the woods. I hadn't gone far when I stopped short. Where the hell was I going? I couldn't follow the road since the burn left nowhere to hide if they came after. The only thing that made sense was to stay in the trees and either wait for the family to go for help or someone else to come by, preferably a ranger. And if I was going to do that, I needed food and water.

I snuck back to my parking spot, stepping toe to heel, careful not to crack any sticks. Barely lit by the faint rays of a newly risen three-quarters moon, the brothers stood in front of my car, one of them holding something in his arms. My hand was so sweaty on the plastic machete handle I was afraid I was going to drop it.

"Gimme that, you're drunk," Younger Brother whispered.

"So are you, asshole," Older Brother said a bit louder.

"Someone's gonna get hurt, and then we're gonna get pinched. Again."

"I'm not gonna hurt him," Older Brother growled.

I let out a deep breath, relieved. The schmuck was just trying to scare me. The best thing to do at that point was to come out and own what I did. I'd apologize, and that would be that.

I barely heard the next whisper from Older Brother. But it was enough to make my heart skip like a scratched CD. "I'm just gonna wing him."

Fuckface might not have been planning a murder, but he was still going to shoot me!

"You're fuckin' nuts, you know that?" Younger Brother almost yelled. "Gimme the light!"

"Screw you, man. I'm taking care of the tires and bouncing."

Younger Brother strutted off into the night with the flashlight, leaving a muttering and swearing Older Brother alone with his gun. Sheathed machete in hand, I crawled away quickly and quietly as I could towards the creek, hoping the rushing water would mask my retreat, and, once I waded across, put them off my trail.

But it looked cold and deep. Warm as the night was, I'd get chilled to the bone if I got my clothes wet. And that fact made me consider if maybe the guy was just bluffing.

Yes, they were noisy shitheads who had no right to disturb my peace. But I was the one who'd picked the fight with them. Which, in their backwards ape culture, they probably took as a direct challenge to their alpha supremacy. Meaning, they'd only let it go if they could save face.

I felt better right away, the horror of being chased by a bloodthirsty madman fading into a petty high school beef. And even if an apology wasn't enough, I'd pay them off; I had close to $200 in my wallet in the glove compartment. Surely, that would go a long way towards healing their wounded pride.

I climbed back up the bank and through the trees, and soon as I could make out Older Brother's silhouette in the moonlight at the edge of my site, I stepped behind a fat conifer.

After taking a deep breath, I called out, "I'm sorry!"

He swung the rifle in my direction but didn't fire. As I knew he wouldn't.

"I was mad about the noise," I went on. "But I shouldn't have touched your truck."

Older Brother lowered his weapon. It was almost over.

"I've got an air compressor if you need one." A whine in my voice I didn't like. "Then I'll go."

Just the hiss of the creek as Older Brother appeared to mull things over. I was about to step out from behind the tree when he raised the gun and fired straight at the trunk. Thank God the bullet didn't go through, though I felt the vibration in the wood, the sharp bang ringing in my ears.

Whether he'd tried to hit me or was only fucking around, one thing for sure, he hadn't accepted my apology.

I dropped to my knees and crawled in a frenzy back towards the creek again. Behind me, Older Brother crashed through the trees. Too late for me to run.

On the banks now, I got to my feet and hid behind another tree. I unsnapped the leather sheath and dropped it on the ground, and the machete trembled in my hand. I held my breath and cocked an ear.

The crashing stopped. Maybe he'd reconsidered. Or given up.

Then, his voice from not far away. "Come on out, nowww!" he taunted in sing song.

No way in hell. And if he got any closer, he'd be sorry.

As he crunched towards me, I lifted the machete over my head. The instant his silhouette appeared, I lunged forward, and swung my arm as if I offering my best tennis serve. I connected with a thunk that vibrated up my wrist all the way along my elbow to my shoulder. He screamed and a shot whizzed past my ear.

I tried to yank the blade away, but it was stuck in the meat of his neck. I was about to knee him in the groin, when, with a gurgle, he fell forward. Jumping back, I let go of the handle as my attacker tumbled headlong into the moonlit shallows of the creek. The rifle flew out of his hands and plopped into the middle of the current.

I stood there a moment to catch my breath, ears pounding, blood pumping like lava, ready to dash off if he moved a muscle. But he didn't. The ripples picked him up and floated him a few feet downstream.

Dead.

No time for shock, mourning, or remorse, as I knew Younger Brother had to have heard the shot. I flicked on my headlamp so I could grab the machete. But the shouting was already too close, footsteps pounding through the trees. If he, too, had a gun, I was screwed.

Something in the mud by my feet glinted. I knew what it was right away. A tent stake!

I leaned over to snatch it and switched off my light. Then scrambled atop the nearest boulder.

Adrenalin pumping, I didn't even think. As Younger Brother raced over, I pounced onto his back like a mountain lion. We fell hard to the duff, and I stabbed him in the cheek with the stake. He dropped backwards onto me, but I squirmed out from under him and kneeled on his chest. Ignoring flailing fists against my thighs, I jabbed the sharp metal into his face over and over—ten times? twenty?—until I felt it sink deep, my fist wet and slick.

Panting hard, I turned on my headlamp. The stake jutted from one of his staring eyes, gleaming fluid leaking down his cheek. Nothing in his bare hands, no weapon at all. But dead as a doornail, just like his brother.

The full horror of the situation still hadn't hit me, but at least I was safe. The only thing left was to collect the weapons, head home, and try to make sense of it all. I wondered if a therapist's patient-client confidentiality applied to taking a life.

As I slid the stake out from his eye, more liquid dripped, and I puked. Like a time-release narcotic, the shock was coming on. I needed to hurry out of there before it kicked in all the way and made me do something stupid.

In a half-trance, I wiped the stake on his pants and stuck it in my back pocket. Then dug in his pockets for the keys.

I scurried downstream, slipping on the mud but catching myself before I fell. Older Brother hadn't gone far, bobbing face down in the shallows like that "dead man's float" they taught in instructional swim. Jamming my foot between his shoulder blades, I grasped the handle and yanked out the machete.

A rush of hope, as salvation was only moments away. Then I remembered the family. My chest constricted as if lassoed. Sooner or later, the cops would show, the parents would give them my description, my car make and model, the plate number. And they'd find me.

Sure, I could argue self-defense. But even if I made bail, I'd still have to deal with court for months, maybe even years, reliving the awfulness again and again. Plus, judges were all activists and juries nothing but partisan. I could easily find myself wrongly convicted for murder. I tried to swallow the lump in my throat. Or even worse, *rightly* convicted.

There was only one way out, and that was to scare the hell out of the family so they kept their mouths shut. I wouldn't lay a finger on them, of course, but I'd have to make some threats. And for that to be convincing, I'd need more than a machete.

Luckily, the moon had risen above the trees, and I could see more clearly. Bracing myself, I waded into the stream, the cold instantly soaking through my pants. I made myself keep going up to my hips to feel around the rocky bottom with my foot. Nothing.

Midstream now, my waist under water. Then the bottom fell out beneath my feet, and I plunged in up to my neck, every muscle in my body knotting against the jarring chill. But my boots touched ground.

I'm not sure why I didn't leave the rifle. It wasn't like it had my prints or anything. But at the time, I guess I felt like I needed it to bully the family. And, yes, groping around for another minute, I kicked something. Shifting with my foot, it was either a stick or what I was looking for.

I tossed my headlamp back onto shore. Drawing a deep breath and holding it, I closed my eyes, dunked under, and grabbed for it. My fingers brushed metal and plastic.

To the surface again, spluttering but triumphant, rifle in hand. Sure, it was too waterlogged to work, but I only needed it as a prop anyway.

I slogged out of the creek, picked up my headlamp from the mud, and stood on shore for a minute to drip dry. Frigid to the bone, there was no time to change clothes. I'd warm up in the car on the way out.

Weapon slung over my shoulder, I squelched back to the campsite, water in my boots. Stuck the machete and stake in the back of the car under the cargo mat and jogged off down the drive. I half-expected to find the family's tent and minivan gone. But both were still there, dark and hushed.

I went over to their tent, water dribbling on the dirt, and flicked on my light. "It's over," I said.

A muffled squeak, probably from the kid. Unlike wild fawns and chicks, human babies don't have the instinct to keep quiet when in danger.

"We need to talk," I said in a calm voice.

"Please don't hurt us!" the woman said.

"I'm not gonna," I said. And then, remembering my role, added ominously, "If you do what I say. Now come on out."

A few long seconds later, the flap unzipped, and the man crawled out dressed in a sweatsuit. He shielded his face against my light with a forearm. Then, clearly noticing the rifle by my side, clasped both hands under his chin as if in prayer.

"I didn't have any choice." My voice came out weakly, almost pleading.

"I know, I know," he whimpered. "They're...?"

"Yes." Not liking how insecure I felt, I slid a finger inside the trigger guard to remind him—and myself—that *I* was the one in charge now. "They came after me."

"Then you did the right thing," the man said, voice steadier, perhaps realizing I wasn't going to massacre him and his family. "I would've done the same."

Maybe he was telling the truth. Maybe he wouldn't rat. But I couldn't risk it. Would you?

"I need your IDs," I grunted.

He squinted in obvious confusion.

"If I know where you live," I said with a hint of menace, "I know you won't tell."

"We're not gonna say a word!" he blurted. "We'll say we were asleep the whole time!"

"IDs." Then I shouted, "Now!"

"If you promise not to—"

Out of patience, I lifted the rifle and swung the muzzle towards him. "I said I wouldn't if you kept your fucking mouth—"

A snuffling from behind the tent. Definitely animal, not human.

Out of the corner of my eye, a big black shadow detached from the night. Bear! Instinctively, my finger squeezed the trigger, and, to my surprise, the waterlogged rifle fired off a shot.

I swiveled my light over to the creature as it turned tail and crashed off into the trees. Not a bear at all but a dumb cow. I'd forgotten that ranchers could graze in National Forests. *That's* what the pile of shit had been.

In the meantime, the man had slipped back inside the tent. I poked my head in to make sure he wasn't up to anything.

He was not. Cradling his nightgown-clad wife in one arm, he wiped long strands of hair away from her pale face with the other. The boy, dressed in a romper, curled in the corner.

I leaned forward. The woman's eyes were wide open...as was a chunk of her forehead.

My shot hadn't gone wild but straight into the tent.

The man turned to me, teeth bared, blind hate in his eyes. When he lunged at me, I fired—on purpose this time—hitting him square in the chest. He dropped like a sack of flour, lay on his back groaning for a moment, and then fell silent.

I'd killed again. And *again*! What was *happening*?!

I staggered backwards out of the tent, gagging. I tried to puke but my belly was empty.

Still, my grisly work wasn't done. I needed to take care of the boy.

I knelt down and crawled back inside the tent. The kid didn't say a word—not a cry, not a sniffle—just stared at me. Through me. Like his unconscious mind knew the safest thing was simply to check out.

Obviously, I couldn't leave him alone in the woods with the bodies his dead parents. And even when this ended, he'd probably never fully come back. At best, he'd become a depressed and isolated mental case. At worst, a school shooter. Whatever his fate, he hadn't done a thing to deserve it; a life over before it'd barely begun.

I took in a deep breath and let it out in a body-wracking shudder. Horrible as it was, I knew what I had to do.

I checked the chamber, and there were two rounds left. One for him...and then. I swallowed, and the tears came.

I'd never asked for this. Any of this. Even without mind-numbing tragedies, the world was a bleak one—being born less like winning the lottery and more like getting drafted for World War III.

And if this could happen to people like me—like this family—then what was the point? We'd both die sometime, anyhow. This way I could at least control how we went out. In a split second, no pain.

I aimed the rifle at the kid's forehead. He didn't flinch. Like a sick dog, maybe he knew I'd be doing him a favor. Only stared at me with those dull filmy eyes, no fear, no sadness, no anger—no emotion at all. Just pods of jelly in a sack of bone.

My hands shook but my finger curled around the trigger. I counted down from three, two, one.

And dropped the rifle. Who was I kidding? I'd done what I needed to survive, but I couldn't kill a kid!

An ember of hope in the ashes in my soul. What if it *wasn't* too late for him? Maybe he wouldn't remember any of this and could still turn out okay with a new family. Kids had survived concentration camps, even being made into child soldiers, with their minds intact. So, why not this little boy?

For the first time that night, I was going to make the right choice.

Slinging my rifle, I crawled past the bodies and took him in my arms. The poor little bugger hugged me. Actually hugged me. Though probably just for warmth. Or some primitive instinct to accept the rule of the new alpha.

I carried him out to my car. Put him in the back seat and buckled him in. He was shivering, so I spread my sleeping bag over him.

"Be right back," I said, but he just stared off into space.

Still dark, moon bright, I jogged over to the brothers' truck and moved it out of the drive to their parking spot. Getting out, I chucked the keys into the creek.

Back at my car, I checked on the kid again. His eyes were closed, but he was still shivering. I got the tarp out of the back and draped it over him, all except his head. Then I tore out of the campsite.

Twenty minutes later, dawn creeping in, and we're almost out of the burn. My plan is to drop the boy outside a fire station and call in from a payphone, if I can find one. Sooner or later, they'll connect him with everything, but by then I'll be out of the country. Not sure if it'll be Canada or Mexico—while I'd stick out less up north, they'd ask less questions down south.

I figure I have less than twenty-four hours before they find the bodies and officially start the investigation. Lucky for me, the only witnesses are dead. And the elderly couple at the wilderness trailhead most likely gone home by now.

The yellow light of dawn seeps into the sky like ointment on an infected wound. I let out a sigh...maybe things will turn out okay after all.

In a few days, I'll send a postcard to my folks to let them know I'm safe. And the kid's so cute and well behaved, he'll be snatched up by some loving parents in no time. And whatever happened, however traumatic for him, it can all be worked out in therapy.

The worst is behind me now, no longer feeling exposed by the open burn but free as a bird. I force a smile. And, incredibly, it stays. Sometimes bad things happen to good people, and there's nothing you can do except— I stomp the brakes and come to a skidding halt, bucking up against the seatbelt.

No critter in the road. Nothing I've forgotten at the campsite. No last-minute regrets, either. Just the clear and undeniable memory of signing my full name into the register at the trailhead.

Long Strange R.I.P.

"Long time no see, Mr. Garcia." Satan slouched on his throne of charred ribcages and femurs at the heart of a vast dim obsidian hall. "Whatever can I do for you?"

The heavy-set white-haired and bearded man—basically Santa Claus in glasses and black T-shirt—stood with his feet planted wide on the ashy stone, sulfurous gases twining around his legs like friendly cats. "You know damn well why I'm here," Jerry said.

"Written any new jingles?" Satan's black lidless eyes oozed like tar as he scratched the mushroom head of the ghoul squatting to his side. "I still get a kick out of that one song. How does it go? 'Set out running but I take my time, a friend of the devil is a friend of mine.'"

"It's gotta stop."

"Is my singing that bad?" Satan flashed hundreds of tiny immaculate teeth, and the thing beside him tittered. "I forgot to congratulate you on the Hall of Fame induction. Quite the honor."

"Leave Vince alone." Jerry stuck out a trembling pointer finger, the finger beside it missing.

"Ah, yes, how is Mr. Welnick? Still tickling the ivories to your satisfaction?"

Jerry shook his head, spraying droplets of sweat that evaporated in mid-air. "You can't keep killing them."

"I quite enjoy their playing." Satan put a hand to his ear. "In fact, that's them now." From somewhere not far away, a faint tinkling of piano mingled with a droning organ and synthesizer chimes.

"One time." Jerry's shoulders slumped. "One time I forgot my insulin. I was just a kid. The band was taking off. Had my whole life ahead of me."

"So did Mr. McKernan. Or shall I say, PigPen."

"The way he drank and with that autoimmune thing, I figured he'd be gone in a few years anyway."

"A deal is a deal." Satan tented his long fingers, each of which sported an extra knuckle. "Whether he was sober enough to know what he was signing is beyond my purview."

"It was only supposed to be one."

"Was it now?" A scroll materialized in Satan's hands. After clearing his throat, he read aloud, "In exchange for another fifty years of life, I, Jerome John Garcia, offer the soul of the Grateful Dead's keyboard player in lieu of my own until the day of my death." With the flick of a wrist, the scroll disappeared.

"Keith and Brent never signed."

Satan sniffed. "It's called power of attorney."

"I had a feeling you'd be up to something," Jerry sneered. "So, when Keith started doping, I kicked him out of the band. But you still got him. On his fucking birthday," Jerry growled.

Tsking, Satan shook his horned head. "Over fifty-one thousand motor vehicle fatalities that year in the U.S. alone."

"And then, ten years later almost to the day, you took Brent." Jerry clenched his fists. "He had a little girl, man."

"Cocaine is a powerful pharmaceutical, as is morphine. Dabbling in either comes with great risk. Combine the two, you're pretty much asking for it."

"You got three for the price of one. It's not fair."

"Are you accusing me of cheating?!" Satan stomped a hoof, and, startled, the ghoul skittered off to hide behind his throne.

"I'm not gonna let you take Vince." Jerry folded his arms across his sweat-stained shirt. "This ends now."

Satan lifted a hairless eyebrow.

Lying in bed at the rehab center, Jerry Garcia woke to a crushing pain in his chest, as if someone had dropped an amplifier on him.

The LSD coursing through his system helped him resist the urge to fight, to call out for help, and instead simply accept his fate. Gritting his teeth, he focused on the ceiling fan overhead as it chugged out its locomotive rhythm, the spinning blades blurring into a mandala.

The glowing bulb at its center pulsed, buzzed, and blew out.

Lungs creaking like an attic door, Vince Welnick crested the grassy hill and stopped to catch his breath. A breeze blew up from the grey Pacific churning below.

Given the choice between emphysema's constant waterboarding or cancer eating him alive, he'd pick the latter every time. While chemo and radiation had knocked out his tumor almost a decade before, the wheezing was only worsening—thanks, in no small part, to his refusal to quit smoking. Of course, having kicked pills and booze, cigarettes were his only comfort. He patted his pocket, knowing full well he'd left his butts at home.

It was true he'd only known Jerry for five short years, but losing him still felt like the death of an older brother, the man's absence leaving a smoking crater in the music scene and his life. Despite all Vince's efforts to convince the guys to keep touring, The Dead was done. Yet the biggest kick in the balls came seven years later when the band finally did get back together—without him. Calling themselves Dead and Company, Vince preferred the spiteful moniker, Dead, Inc.

After a half decade playing to packed stadiums, gigging in dinky clubs with random jam bands was humiliating for Vince. Every time he got up on stage and stared out into a crowd of hundreds—instead of tens of thousands—he died a little inside. Gradually, he stopped performing. Hell, it'd been almost a year since he'd last sat down in front of the keys.

All hard pills to swallow, but he was finally at peace. He'd played his part in the most successful touring act in history and played it well. Naturally, it could only be downhill from there.

Speaking of hills, Vince couldn't remember the last time he'd hiked along the coast. With eye-popping greenery swooping down to the rocky shoreline and foaming breakers, it was really a stunning view, the perfect place for the task at hand.

Gripping the kitchen knife with sweaty palm, he lifted the blade to his throat. "Tune up, Jerry. I'm coming home."

Levi Cures The Plague

I swung open the pasture gate as the pink summer sun cleared the sugar maples. Sarah, Rebecca, and Rachel, my three spotted goats, cropped the bright grass at the center of the fenced-in acre, the morning air earthy and clean. Time to herd them inside the barn for milking.

A shadow in a clump of tall grass by the edge of the wire fence caught my eye. As I got closer, the breath froze in my chest. Schlomo, the half-feral tom cat who'd kept me company the six years I'd owned Adamah Farms, lay stretched out on his side. His fur was shredded and bloody, pink gore and white ribs exposed, hazy blue eyes staring off into nothing.

Stifling a sob, I knelt in the dewy grass, soaking the knee of my jeans, and gently picked up poor Schlomo's cold, stiff body. A string of blood stretched out like taffy from his torn throat, stuck to a single green blade, and then broke off.

Little guy hadn't come home last night, but that was nothing unusual. Yet my farm is an inholding in Adirondack Park—six million acres of forest preserved by the state as "forever wild"—which meant there were fisher cats, coyotes, catamounts, and even the occasional wolf roaming around. The fleet-footed kitty had evaded all of them for years, while making an unfortunate dent in the local bird, squirrel, and chipmunk population. Until, finally, his ninth life had come and gone.

Heart heavy, cradling Schlomo's corpse against my flannel, I went into the old red barn and set him on my work bench next to the milk buckets and bales of wire. I'd give him a proper Jewish burial at the edge of his beloved woods, but I had other chores to tend to first. I slipped him into an empty feed sack, grabbed a wicker basket and bag of cracked corn, and left the barn.

I stepped over the waist-high portable electric fence enclosing the twenty-by-twenty patch of lawn on the woods-side of the barn, chicken hutch in the middle, fifteen laying hens clucking and pecking by my boots as I tossed them handfuls of corn. I opened the wire cage and walked up the ramp, stooping to enter the tiny hutch where I gathered six fresh eggs from the straw-covered shelves and set them in the basket.

Of all the morning's chores, the next was always the hardest. Butterflies in my stomach, I paced the path through the unmown crabgrass to the log cabin. Climbed the three steps onto the porch I'd stacked with cords of split pine, birch, maple, and oak, and knocked lightly on the door. Then shook my head, weird to be seeking permission to go inside my home, one I'd built with my own two hands.

No sounds from inside, just the creek purling a stone's throw away, its cold waters stealing into the brightening forest. I knocked again.

If my guest had been anyone else, I would've just gone in. But this was the famous healer Levi, and not a person you wanted to sneak up on.

I turned to go back to the barn, my living space since accompanying Levi on the cross-Atlantic freighter from his ancestral Lithuania three months before. It wasn't like I was sleeping in the hayloft, or anything, as I'd recently fixed up half of the one-hundred-forty-three-year-old historic building as guest quarters complete with finished bedroom, kitchenette, and bathroom. Only thing is, I'd figured Levi would been the one staying there. Yet somehow, from the moment we got back, Levi took over my cabin.

So, the barn it was. And for those of you who think that's pathetic...Believe me, if you knew the man—much less his history—you'd have done the same.

Before I took more than a step, an answer through the door, booming yet not shouting, like a stage magician throwing his voice. "Ya?"

It was Yiddish, the only language Levi chose to speak, although he clearly understood every word of my English. Luckily for me, growing up Jewish in Brooklyn next door to my grandparents meant I had a decent grasp of the old tongue.

"Levi?" I still didn't know if Levi was his first or last name, so I never added a Mr. Frankly, it made me nervous to talk to him at all. Especially with the bad news I was about to give him. "The sea salt you wanted..." My throat caught, and I dry swallowed. "Store's closed."

Levi hadn't told me why he needed it, why regular table salt wouldn't do, and I hadn't asked. But wasn't this why I'd woken him from his slumber in the catacombs of the ruined synagogue at the heart of the Dainava forest, so he could go on exploring the secrets of the universe? It'd been tough enough for Levi as a practitioner of the occult in mid-nineteenth century Eastern Europe. But the fact that he was a Jew—if one renounced by all who shared his faith—meant he'd been constantly on the run from those who wanted him dead, including brutal pogroms that had slaughtered countless others of our Tribe.

A few long, heavy seconds of silence. Figuring Levi had gone back to work or sleep—

I had no idea what he did in there—I turned away yet again, still having to milk the goats, weed the carrots, the hundred other things that needed tending on a farm in August.

Then the door swung open. Levi stood there stark nude with his tall, rangy, slightly stooping physique, cords of muscle running like tree roots beneath sun-browned wrinkled flesh. The top of his spotty egg head was bald as a stone, in the back a shock of bone-white hair flowing over ropy shoulders, a bird's nest beard halfway down his thatched chest. I did my best not to let my gaze wander any lower, but from the glimpse I caught, let's just say the rabbi who'd circumcised centuries before had had his work cut out for him.

"Farvas?" *Why?* Levi growled in an accent thick as the maple syrup I harvested each spring from my sugar bush.

I met his eyes, a feat easier said than done. Above a scowling thin-lipped mouth, long slightly crooked nose, and tan leathery cheeks, a pair of close-set hawk's eyes pinned me like I was a rabbit caught out in an open field. As always, their color was hard to pinpoint. Swamp green at the moment, though other times pale turquoise. I'd even once seen them a burning gold. He glared at me below eyebrows bushy with corkscrew hairs like those of a madman. Which I sometimes wondered if he was, that I'd made a mistake in reciting the Kabbalistic prayers that roused him from his sleep.

"It's closed," I shrugged, doing the trick of looking between his eyes to avoid that withering stare. Truth was, the general store had been open. But the second I'd set foot inside, the sixty-something proprietor had been hacking up a lung, obviously infected with the latest variant. And so, despite my N95 mask, I turned my asthmatic ass around and headed home. "But there's eggs." I held out the basket like a peace offering.

" *Why?*" Levi asked again—my mind instantly translating the Yiddish—a bit louder this time.

Terrified he'd sniffed out my lie, I darted my eyes past him into the cabin. All sorts of green plants, unlit Shabbat candles, and, it looked like, bones, strewn across my Bubby's walnut dinner table.

"Everyone's sick!" I snapped, and then immediately cowered before him. "I'm sorry, Levi. It's like they're *all* sick, all the *time*."

Levi ignored me, yanking his black wool cloak from the peg on the door and draping it over his well-preserved body.

"*Your little plague has become tiresome,*" Levi sighed.

I wasn't sure if he called it a "plague" because that was his only point of reference from the olden days. Or because he was making fun of this new virus, which, while killing over a million Americans and probably tens of millions worldwide, permanently disabling countless more, was nothing like the Black Death, smallpox, or the other contagions Levi had lived through. I wasn't even sure if he was susceptible to the sickness, or any for that matter. My guess is viruses and bacteria are as flitting gnats to ones such as Levi, who swim far deeper currents than the surface ripples the rest of us call life.

"I'm with you on that," I said. Unfortunately, not only didn't the residents of Moss Hollow take the pandemic seriously, they insisted the whole thing was a hoax. A worldwide conspiracy to subjugate the citizenry for some grand nefarious purpose they could never quite articulate, with not a few blaming us Jews. Even though almost everyone in town was sick again with the latest highly contagious strain—and pretty badly, since few were vaccinated—with three more dead that week to add to the previous two years' toll of forty-seven. What with my asthma, I avoided town as much as possible, making only bi-weekly trips in for animal feed, dried goods, and necessary odds and ends.

"*Gather the sick tomorrow evening,*" Levi said, spearing me with those angry eyes, now a stormy grey. "*And I shall heal them.*"

My jaw dropped. I had no doubts about Levi's abilities, of course. Indeed, his powers were the reason I'd tracked him down in the swampy wilds of Lithuania, in hopes that some of them might rub off on me after a lifetime of social, financial, and other failures. My surprise was simply that he'd be showing his face in Moss Hollow for the first time.

"*But first you must fetch the salt,*" Levi grumbled and strode out the door barefoot, presumably on another of his herb walks, or whatever it was he did out in the forest every day except Shabbat.

I had work to do, including burying my cat. But if Levi could really cure the whole town, how could I not make that my priority? It wasn't like poor Schlomo was going anywhere.

Levi loping off between a pair of fat oaks, I paced the pinewood floors and faded hook rugs of my rustic cabin, past my father's leather chair, my zaydee's antique rolltop desk, the iron woodstove fitted into the stone fireplace. How could I get all those hillbillies into one place at the same time?

In any normal town, a pop-up medical clinic would've done the job. But even the sickest and frailest Moss Hollowites were choosing to die gasping in their beds instead of admitting they were sick at all. Clearly, I was going to have to trick them.

But how? A chili dinner? A night of bingo?

Then I had it. And hurried to the phone, a landline on the desk, as my cell didn't work hardly at all in the sticks.

I dialed the number of the only local I could call an ally—if not quite a friend—Constable Phil. Though the friendly, back-slapping loudmouth had a good thirty years on me, we bonded over our common roots in New York City; I, from a conservative Jewish family, him, Greek Orthodox. That and the fact that we weren't in denial about the pandemic and therefore hadn't gotten sick.

"Hello?" Instead of Phil's raspy voice, a woman's soft one.

"Oh, I'm sorry," I blurted, "must have the wrong number."

"Who are you looking for?" The voice was quiet and breathy, like a breeze in the maples.

"Constable Phil."

"He's out on a call right now, but I'd be happy to take a message."

"Can you tell him Aaron called?" I was impatient to hang up and get everything ready for the next day.

"Sure, what about?"

I paused. "Who's this?"

"His daughter, Ellie. I'm in town for a few weeks." Silly as the thought was, my impression from the liquid tones of her voice was that she had to be pretty. "He's gonna want to know why you called."

"Alright..." Twining the cord around a dirty finger, I explained how I was hosting a raffle Thursday night at the Meeting House and would be leaving free tickets in everyone's mailbox. But to claim the five-hundred-dollar prize you'd have to be there in person. "Think Phil would be up for hosting?"

"You're not charging for tickets?"

"No..."

"So, you're just giving away five hundred bucks?" she asked, flatly.

Damn, it was a good point. I'd been so busy scheming to get everyone together I hadn't offered a plausible reason for my seeming generosity. Drops of sweat ran down my forehead, and I wiped them away with a sleeve of my flannel.

"You're that farmer out by the Park, aren't you?" It sounded like an accusation.

"I am." Wincing, I wondered how much Phil had told his daughter. Whether he'd let on that I was the town outcast barely eking by, all alone on his dumpy little farm.

"Dad says you've got the best eggs in the 'dacks."

"I don't know about that." I couldn't help but sniff at her use of the tourist abbreviation.

But speaking of eggs, it'd be a good time to boil up a few for Levi, the only food I'd ever seen him eat. Pinning the phone between my ear and shoulder, I grabbed a saucepan from the hook, filled it halfway with sink water, set it on the gas stove, and turned on the burner. "Though I do try to keep my hens happy."

"Happy hen, happy men," Ellie said, I assumed as a play on the old, "Happy wife, happy life."

"So I've heard," I said, a note of sadness creeping in at the fact that I hadn't had a date in years, which I quickly covered up with a laugh.

"Oh, I get it. The raffle's like an ad for your farm."

Dingdingdingdingding! "Yeah, of course," I went along with her genius idea. "To advertise fall shares for my CSA. You know, Community Supported Agriculture"

"I'm familiar. And he's in!"

I was confused. "Wait, is Phil there?"

"No, but you know how much my dad loves a crowd."

It was true, Constable Phil was quite the yapper. Luckily, everyone loved his stories, particularly about his years as an NYPD beat cop.

Just one nagging worry as I grabbed six brown eggs from the fridge. The kids. Again, I didn't doubt Levi could cure these folks of a simple respiratory virus. But it would still be an experiment, and I'd sleep a lot better knowing Levi tested it on the adults first.

Which meant I'd have to mention on the raffle flyer that no children were allowed. Moss Hollow's underage population was probably around three dozen, with maybe a third of those old enough to stay home by themselves. But what about the younger ones? I plunked the eggs in the saucepan and clanged on the lid.

"You wouldn't know someone willing to watch about twenty kids during the raffle?" I asked, hoping against hope. "The schoolhouse has a playground."

"Are you kidding?"

I hung my head, knowing I'd gone too far. "I could pay—"

"No, this is perfect! I'm a tutor and was looking for a way to pick up some students."

68

"You sure?"

"Trust me, you'd be doing me a favor."

"Okay!" In my excitement, I flung out a hand and singed my pinky against the hot pan. But even a burned finger couldn't dampen my mood. Over the previous six years—especially the two of the pandemic—I'd seen nothing but stingy selfishness from the vast majority of Moss Hollow residents, the opposite of the small-town neighborly vibe I'd hoped for after escaping the city.

Ironically, it took an outsider to finally make me feel welcome. "I'll drop off a flyer with the details and two tickets for you and Phil."

"Sounds great," Ellie said. "Thanks so much for doing this. It's a really sweet gesture."

"Of course. And thank *you*." Her kind words almost made me forget my burnt finger as I went to hang up the phone. "Oh yeah," I said before I did. "You don't, by chance, have any sea salt?"

After milking Sarah, Rebecca, and Rachel and letting them back into the pasture, I went into my tiny barn bedroom, sat at the desk, and flipped open my laptop. I put together a template for the raffle tickets, numbering each up to one hundred—the rough number of townies still alive. I connected the laptop to the printer, which spat out the dozen sheets, and I cut the tickets with a rusty scissors.

Next, the flyer. A half hour of tinkering later, the final heading read: $500 **RAFFLE DRAWING AT THE MEETING HOUSE - THURSDAY @ 7 PM**

Underneath, I included a photo I'd taken years before of the old white and green peak-roofed historic building. Then below that: MUST BE PRESENT TO CLAIM PRIZE! (18+ ONLY, FREE CHILDCARE AT SCHOOLHOUSE)

Then, at the bottom: BROUGHT TO YOU BY ADAMAH FARM. SIGN UP NOW FOR FALL CSA SHARES.

I set the printer for fifty black and white copies, hoping the ink would make it all the way through, and left the bedroom to where poor Schlomo lay in his canvas burial shroud on the workbench.

Shaking my head, frog in my throat, I tried to tell myself he was just another farm animal. That I didn't get all upset when I killed a chicken or a goat died. But the truth was that Schlomo had been more than a farm animal or even a pet. He'd been a friend.

"Tonight, buddy." I laid my hand on his rigid form. "I promise."

Once the flyers were ready—the last dozen or so streaky but readable—I got into my rickety blue Datsun pickup and started the ignition, the smell of French fries wafting up from the recycled vegetable oil I used for fuel. I rolled down the narrow, rutted driveway along the pasture and then into the forest out of which my hardscrabble farm had been hacked a century and a half ago by some French hermit. A good thing, as the only reason I'd been able to afford the place was because the trees had half swallowed it back up.

Past the open metal gate, onto the smooth wide county road, through the last half-mile of Adirondack Park. Where public land ended and private began was painfully obvious, sloppy swaths cut out of the hardwoods for lumber, firewood, and ATV/snowmobile trails.

I reached the driveway for Winslow's cattle farm and got out to stick the flyer and three tickets—one for him, his wife, and teenage daughter—in the mailbox, the vinegar tang of fermented cow shit sharp in my nostrils. Back in the truck past more logged-out woods to drop flyers with the appropriate number of tickets at every mailbox, some right in front of the ramshackle cabins and trailers, others at the end of dirt driveways snaking into the trees.

Another twenty or so mailboxes as the cabins turned into brightly painted two and three-story houses closer to town. Then into Moss Hollow itself, past the iconic red schoolhouse, rundown general/hardware store, post office, stone church, Mickey's, the town's one eating/drinking establishment, and through the crossroads featuring the pride of Moss Hollow: the stately, perfectly preserved Meeting House, circa 1806.

I delivered to the dozen or so houses down Main Street. At the town limits where the dirt road skirted another ten miles of uninhabited Park into the neighboring village of Goshen, I pulled A U-turn. Then doubled back to Old Swamp Road and the former farms tucked back in amongst the thickets of leafy trees.

At the dead end by the turnaround sat the constable's yellow farmhouse with its newly mown lawn, which he'd kept up surprisingly well the three years since his wife's passing. I opened the mailbox, and, sure enough, a pound sack of sea salt along with a note in a neat flowery script: *Dad said he's good to go for the raffle, and we'll take it from here! -Ellie*

Smiling, I grabbed the salt, folded the note to put in the back pocket of my jeans, shoved in a flyer and two raffle tickets, and closed the mailbox. Then opened it again to slip in eight more tickets.

As I got back into the pickup, motion from the corner of my eye. The front door to the farmhouse opened and a very short—under five feet, for sure—dark-haired woman, barefoot in long white flowing dress, stepped out on the porch. She waved. Ellie. My heart thrumming like a grouse's wings against a hollow log, I waved back. But somehow instead of going over to talk to her, as a single man like me should, my legs brought me back inside the truck.

Driving away, I asked myself why I'd left without saying hello. Sure, I was nervous after years of isolation. But it had to be more than that.

As I sped through town kicking up a rooster tail of dust, I wondered if it was maybe because I figured that the phone call and wave from across the yard were as good as things were going to get between us. Either she wouldn't be interested, and I'd have to add on yet another rejection to the list. Or worse, she'd totally be into me, and *I'd* soon feel trapped. Or even more terrible, we'd fall in love, have a few incredible years together, only for her to get sick and die, leaving me torn and broken.

"Thanks, but no thanks," I said out loud to no one as I trundled along the dirt road through the thick forest, chasing the smeary sunset.

It was dark by the time I got back to the farm. A bright green light flashed from the cabin windows along with a deep bone-shaking rumble I could almost but not quite hear. I might not have love, but I was grateful to have Levi with me working on a cure.

I shooed the chickens into the hutch and went into the barn. I tried not to look at Schlomo in his sack on the workbench, promising myself I'd bury him in the morning. Then into my cramped makeshift bedroom, stripped off my clothes, and dove into bed. Perhaps the greatest gift of farm work is that it leaves me exhausted at the end of the day, and I fell asleep within minutes.

I opened sticky eyes to early morning sunlight oozing through the one window and a warm weight on my chest. What the—

Yelling, I rolled out of bed and fell hard on my side on the wood floor. With a friendly meow, a black cat leapt off the bed to nuzzle against my chin. I grabbed the animal by the nape, knowing it couldn't be him. Just another stray that showed up at the strangest time imaginable.

But I inspected his face down to the white patch around his muzzle and his whole body. It sure as hell looked like Schlomo. Except this one's throat was intact, not torn to shreds. And his fur was perfect, not so much as a cut from head to toe. I let out a breath. Not Schlomo. Unless...

Levi! He'd brought him back to life! Perhaps as a thank you for all I'd done for the man.

Tears of joy streaming down my face, I kissed my friend on the top of his fuzzy head, set him down on the floor, and went to the mini fridge to pour him a fresh bowl of goat's milk.

I would've gone to run and thank Levi, but clearly he'd been hard at work all night reviving Schlomo, and I needed to let him rest for his task later that evening. I went to the coop to pick out the four largest eggs and left the basket on the cabin porch.

Over the next several hours I hoed the carrots, beets, and cabbages and replaced the drip irrigation pipe around the chard. Around noon I knocked on the cabin door—the eggs still in the basket—but Levi didn't answer. I harvested peppers for the next couple of hours and then tried again at the cabin. Still no answer.

I herded the goats into the pasture, and, after locking the chickens in the hutch, moved the portable fence a few yards to a fresh patch of grass. By five, I figured it was time to bring Levi into town. I wasn't sure if he had any preparing to do at the Meeting House—I didn't know the details, it wasn't for me to ask—but I certainly didn't want him to be late.

My knock unanswered yet again, I went inside. Empty. The bedroom door was open, but Levi wasn't there, just the piece of bare plywood on which he slept. No one in the bathroom, either, though I was pretty sure he took care of all that in the woods.

Apparently, Levi had found his way into town without me, maybe hitched a ride with some farmer. The *asshole.* Alarmed, I scanned the cabin in case he was there hiding, petrified he'd heard my thoughts. Silly, perhaps, but you don't know Levi like I do.

I hurried out to my truck, telling myself Levi needed my help. Of course, if that'd been the case, he would've asked for—no, demanded it. Truth be told, I think I just wanted to see him work his magic.

Down the driveway, through the gate, to the county road. Then three miles outside town, the pickup staggered and tilted. I choked the wheel, and, resisting the urge to stomp the brake, gently feathered the pedal until I came to a stop on the side of the empty road. A goddamn flat.

Muttering curses, I got out of the truck and knelt down to see how bad it was. A nail had been sunk deep into the tread—probably from the previous day's trip into town—leaked all evening and finally gave out.

I went around back and lugged the spare from the bed. It, too, was soft, a six-inch gash along the wheel well. And let it drop back into the bed.

It wasn't the first time I'd had vandals—on Halloween, the high schoolers had the irritating tradition of egging my barn with my own supply—but this was certainly ratcheting things up. Of course, everything had gotten worse during the pandemic, which I knew more than a few Moss Hollowites blamed on "the globalists," a term often used interchangeably as code for Jews like me.

I grabbed my headlamp from the glove compartment along with my N95 and hand sanitizer from the passenger seat and started off at a jog. I covered some ground, but after maybe a half mile I got winded and had to stop to catch my breath. Farm work made me good at moving heavy stuff around, but I was still forty pounds overweight, not to mention the asthma. I took a toot from my puffer and speed-walked down the dirt road as the sun set in marmalade, praying I wouldn't miss the show.

About an hour later, I made it into town. My cell said 7:12, which meant everyone who was going to had probably already shown up at the church. But maybe Levi hadn't worked his magic yet, and I still had time.

A guitar strummed from behind the dark schoolhouse. Curious, I peeked around the corner. A cozy, rock-ringed campfire was burning, maybe twenty kids, from toddlers to teens, sitting or standing around the fire, the older ones feeding the flames with sticks.

Ellie was singing about the River Jordan in a high, slightly off-key voice, "Look at that cold Jordan, look at its deep water." Boring Jesus stuff, but for some reason I couldn't put my finger on, it my made heart ache. Breaking myself out of the spell, I turned away and hustled down the road, dozens of pickups parked on the shoulder.

Draped in his black cloak, Levi stood in the middle of the crossroads looking ten feet tall, a combination of the low light and the fact that his bare feet floated inches off the dirt. I'd never seen him do anything, well, *magical* before, and as much as it unnerved me to see him levitate, I couldn't look away.

The Meeting House itself was engulfed in a deep green haze, like smog but thicker. It pulsed like a strobe shot through with flashes of black lightning. Some sort of healing vapor with the slightest whiff of menthol.

The night was silent, and no sounds from inside the Meeting House either. Just that bone-deep throb I'd felt earlier at the farm. I stood there agape, marveling at Levi working his famous powers, proud of myself for making it all happen.

After only a few minutes, the green fog dimmed and faded, and Levi settled down onto the street. With a downward chop of one hand, the mist broke apart, its tendrils swirling off into the dark forest.

Levi strode over to stand before me, eyes glowing with a green fire. "*It is done*," he muttered in his native Yiddish, and set off down the road.

"Thank you, Levi!" I waved after him as he blended into the night.

Time to see how well he'd performed. Even if he'd only managed to heal a few of them, it would still be a miracle. Maybe I could convince him to try again with more people. I pictured Levi standing on second base in Yankee Stadium, curing tens of thousands of coughing, sneezing, wheezing fans in one fell swoop. And while Levi, the star player, would get the applause—rightfully so—I'd know some of it would also be for me, his manager.

I put on my mask and walked up the stone path to the Meeting House. But when I tugged on the tall front door, it wouldn't budge. Luckily, I knew a back way in and snuck around to the kitchen entrance. It was unlocked, and I strolled through the outdated industrial appliances and swung open the door.

It smelled like it always did in the high-ceilinged hall, a mixture of dust, mold, and body odor. I stopped short. Five rows of metal folding chairs, all empty. Not a single freaking person had shown up?!

But then I got closer. And it was as if I'd forgotten how to breathe. I stripped off my mask and fumbled for my puffer, taking three deep draws before my lungs remembered how to take in oxygen.

People *had* shown up for the raffle. Most of the town, it seemed, based on the several dozen piles of fine grey ash on nearly every chair, the floor, and along the sides of the room. And one on the stage behind the podium that could've only been Constable Phil.

Levi had, indeed, ended the pandemic in Moss Hollow. Not by curing the sick of the virus, as I'd wanted. But by burning every single one of the infected to a crisp.

Drain

As I lay in bed, leafing through my old hardcover copy of *Talking To Heaven*, a tickle on my wrist. Some sort of beetle the size of an apple seed, flat and brown, crawled up my arm as if out for an evening stroll. I shrieked and blew it onto the nightstand.

I'm guessing it's because I've lived in the city my whole life that I've never been a fan of bugs. Spiders hunched in dark corners. Bloated worms rotting on the sidewalk. Fruits flies buzzing around the sink in a cloud of filth. I know insects are a part of nature, but so are viruses—just because something's natural doesn't mean it's good.

I snatched a tissue from the box, draped it over the thing as it tried to scurry off the edge of the nightstand, and smashed it with the spine of my book. Wadding up the tissue, I flushed it down the toilet. And flushed again.

Back in bed, I closed my eyes and tried to sleep. But an Internet factoid kept creeping into my mind, how the average person supposedly swallows eight spiders a year in their sleep. Throat scratchy, I scurried to the bathroom for a glass of water and an Ambien, then burrowed under the covers and fell asleep.

The next morning, I awoke having all but forgotten about the encounter. I held a session across town, browsed the aisles at a used bookstore, and spent my usual quiet evening at home, this night with a filet of salmon, pint of mint chocolate chip, and a *Twilight Zone* marathon on the SyFy Channel.

Three days later, while stripping my bed sheets, another of the disgusting bugs bumbled across my mattress like a cursor on a computer screen. Without thinking, I brushed it on the floor with the back of a hand and stomped, mashing it into the carpet with the heel of my slipper. I lifted my foot to make sure it was dead. Motionless, it stuck to my sole.

I took off the slipper and brought it over to the computer. Typed "indoor insects" into the search engine and sifted through a nightmare gallery of cockroaches, pill bugs, and centipedes before I had a match. A wave of nausea swept through me. It was a goddamn *bedbug*.

Weren't bedbugs for messy people? But my apartment was spotless! Which meant they were coming from someplace else, probably that meathead down the hall, the stink of a locker room seeping out from under his door.

I did more research and learned the nasties had become increasingly common over the past few decades, for whatever reason. The only good news was that, although they could bite—sucking blood like mosquitoes and ticks—they weren't disease carriers. Some consolation.

Though it was almost midnight, I called my landlord, demanded that he send an exterminator the next morning, and hung up before he could make any of his excuses. I yanked off the bedsheets and shoved the mattress on the floor but didn't find any more of the bastards. A couple of Ambien later, I curled up on the living room couch under the afghan, and, scratching the occasional imaginary itch, watched *I Dream of Jeanie* reruns until I fell asleep.

A ring woke me late the next morning. It took a few confused seconds to figure out it was my doorbell—sadly, it'd been that long since I'd had a visitor. I jolted up from the couch and raced to the door, eye against the peephole. A man in a red and blue uniform stood there.

The exterminator told me I'd need to "vacate the premises" for the next six hours, which was perfect since I had a session, anyway. I got dressed and left, relieved to be escaping the infestation, if only for the day.

My client was a tiny, quivering Lithuanian widow whose sprawling Victorian smelled like onions. She wanted to speak with her husband, gone for almost twenty years. Her cold dry hand clutching mine, I tried to establish contact for nearly two hours but to no avail.

"The spirit world is elusive," I told her with a shrug. "We can try again tomorrow."

When I asked for my modest fee, she grunted up from her chair, shuffled to the closet, and came back gripping a broom. Jabbering in a foreign tongue, the awful woman literally swept me from her kitchen, down the hallway, and out the front door, which the ingrate slammed in my face.

Teeth clenched against my rage, I called a cab to take me to the pharmacy so I could refill my old Xanax prescription, which, thankfully, was still good. I popped one on the way out the door, and, calmer than I'd felt in days, strolled the sunny sidewalks for some window-shopping.

To distract my mind away from my vermin-filled home, I killed a couple of hours at a coffee shop, sipping a latte and browsing tabloids. A scruffy teenager played an acoustic guitar in the corner, fingers scrabbling over the strings like a Daddy-longlegs. It might've been the amplifier, but when he sang a second voice in the background, faint and trembling, wove in off-key harmonies.

Before long, six hours had passed, and it was time to go back to my apartment. But I didn't want to. I dug my cell from my purse and called Arianne.

"Can you hold on a sec, hun?" Arianne said. I leaned against a lamppost, phone against my ear, listening to roaring laughter and what might've been a brass section. "Okay, I'm back."

"So good to hear your voice," I blurted, tearing up, happy to be speaking to the only person in the city I could honestly call a friend. "First—and you won't believe this—I found a bedbug in my apartment. An actual bedbug! So, of course, I got the place fumigated."

"Really," Arianne said, barely audible over blaring trumpets.

"And then one of my clients wouldn't even—"

"Don't you dare!" Arianne screeched in my ear.

I held the phone away from my face. "What?"

"Not you, hun. Someone else," Arianne said. "Know what, babe? This really isn't a good time. I'm in New York. With Gil." She whispered the last part.

I didn't know who Gil was but figured he had to be Arianne's latest paramour. "Sugar daddies," she called them, which she explained wasn't sex work because *she* chose *them*.

"I'm really having a hard time here," I almost sobbed. "Could I maybe stay at your—"

Arianne sighed irritably. "I can barely hear you. How about you fill me in when I get back, okay? Love ya!" A smacking kiss, and she hung up.

I stood there with the phone in my hand beside the swarming traffic, berating myself for expecting anything—anything at all—from that selfish creature.

When I got back to the apartment, the exterminator was gone. The smell wasn't bad, just a faint trace of something metallic. I opened the windows to let in the cool early autumn air, switched on the ceiling fan, and lit a few vanilla candles.

My heart crammed in my throat, I tiptoed into the bedroom as if sneaking up on an unfaithful lover. Holding my breath, I inspected the top of the mattress, flipped it over. Reluctantly, I knelt down to look under the bed. All clean. I let out a sigh.

Every day for the next week I scrutinized my bed, carpet, dresser drawers, and closets for signs of the invaders. Nothing. They were gone. I could relax again.

Four mornings later I woke to find one of the horribles squatting on my pillow, inches from my face, like a mint left behind by housekeeping. Gagging, I carried the pillow at arm's length over to the balcony, sliding the torn screen door open with my foot. Then tossed the whole thing over the railing to watch it plummet seventeen stories to the street below. Suddenly exhausted, I crumpled into a ball on the cement. I cried a little.

The exterminator came back that afternoon. "Sorry," he said with a sheepish smile. "Must've missed some eggs on the first sweep. Mind if I take a look?"

"That's your job, isn't it?" I snipped, not about to be taken advantage of again.

Sliding a flashlight from a hip holster, he went into the bedroom while I vacuumed the living room carpet for the second time that day.

After maybe ten minutes I noticed him standing there looking at me. I shut off the vacuum.

"I didn't find anything," he said, almost accusingly.

"Must not have looked very hard," I shot back.

"Sure they were bedbugs?"

Annoyed now, I clenched the handle of the vacuum. "Positive."

"There's no sign of them." He scowled, as if blaming me for his own subpar work.

"You think I'm making this up?"

He paused a bit too long before answering, which made me furious. "I don't know, lady." He shrugged. "If your landlord's paying for it, I'll bomb the place again."

Satisfied, I nodded. "Make sure you get them all this time," I spat, and fled the apartment to catch a film.

The next week, I discovered two of the monsters on my headboard. The room swam for a moment before I got ahold of myself. Then I punched each of them dead with a bare fist, blood trickling from my split knuckle.

On my hands and knees I inspected the carpet. What if they were breeding under there? I crawled to the corner to see if I could pull up an edge. No, but there were a few tiny brown turds. For Christ's sake, not only did I have bedbugs, mice were setting up shop, too!

I must've sounded like a madwoman when I called my slumlord, as he kept telling me to "settle down," that he couldn't understand what I was saying.

I calmed myself enough to insist he send over another exterminator right away or I'd "burn the place to the ground." Needless to say, I took a double dose of Xanax.

By noon, a new exterminator in a brown jumpsuit showed up, and I checked in to a four star hotel. Despite my meager bank account, I needed to feel clean, if only for a night. You better believe I scoured every inch of that room to make sure it was pristine before I lay down on the ivory comforter.

I slept okay despite the occasional grunt, groan, or sigh from the bathroom—like someone relieving himself—startling me awake a few times. My phantom urinator aside, I was comfortable in the plush and immaculate room, and in no rush to head back home. I ended up staying for three nights, which cost almost a thousand bucks, part of a good month's income. And it hadn't been a good month.

Finally, nowhere left to hide, I trudged back to my apartment, dread scalding my insides as if I'd swallowed a pot of hot soup. I unlocked the door and sniffed the air, encouraged by the strong metallic stink. Chewing my lower lip, I marched straight into the bedroom.

I'm proud to say I didn't make a peep when I found five of the sons of bitches cavorting on the nightstand. One at a time, I crushed them between my fingers and smeared their carcasses against the wall as a warning to the others.

Obviously, getting rid of the wretched beasts was beyond the ability of some rip off exterminator. Like everything else, it was going to be up to me. I dry swallowed another couple of Xanax.

Back on the Internet, I spent hours reading up on the crawling freaks, eventually clicking on a page with close-up photos of insects that looked like—but weren't—bedbugs. A cousin of bedbugs, bat bugs lived in caves and fed on the blood of roosting bats.

I thought back to the poop I'd found in the corner. Could it have been from a bat instead of a mouse? Had one found its way into the apartment— through my torn screen door, maybe—bugs hitching a ride on its veiny wings?

I did some more research, learned how there were over a thousand species of the hideous flying rats, how they were supposed to be so great because they pollinated flowers and ate mosquitoes, and how millions of them were dying from some fungus that grew on their faces. Good riddance.

As the night grew late, I found myself on a website about vampire bats, the South American species that drank cow's blood...along with the occasional sleeping human's.

When I finally fell asleep, I dreamt of Casper, my childhood kitty, twining around my legs. Except when I bent down to pet him, a torrent of yellow maggots spilled out of his empty eye sockets and piled in a squirming mass around my ankles. I woke drenched in sweat, ran to the bathroom, stripped off my nightgown, and examined my entire body for bites. All clean, false alarm.

Curious what the dream meant, I logged onto Occultopedia.com, which explained how cats could be familiars for vampires. I laughed out loud. Still, for no other reason than to occupy my mind, I kept reading and learned that familiars didn't have to be cats, they could be any sort of creature. Like insects, I wondered?

Yes, I'm a medium who was born with the ability to speak to the dead. That doesn't mean I believed in vampires. I turned off the computer, checked my sheets and pillows—all clear, thank heavens—took two Xanax and two Ambien, and shut off the light.

I woke again in the middle of the night scratching my neck. Hit the light, flung off my nightgown mid-sprint to the bathroom to stare at my pale goose-bumped flesh in the mirror. Eyes blurry from sleep, it took me a few seconds to make sure it was real.

Lifting my chin to get a better look, I traced a finger over a pair of red spots on my jugular vein. The bites, two inches apart, almost looked like fang marks. Dizzy, I sat down hard on the closed toilet lid.

I'm not naïve, but years of communicating with the dead taught me to have an open mind. If there are lost souls among us yearning for contact, then are the undead really that much of a stretch? Clearly not, I finally accepted.

It was three in the morning, but I had to tell the world what I'd uncovered. I called Arianne, but of course it went to voice mail. I rushed over to the computer and, typing in a frenzy, dashed off emails to the local TV, newspaper, and radio outlets explaining my revelation.

How it's not only bats that can be a vampire's familiar but bat bugs, too. How the bats find their way inside a home, carrying the bugs, which siphon off the victim's blood and crawl back to their master to feast.

After all, if you're a hungry vampire, why go to the trouble of a restaurant when you can get home delivery, lying in bed (in coffin?) as you pop one blood-filled insect after another into your mouth like bonbons? I implored the journalists to do their jobs for once and report on what was happening, before it was too late.

I shut the computer and paced around my apartment, smacking the side of my head, trying to get the thoughts to flow. I had to accept that, even if the authorities got involved, it wouldn't be in time to save me. As always, I was on my own. I scratched the bites on my neck until they bled.

Obviously, it was pointless to try to stop the bat from coming in. The bugs were already there, breeding under the carpet, behind the furniture, in the walls. Like unwanted houseguests, as long as I kept the refrigerator full—in this case, my veins—they weren't going anywhere. I laughed at the idea of the vampire bugs as some deadbeat relatives mooching off my hospitality. And kept laughing, until the answer came to me.

My plan was simple but brilliant. I'd go out and buy a bottle of wine and drink a few glasses. Then I'd let the little shits suck down my alcohol-tainted blood and bring it back to their boss, who'd spit out his spoiled meal, call off his minions, and never trouble me again. If the tactic worked, I could share it with others, and maybe we could start to rid the city—the world?—of the bloodsuckers.

Sure enough, I found a couple of them on the nightstand the next day. Having them where I wanted, I just smiled. Defiantly, I polished off the rest of the wine along with a double dose of pills.

There were a few more on the bedspread the next morning, but I refused to panic. I went out and bought some scotch, took slugs from the bottle until I passed out.

I woke up hours later and found a spot of blood on my nightgown just above my left breast. Still numb from the alcohol, I watched myself go through the motions of taking off my gown, running cold water over it from the bathroom sink, and dabbing the spot with a paper towel. Then fell to my knees with the futility of it all.

It had been stupid to think that the vampire would somehow be put off by my blood alcohol level. For all I knew, it was a treat for him, like a sweet after-dinner Riesling. There was no beating this, no happy ending.

Nude and in a daze, I walked out to the balcony, nightgown in hand, and gazed down at the city, yellow streetlights strung out like a garland of fireflies. He was out there somewhere, laughing at me, knowing that I belonged to him—knowing that *I* knew it, too—and there was nothing I could do about it.

My chest felt tight, like a mousetrap ready to spring. I wanted to cry, but I couldn't. I stared at the dark honeycomb windows of the apartment building across the street, wondering if any of them housed my vampire.

From a dead calm, the wind picked up. It blew through my hair, whooshed in my ears, almost like someone muttering. It was.

I couldn't understand, at first. As always, it seemed to come simultaneously from inside my head yet miles in the distance.

The wind died down. I shut my eyes and concentrated.

"Very close now," the paper-thin voice of an old man rasped. A warning? I couldn't recognize the speaker, but the accent sounded a lot like my Lithuanian client whose dead husband I'd failed to reach earlier that week. Seemed I'd made contact, after all.

I stared at the inner wrist of my hand clutching the blood-spotted nightgown, blue veins branching beneath translucent skin, anesthetized to the fear.

"Almost here," he said.

The dead had no reason to lie, and I was grateful to him for his counsel. I knew then what I had to do.

I flung the nightgown over the balcony, it floated to the street below like a white flag of surrender. With both hands, I gripped the cold railing and leaned forward.

A buzzing from the bedroom. My cell phone. Automatically, I walked inside, lifted it from the nightstand, and fingered it to life. I had a text and a voicemail.

The text was a dimly lit photo of Arianne with an older man. She wore too much eyeshadow, dyed yellow curls piled atop her head in a parody of elegance, evening gown cut desperately low. The man had a full head of white hair and was dressed in a tuxedo. He looked at something off camera, hand resting on the inside of Arianne's upper thigh.

In her voicemail, Arianne explained how she and Gil would be coming back into town that weekend and that she wanted me to meet him.

"Gil's very generous, you have no idea. I really hit the jackpot." A few seconds of silence before Arianne went on. "But he's got these quirks. And part of our arrangement is that I take care of them. So..." Arianne sighed. "I showed him your picture. And, well, he's interested. Which is why I need you to do me this one teensy favor and—"

Disgusted, I flung the phone across the bedroom, Arianne's voice still whining out demands from the carpet. Was she serious? As if I'd ever—

A thought jolted me like a cattle prod, and I leaned against the wall for support. Oh my God. Oh my God, it was *her*. It'd been her all along.

All the times I'd held that needy little floozy in my arms, consoling her after the latest guy tossed her away like a used tissue. The hours I'd spent listening to her drunken blubbering over the mess that was her life, her fading looks, the wrong choices she somehow couldn't stop making.

All the times I told myself she was a bad friend, how she took and took and never gave back. That the next time she banged on my door late at night, I'd ignore her.

But I never had the guts. I always let her in.

My neck tingled where I'd been bitten, and I scratched. When I took my hand away, my nails were streaked with red, like a sexy polish.

Unable to resist a sudden impulse, I plunged my fingers into my mouth and slurped up the blood.

Coppery sweet with a dash of salt, I was horrified to find that I was delicious.

Doing Without

March 7

All the diet gurus say I should keep a journal about my eating. Pretty dumb, but I've been trying to lose weight for ten years, and nothing's worked. At forty-one and 236 lbs., if don't do this now, I probably never will.

First step? Skip the after-dinner ice cream.

March 10

No dessert on Tuesday and Wednesday, but today I had a scoop with Jamie's birthday cake. Since I don't have the self-control to keep the stuff in the house, I dumped the rest down the sink.

March 16

Almost a full week without sugar, and I've lost two pounds! Then, this morning, I found myself rooting through the cabinet for a jar of honey. Like an addict, I scraped up the last spoonful and licked it down. That aside, the cravings aren't bad as they were. Just need to keep away from anything sweet, and Jamie's been very supportive about that.

March 19

Down another three to 231! Go me! Thing is, every time I drink I want sugar.

The verdict? No alcohol for a month!

March 24

Down four more pounds. I know I'm hardly svelte, but this is kind of a big deal for me. Jamie keeps telling me how good I look, and I swear I have more energy.

April 2

Haven't lost a single damn pound in over a week. Must've plucked the low hanging fruit, and if I don't do something else, I'll be stuck at 227 forever.

Going to have to ditch carbs. Ice cream and beer were just diversions, but is life even worth living without pasta, pizza, and potato chips?

April 13

I can't believe it, but the carb cravings are gone. Okay, not totally, but I'm enjoying meat and vegetables and beans and nuts more than I ever thought I would. And I'm down to 220!

April 19

213 and Jamie can't stop touching my new bod.

The other day I realized I'm using way too much salt and spices. So, I've been doing without, and, while at first everything was bland, the other flavors are now coming through. Almonds, which I'd never eaten except in a candy bar, taste like tropical flowers blooming in my mouth.

April 29

Weighed myself for the first time in weeks. Not only am I under 200, I'm an even 196!

Jamie says I'm turning into an anorexic, but that's silly. I'm not avoiding food, just realizing a lot of my eating was from stress or boredom. Trying smaller mouthfuls, more chewing, pacing myself instead of scarfing everything down. Only three small meals a day, and I'm totally satisfied.

May 23

Not weighing myself anymore but definitely in the best shape of my life.

Except the deeper lesson hasn't been about eating but craving sensation. In this modern cyberworld it's all about that dopamine hit, the noise and flashing colors killing our attention span. That's why I'm quitting all TV and movies and cutting off the internet.

Never seen Jamie more upset over nothing. I don't know what's going on with us anymore.

May 27

Jamie moved out last night. Why? Because I don't want to have sex all the time. The hyperstimulation drowns out everything else, and I just wanted a break.

Sad as I am, it's probably for the best. Jamie and I aren't compatible now. In fact, I'm starting to suspect relationships are only another kind of addiction.

June 2

Been talking on the phone to Mom and Dad a lot. Isn't conversation a crutch, too?

June 7

Boss wasn't keen on my week of silence, so next day came the pink slip. And while I know I should feel super anxious, I don't. Never liked that job anyway.

How much money do I even need? My food and electric bills are a quarter of what they were before. Biggest expense is rent. Which makes me wonder.

July 3

Landlord kicked me out after I tried to sublet the place so I could live in my tent in the backyard. No big deal, found a nice campsite in the woods near a pond. Speaking of which, I've shed so many of my addictions that one craving stands out like a sore thumb: water. But if I just eat fruits and leafy greens and don't move around a lot, I don't need more than half a liter a day.

July 25

Eating only a few leaves of kale, but I'm still thirsty. Luckily, I've been down this road before with everything else, and I know I'll get used to it.

August 5

Still not solved the water problem, but meditation takes my mind off it. I don't even read now, because when you strip away the distractions, all the entertainment you need is to breathe in and out, in and out.

August 14

Harsh realization this morning. The joy I get from meditative breathing is just more attachment. But when I sit very still, I can slow my heart beat down to where I don't need to take so many breaths.

August 17

Trying to hold my breath, counting up to ninety seconds.

August 21

Working on two minutes.

August 24

Reason I couldn't get to two minutes was it was too easy to sneak a breath. Until I started dunking myself in the pond, and problem solved! Now going for two and a half.

August 27

My body keeps pushing itself up to the surface when it gets low on air. So, I'm tying a rope to my ankle attached to a rock, which I'll only untie when I'm really out of breath.

September 5

Hard but made it to two minutes and forty seconds. I know I can get to three. A little risky, but so what?

After all, isn't consciousness—life itself for that matter—the worst addiction there is?

The Connecticut Witch Panic

1651, Wethersfield, Connecticut

The gallows cast its shadow on the whitewashed walls of the courthouse. At its foot, close to a hundred men, women, and children gathered silently on the frosty dead grass.

Side by side on the wooden platform stood a figure in drab shirt and pants and another in homespun dress, burlap sacks over heads, nooses around necks, hands behind backs. Next to them, a large man in black hood and robe set his hand on a wooden lever.

At the far corner, an elderly man in white wig and dark suit with broad white collar spoke solemnly to the prisoners. "Jonathan Reece. Joan Reece." Then, turning to the villagers, in a louder voice, "Having been found guilty of entertaining familiarity with Satan, the grand enemy of God and mankind, you must be hanged by the neck until death."

Muffled moans from the accused. The crowd pressed forward, unblinking eyes locked on the spectacle before them, not a few of them grinning. Towards the front, an elderly woman clutched a young boy by the shoulders, tears streaming down his chubby cheeks.

The judge nodded to the hooded man, who, without fanfare, yanked back the lever. The platform swiveled and dropped the captives to dangle, bare feet kicking inches above the grass.

Gasps, groans, and titters of laughter from the townsfolk. Sobs from the little boy. After a minute or so, the bodies hung limp, liquid dripping from their toes, swaying at the end of the ropes like fish at market.

Present day

Theo, shaking mad, tore his gaze away from the fireplace in the cozy den of his parents' modest home.

"So, my great-great-great-great-great-great grandparents?" he asked Pop-Pop, the older man's thin body, swimming in its cardigan, sunk halfway into the couch.

"Add one more great, and you got it," Pop-Pop said.

"Why didn't anyone tell me?"

"Your folks didn't want to upset you." Pop-Pop blew the steam away from the mug in his hands.

"I'm eighteen, not some little kid."

"Maybe they were afraid you'd overreact," Pop-Pop said softly.

"Why?!" Theo burst out. "How many times do I have to tell everyone that was a one-time thing—" and then took a deep breath, bowing his head in embarrassment. "I've been working on it."

With the sleeve of his fleece Theo wiped a circle of frost from the window. In the dusk, a tangle of yellow Christmas lights glowed in the branches of the lone spruce in the snow-crusted suburban yard half a dozen miles south of Hartford. One incident of chasing and *barely* rear-ending a guy who'd almost run him off the damn highway. Most of a year and six anger management classes later, he still couldn't live it down.

"I know you have. That's why I'm telling you now." As always, Pop-Pop was calm and engaging around him, no knitted forehead or silent scowl like his parents.

Theo plopped down on the couch, his lean one hundred and sixty pounds shifting the elder on his cushion. "Were they healers? Herbalists?"

Pop-Pop shook his head, which, despite approaching ninety, was still covered in a thick thatch of snowy hair. "Nothing but petty jealousy and score settling. As always."

"I thought they just went after women."

"That was most of it in the States. But in some parts of Europe the numbers were actually reversed." Grandpa took a careful sip. "And hereabouts, of the dozen they executed, almost all were men."

"Was this during the Salem trials?"

"Earlier. By a few decades."

Theo shook his head. A local, real-life horror movie. "Why didn't I hear about this at school?"

Grandpa laughed, bony shoulders hunching up and down in his sweater, which turned into a thirty-second phlegmy coughing fit. "The typical excuses. Leave the past in the past. Let bygones be bygones. No point in opening up old wounds."

"But if people don't know what happened, who's to say it won't go down the same way again."

Grandpa smiled admiringly at his grandson, and on that cold December evening it warmed Theo in a way the fire never could. For the first time Theo wondered if maybe his family being too poor to pay for assisted living was a blessing. And while Theo was happy to be out of the house for his first year of college, Pop-Pop was a major reason he'd picked a school less than an hour away.

Pop-Pop craned back his head to drain the last of his mug and set it down on the arm of the couch. "As Mr. Twain once said, 'History doesn't repeat itself, but it often rhymes.'"

The old man reached out a hand to Theo, a sign he wanted to get up. Theo took it and pulled his grandfather to standing with mutual grunts.

"Sleep tight," Pop-Pop said, and shuffled off towards his bedroom, leaving Theo with the fireplace flames eating away the cordwood.

It was Friday night, and Theo was due back at school on Monday. He was *supposed* to be reading another hundred pages from his journalism textbook. Instead, he hunched in front of his laptop at his old desk in his tiny childhood bedroom—rock posters on the wall, cross country trophies on the shelf over an unmade twin bed—and typed "Connecticut witches" into the search engine.

After scrolling past a bunch of Salem stuff, he clicked on an article from the New England Historical Society titled, "The Hartford Witch Panic." He took a long swig of beer and started to read.

In the early 1660s, a pre-teen girl came down with bad stomach pains after eating soup made by an elderly woman neighbor. Sweating, moaning, and convulsing in bed, the girl claimed the old lady was a witch attacking her insides. Soon, the girl died.

An autopsy found "unnatural" causes, though it was almost certainly accidental food poisoning, common in the days before refrigeration or even germ theory. Constables were sent to arrest the woman, but she'd already skipped town. And it seemed that unconsummated wrath set off a chain of witch accusations in the capital city.

Theo swiveled around in his chair to face the closed closet door. Without much effort he conjured up the heavy sense of dread he'd felt as a kid, refusing to sleep until his parents shut it against the monsters. That was pretty much how those superstitious people had lived every day. Shaking his head, he turned back to his computer and kept reading.

Over the decades, the hysteria swept up and down the Connecticut River to the neighboring towns of Farmington, Windsor, and Theo's native

Wethersfield. Luckily, in most cases, cooler heads prevailed, followed by acquittals. Though, sadly, not before nine men and two women were hanged, including Theo's great greats, listed by name in the article.

Finally, by the early seventeen-hundreds the mania lifted, and the law that made witchcraft a capital offense got scrubbed from the books. The article ended by recounting how descendants of the victims—no names, though Theo couldn't help but wonder if they were talking about Pop-Pop—had tried to get the state legislature to issue a formal apology, except it never got the votes to pass.

The findings, instead of giving Theo closure, only made him angrier. Hot as if with fever, he paced the creaky wooden floors of his room, mumbling curses.

Murder. Tearing families apart. Poverty and outcast status passed down through the generations. Even to the present day, what with Theo's father as a lowly toll booth attendant, and mother, who, as a nanny, had spent more time with rich people's kids than her own.

Forcing Theo to grow up wearing thrift-store clothes, playing with last year's toys. Lame camping trips to Maine instead of ski vacations to Aspen like his friends. No brand-new car when he turned sixteen, just a rusty bucket of bolts he was still driving years later. And, if it hadn't been for his cross-country scholarship, he wouldn't even have been able to get into a top-rated school without massive debt.

Burning like a pot left too long on the stove, Theo remembered the lessons from anger management: Feel the emotions, don't repress them, and then find a positive outlet to let them go.

As a journalist in training, he had a free subscription to Lexis-Nexis, the search engine for databases around the world. Making himself sit down again, he typed, "Wethersfield Connecticut judges."

Before long, he found a spreadsheet of judges back to when the state was officially settled in 1633. One name, Whitley Alaister, was listed over and over from 1648 until 1697. Theo double-checked the date of the

Wethersfield hanging—1651—and did a celebratory fist pump. He'd ferreted out his witchfinder, the shedder of his own blood.

Energized, Theo traced the Alaister name through the next two centuries, many who'd been prominent in local politics, business, and education. No surprise there, exploiting blood money to make a name for themselves. Not simply bad deeds gone unpunished but handsomely rewarded.

He got up and skated across the room in his socks, eager to tell Pop-Pop what he'd found. But as he opened the door to the quiet hallway remembered it was the middle of the night. And quietly closed it to sit back down at the computer. Besides, Theo had a feeling that the older man might not think it a worthwhile angle to pursue.

To his frustration, the trail ran cold in the early nineteen-hundreds, at which point the Alaister name almost completely disappeared, save a handful of obituaries of day laborers and seamstresses. And then, towards the end of the century, a few convictions for possession and distribution of narcotics as well as solicitation, aka sex work. He grinned. Could it be that karma had finally caught up with the monsters?

And then, through the eighties and nineties until the present day, only one hit. A 1991 Wethersfield High graduation announcement for one Charlie Alaister. Over a decade before Theo, which would make Charlie almost thirty. Could this be the last living descendant of the bastard who'd set the whole dark chain in motion?

Soon, Theo found three Wethersfield addresses tied to the name. And—Theo's rage flaring like a splash of water on an oil skillet—all in ritzy neighborhoods. Did this guy even know what his people had done? If he didn't, Theo was going to tell him. And if he *did* know, it was past time for accountability.

Theo barely slept that night. Tossing and turning as if in a rotisserie oven, the mattress a baking rack, the blankets sizzling tin foil, dreaming of Mom, Dad, Pop-Pop, and himself tied to stakes and burning alive.

Theo woke before anyone else, the house dark and quiet. After his car finally started on the third try in the frosty dawn, he typed the first address into his phone and set off. It took only ten minutes to leave behind his middle-class neighborhood with its ranch homes, small yards, and older sedans and pickups to another with three-story houses, huge snowy lawns, and fancy SUVs and sports cars. Even the Christmas decorations went from a few sad strings of lights to dazzling, candy-colored spectacles.

"Your destination is on the right," the phone told him, and Theo parked at the curb of a big red brick colonial, tennis court out front, Lexus in the driveway. He waited until the sun came up in bloody bandages, and, at seven a.m. on the dot, got out. Breath fogging in the cold, a little nervous and unsure what he was even going to say, he walked up the driveway to the wreathed front door.

He rang the bell and an older woman in a robe answered, greying hair and smile lines putting her in her early seventies. She smiled pleasantly and lifted her manicured eyebrows expectantly.

"Hi, does Charlie Alaister live here?" Theo asked, knowing he should smile back but somehow not able to.

She cupped her hand to an ear. "Come again?"

"Charlie. Alaister."

"I'm afraid not, dear. But maybe I can help you find—"

"That's okay, ma'am. Sorry to bother."

Theo turned on his heels, and, hands in pockets, slunk back to his car. One down, two to go.

The next address was fifteen minutes away in a part of town Theo had gone apple picking as a kid but was now, to his dismay, dotted with sterile McMansions. His target was a baby blue Victorian with turrets and arches strung with garish red lights, a giant inflatable Santa in the wide-open yard. A Land Rover, Tesla, and one of those ugly Porsche SUVs sat in the open garage. Could this be the place, the well-feathered nest of his family's predators?

Head held high, Theo strode up the path, morning air thawing somewhat as the sun rose higher. He poked the doorbell, and a dog yipped on the other side of the door. It opened to a husky boy in a sweatsuit, probably around twelve, with a yapping pug in his arms. Could this be Charlie Jr., next in line to inherit the dirty cash? An image flashed through Theo's mind of grabbing the kid and stuffing him in the trunk of his car for a ransom.

"Hi, your parents home?" Theo asked through a fake smile.

The kid nodded, sucked in a deep breath, and yelled out, "Daaaa—aaad!"

Moments later, a thirtysomething man, blond ponytail over a zip up hoodie, in faded jeans—a "cool Dad" who probably skateboarded and played video games—came to the door. He squinted. "Oh, you're not the Amazon guy."

Theo shook his head, searching the man's brown eyes for that spark of evil. "Does Charlie Alaister live here?"

"Wrong house, my dude."

Theo's shoulders slumped in disappointment. "You sure?"

The man nodded apologetically.

With a mumbled, "Okay, thanks," Theo moped off to his car. Two strikes. One more and he was out. And what was he supposed to do then? With the burden of knowledge on his shoulders, it wasn't like he could just drop it.

The next address was at the far edge of town in a neighborhood he'd never actually been before but knew was wealthy. His phone showed two routes to get there, one a straight shot from downtown. But from where he was, the winding route along the edge of the state forest was actually closer, only twenty minutes.

A few miles later, Theo passed an UNMAINTAINED ROAD sign, and Theo left all human habitation behind to bump along a pot-holed dirt road past thick naked oaks and maples and then an icy swamp. It was pretty in a lonely kind of way. After maybe fifteen minutes the road was paved again where the forest opened into snowy fields behind a high fence. Probably farmland once upon a time, now a handful of sprawling estates. He stopped at the dead end of a cul-de-sac where one of the driveways snaked along a dark patch of hemlocks, gate open.

Something inside of Theo told him he'd found his man. Of course, people like the Alaisters would live in a place like this. He shifted into gear and puttered up the driveway to a hulking ivory farmhouse—at least five thousand square feet—with three chimneys, the center one smoking. No Christmas decorations and behind the house was a well-kept barn, probably the garage, and behind that a carriage house.

Now that Theo was close his stomach churned. But there was no time for cowardice. He made himself get out of the car, walk up the shoveled and de-iced path to the massive front door, and banged with the brass knocker. Waited a minute, but no one answered. He knocked again, noticing, for the first time, a security camera overhead. Finally, the door opened, and a lean, dapper late-fifties man in a suit frowned down at him.

"May I help you?" the man—Charlie's father?—sneered.

Theo's heart thumped what felt like mere millimeters under his fleece. "I'm looking for Charlie Alaister."

The man sniffed. "How did you get up here? This is private property, you know."

"The gate was open. I need to speak to him."

A disdainful chuckle. "About?"

It was clear in an instant. This was the butler. "Family emergency," Theo lied without missing a beat.

"Is that so." The butler eyed him closely, as if trying to pick out a resemblance.

"We go way back," Theo said, truthfully enough.

A long stare and then a world-weary shrug. "Charlie's out back in the carriage house." He gestured vaguely with a hand.

Theo thanked him and set off behind the farmhouse along the path past the barn. He could barely believe that in less than a minute he'd be face to face with his mortal enemy. Butterflies swarmed in his belly.

The carriage house was teeny, no more than fifteen by fifteen, a couple of bushes out front, dead ivy climbing the white walls. Probably Charlie's man cave or art studio, whatever mega-wealthy people did in their heaps of spare time.

Theo had just gotten to the door when his cell buzzed from his pocket. He grabbed it. Mom. Declining the call, he put the phone on airplane mode.

This was it. Running on the clean burning fuel of righteousness, he couldn't remember the last time he'd felt so alive. He knocked, wondering if maybe his first move should be to punch the a-hole in the teeth.

A short, stocky woman with squarish face, wide-set sky blue eyes, and messy black hair draping the shoulders of a worn flannel shirt stepped outside, closing the door behind her. Not his type—he preferred tall blondes—but right up his roommate Gar's alley, who'd probably call her "juicy."

"Well, hello," she smiled up at him as if expecting company.

"I'm looking for Charlie," Theo said, a bit confused. "Charlie Alaister."

"Pleased to meet you." The woman held out a hand.

Theo stood there gaping. All this time, Charlie had been a woman? Finally, he remembered to take her hand. A jolt of static electricity made him jerk away with an embarrassed laugh.

"And who might you be?" she asked, almost flirtily.

"Me? I'm Theo—" he stopped himself before saying his last name.

"Nice to meet you, Theo." Charlie said, an amused—or was it, mocking?—glint in her eyes.

"You live here?"

"Live and work." She cocked her head. "Mostly work."

"What do you do, exactly?"

"Take care of the big house."

"You're the *maid?*" He hadn't meant it to come out that way, but none of this made any sense.

"Domestic cleaner." She furrowed her brow a second before smoothing it out. "Now, what can I do for you, Mr. Theo?"

At this point, he had no idea. This wasn't some rich dude rolling in ill-begotten dough but a disheveled toilet scrubber living in a shack. All the steam blown out of him, he thought about coming up with some excuse and going home.

Except this wasn't about him. It was about his family. And every family that'd borne the brunt of this particular rotten family tree...or been hung from its branches.

"Do you know who Whitley Alaister was?" Theo's voice shook in the glory of the moment.

"I do." Her eyes flared a split second before icing over again.

Theo waited a dramatic second before the killing blow. "Then you should know that your family murdered mine."

Charlie didn't flinch. Not even a blink. All she said was, "Come inside for a cup of tea?"

Caught off guard yet again, Theo could only nod and follow.

Inside was a small table with a couple of chairs, kitchenette with microwave and hotpot, neatly made twin bed in the corner, and open door leading to a half-bath. All about the size of Theo's dorm room.

Charlie gestured to one of the chairs, and he sat as she filled an electric kettle at the sink.

"Tell me what happened." She leaned her ample butt against the counter, staring him down with those frigid blue eyes.

Without preamble, he ran through a quick summary of the Hartford Witch Panic, Judge Whitley, his great-greats Jonathan and Joan. By the time the kettle hissed, Theo had laid it all out there and waited cross-armed for her reply.

Without a word, Charlie took two mugs from the draining board, fished around in the cabinet for a box of tea, and dropped a bag in each. She poured the water, brought the mugs to the table—as if he'd touch anything she served him—and sat down across from him with that same patronizing smile.

"You've got nothing to say?" Theo sniped, clenching his fists so hard the nails dug into his palms.

"What's there to say?" She sipped from the mug, steam blurring her face.

"Seriously?" Theo felt himself revving up again and took a deep slow breath through his nose to keep from redlining.

"Those were dark times."

"For some more than others," he shot back.

She shrugged a shoulder.

Okay, now Theo was pretty sure she was messing with him. "I'm here telling you you're the descendant of homicidal maniacs, and all you can do is sit there?"

She set down her mug softly. "Did I deny any of it?"

The slightest release of tightness in Theo's chest. Maybe they were getting somewhere.

"We're all the product of our environment, the times in which we live," she went on. "These were uneducated religious fanatics who blamed every bad thing on 'spirits.'" She used quote fingers for the last word.

Theo slumped in the chair. "And that makes it all okay?"

"Not by today's standards." She picked up her mug. "Just like centuries from now people will be horrified by things we're doing."

Theo was so angry he could only laugh. "Why don't you care?"

She set the mug down a little harder this time, smile gone. "What exactly would you like me to do? Invent a time machine so I can stop it from happening?"

Theo didn't know what to say. He just knew this woman was full of crap.

"Black people, Jews, gays, women, all treated badly throughout history," Charlie droned on. "Still are some places."

"I'm definitely not saying it's anywhere near the same—"

"Now, hang on a second," she steamrolled him in that calm, almost lazy voice of hers. Far more irritating than if she'd yelled at him, her self-control making him a petulant child in comparison. "Guess who else has gotten the short end of the stick?"

Charlie didn't wait for an answer. "Disabled people. Overweight people. Short people. Unattractive people. Weird people. Anyone who doesn't fit the mold has always been—probably always will be—pushed to the margins of society, if not outright attacked."

Theo was speechless. The amount of ignorance this woman was spewing would take him hours to unpack.

"I don't know you, and I'm sure you're a perfectly decent person," Charlie stood up, seeming a lot taller than before. "But I'll bet you cash money that you look down on folks who aren't like you."

Theo could only shake his head. If this was a man, he definitely would've socked him in the jaw.

"So, tell me, Mr. Theo, what exactly do you want from me?"

In a flash, it came to him, what had been obvious the whole time. "An apology. I just want to hear you say you're sorry."

She nodded, and Theo sighed. He'd done his part to stand up for his people, his enemy had ceded ground, and now they could both move on.

Then Charlie narrowed her eyes. "You don't want an apology."

Theo let out a long, frustrated groan. He should've known.

"You want me to feel guilty." Charlie wrinkled her button nose in an ugly way, though her voice stayed cool. "But your real motivation? You want to feel superior."

Theo swatted his forehead. This woman was like a brick wall.

"I'm not going to beat myself up for something that happened—what—four hundred years ago?" Charlie sneered.

There could be no appropriate response to such blind idiocy. His emotional oven fully pre-heated, Theo launched to his feet, snatched his full mug, and chucked it hard as he could a few inches over Charlie's head. It hit the wall and shattered, dripping tea from the dent he'd made in the plaster.

Charlie pursed her lips, clearly unimpressed by the tantrum, and then leisurely got up to go to the bathroom. Theo faced her as she went, half-expecting the sociopath to come at him with a baseball bat—maybe even a gun—and tensing to make a run for it.

She did come out with something in her hands. A broom and dustpan. Which she brought over to the mug fragments and swept them up.

"Now, if you'll excuse me," Charlie said in a bored voice. "I've got more messes to clean up."

Theo, face hot with ire and shame, slunk out the door, and slammed it behind him.

Theo took the short way back along the suburban main road to the center of town, yelling over the classic rock station all the things he should've said to Charlie to make her take the least bit of responsibility for her family's trespasses.

He whizzed by the big Christmas tree in the town square, rainbow lights vainly trying to inject false cheer into a bleak world. Okay, maybe he'd overreacted a bit by throwing the mug, but did the ice princess really think she could shrug off karma that easily? All the pain, suffering, and death her people had caused, and she wanted to act like it was ancient history?

Theo rolled up to his parents' house, trying to remember how many beers he'd left in the fridge. An ambulance was pulling out of the driveway. His breath caught and he came to a sudden stop in the middle of the road. Mom in a coat over her bathrobe was getting into her old Chevy sedan. She turned towards Theo, and, in the hang of her head Theo knew what'd happened.

In slow motion, he parked at the curb, turned off the music, and shut his eyes tight. When he opened them again, Mom was knocking on the window, a spacey look in her own runny red ones. He opened the door.

"He didn't make it," was all she said.

Pop-Pop was gone. Theo's favorite person in the world. The only one in the family who actually understood him. Who even seemed to *like* him. And just like that, Theo's link to the past—to who he truly was—was gone.

As Theo shut off the car, he knew he should cry, mourn in some way. And he *was* sad, no question. Though the sadness was only a mild spice in his bubbling stew of rage.

It being Sunday, Theo drove to campus that night, his excuse that he had a big exam in the morning. Truth was, he couldn't bring himself to stay in the house without Pop-Pop.

Theo, of course, came back a few days later for the funeral. A small, quiet service at the local cemetery, bitter wind gusting through the bare sycamore branches, grey clouds promising snow. Just a few uncles, aunts, and distant cousins from out of town and a handful of friends of the family.

Dad, stuffed into his old black suit, gave a syrupy eulogy by the grave—the typical cliches about Pop-Pop being a "kind and decent man," "loving father and husband," joining his late wife in heaven—Mom nodding mindlessly at every word like one of those bobble head dolls. Afterwards, people kept coming up to Theo to say Pop-Pop had had a "good run," as if the words were written on some script passed around. Theo only nodded, biting the inside of his cheek to a pulp to keep from saying something mean.

When it was all over, Theo went back to the house with Mom and Dad for the wake and sat around as people stuffed their faces until everyone left around sundown. He hung out watching eighties sitcom reruns with them until about ten, when he announced he was heading back to school. Eyes glued to the TV, Mom half-heartedly told him he shouldn't drive with the forecasted snow. He promised he'd beat the storm, and his folks didn't argue.

Outside in his jacket, the temperature had dropped below freezing, steely clouds bunched low in the sky. A few sad flakes drifted down like confetti from a party he'd missed. But he had decent tires, and there wouldn't be much traffic where he was going. Indeed, when he stopped for gas, there was hardly anyone out.

Theo took the main route out of town to the unlit outskirts as the snow fell harder, coating the road. Instead of following the cul-de-sac to the end, he parked a way off by the edge of the fence. After slipping on the ski mask and gloves, he got the half-full gas can out of the trunk, heart hammering in excitement.

Cocking an ear to make sure no one was coming down the dark road, he tossed the can over the fence, shimmied up it, and slid down the other side. Can in hand, he crunched along the crusty snow quickly being buried by a fresh layer, which would perfectly hide his footprints. He had a flashlight but didn't need it, the snow reflecting more than enough light from the newly risen half-moon. Soon, he reached the patch of hemlocks, and he slunk through the shadows behind the main house—only a few of its windows lit—past the barn, to the dark carriage house.

Blinking snow from his eyelashes, he popped the cap on the spigot and held back a giddy chuckle. Obviously, he wasn't going to hurt anyone—he wasn't that kind of person. Just send a little message impossible to ignore.

He doused the bushes in front of the tiny outbuilding until the can was empty, the noxious sweet smell making his eyes water, then reached into his pocket for the matchbook. He almost didn't light it, Pop-Pop's voice warning him not to give into his anger. The thing was, he didn't feel mad at all but cool as a cucumber. This wasn't blind fury, it was rational calculation. A reminder that the suffering of people like him—like Pop-Pop—could only be ignored at a cost.

Theo struck the match, lit the rest of the book, tossed it flaring into the bushes, and stood back. A hot whoosh, a flower of flame, and he bolted into the hemlocks. Then he stopped to look back to admire his handiwork. And his jaw dropped.

Not only had the bushes caught, so had the dead ivy on the walls. Not thirty seconds later, the whole side of the house was ablaze.

Theo's mouth went dry, the sour taste of gasoline in the back of his throat almost making him puke. He had to warn her.

That's when the front door flew open, and Charlie, barefoot in flowing white nightgown,

walked out. Not ran but walked, as if for a midnight stroll, to stand back a few feet and stare at the flames.

Relieved he hadn't killed anyone, Theo loped through the trees, slipping a few times though not falling, until he got to the fence. He scrambled up and over and sprinted to his car. Tossed the empty can in the trunk. Swiped the inch of fresh snow from the windshield. Got in, stripped off his ski mask, and turned the ignition. The car wouldn't start.

Pushing back the first tingles of panic in his gut—it usually took the old beater a few times in the cold—he tried again. No dice.

Mouth dry, he made himself wait ten seconds to avoid flooding the engine. If it didn't start soon, the battery might be dead. In which case, his goose was cooked.

Jail. Expulsion. Shame.

Holding his breath, he turned the key again. To his elation, the engine grudgingly turned over, and the car roared to life.

Letting out his breath in a grateful dragon's plume, he flicked on the headlights, switched the heat to high, and got moving. Snow really dumping, visibility little more than ten feet, he drove slowly. The good news was his tire tracks on the way in were already gone, as the new ones would be minutes later.

While the quickest route back to town would also be the safest, fire trucks and police were probably on their way. So, he took the fork along the forest—close to four inches already piled on the unmaintained road—plodding along at fifteen miles per hour.

Charlie would, of course, know who did it. And would almost certainly sic the cops on him, since that was what people like her had been doing to people like him for centuries. Except no one had seen him, and even if there were cameras, his face was hidden under the mask. Plus, once he got back to campus, his roommate Gar would almost certainly be his alibi in exchange for an eighth of weed. Indeed, there was only one thing directly tying him to the crime, and that was the gas can.

Theo pushed on through the blizzard until the trees thinned out into the swamp, where he came to a slow stop in the middle of the road. He got out—car still running—popped the trunk and grabbed the can. Shivering against the biting wind, he trudged over to the water. Almost entirely iced and snowed over, there were patches where dark water still showed.

He swung the can back and let it fly towards one of the open spots about twenty feet out. To his dismay, it hit the ice a couple of feet short but then slid the rest of the way to plop and sink into the water. With a fist pump and a cheer, Theo hustled back to the car.

Inside again, he cranked the heat to max as his whirring brain downshifted to something near calm. He'd done the hard part. In less than twenty minutes he'd be back on the plowed road. And in no more than an hour and a half, in his dorm room snuggling under the covers. Boy, would he be glad when the night was over.

Theo was about to get moving again when a patch of white in the rearview mirror caught his eye. Squinting, he let out a hoarse yell. Someone was in the car!

He fumbled for the overhead light and switched it on. Incredibly—impossibly—Charlie, dressed only in her white nightgown, smiled at him from the backseat.

"How-how?" Theo stammered, twisting around to make sure she was really there, the sheer fabric draping her curves.

"Drive, and I'll explain," Charlie said serenely.

"I'm not going anywhere with you." Theo racked his mind to make sense of it all. Of course, there was only one answer. She'd seen him set the fire, beaten him back to the car, and been hiding there the whole time. She didn't have a weapon he could see, though he sure wished *he* did.

Charlie sighed impatiently. "If I wanted to hurt you, don't you think I would've already?"

If that was true—and he wasn't sure it was—then she was going to make him turn himself in.

"And we don't need police for this," she said, as if reading his mind. "The snow put out the fire pretty quick. No harm that a coat of paint won't fix."

A huge weight lifted from Theo's chest, and he bowed his head in thanks. "So, what do you want?"

"Just to talk."

"To talk."

She nodded in what seemed like earnest this time. No more condescending tea-time smirk.

He shrugged. It wasn't like he could kick her out in the middle of a snowstorm. What other choice did he have but to go along with her demands? Worse come to worst, he could pay her off—he had almost two grand in his checking account.

Setting the gear to drive, he tapped the gas and went up to exactly ten miles per hour on the unplowed road.

"Listen." Charlie took a deep breath and let it out. "You're right about what my family did. It was wrong."

"Okaaay." At this point Theo wasn't even sure he cared about an apology. Hell, he wished he'd never even looked her up. All he wanted was for it to be over.

"I just want you to know it was never personal," Charlie said softly. "Picking your family, I mean."

Either the heat was on too high, or Theo was getting pissed again. Instead of saying something to set her off, he chewed his lip like a gummy worm.

"It had nothing to do with you," she cast her eyes down, "and everything to do with us."

Okay, *now* Theo was listening.

"See, we Alaisters came over from the Old Country to escape certain...accusations."

"What kind?" Theo blurted, out of patience.

"That we were witches in league with the Devil."

"Well, were you?" Theo half-joked.

"Witches are for scaring children," Charlie scoffed, rolling her eyes. "But the lies followed us. And became a problem. When we couldn't shake the reputation, we pointed the finger elsewhere."

"At my family." Snowflakes whizzed at the windshield like Theo was piloting a craft through hyperspace, wipers barely sweeping the snow away before the next blast.

"It was wrong," she said. "But are you honestly saying you wouldn't have done the same?"

Of course, he wouldn't have. At least, he didn't think so. "A moot point. Your family did this to mine. And there's been no justice."

Charlie was quiet a moment, eyes closed. "What's the difference between justice and revenge?"

Livid, Theo sucked in a breath to tear apart the idiotic statement, but she beat him to the punch.

"We tried to pay our debt," she hissed, eyes flashing. "Gave to hospitals, schools, homeless shelters, soup kitchens. I, personally, have kept my hands clean for a long, long time. Even if it meant living like—like some peasant."

An almost complete whiteout through the windshield, Theo nudged the car along through at least six inches of drifting snow. Then the thought hit him. "How did you learn about the history?"

Dead silence from the back, just the smack of wipers and slush of tires. Theo flicked his eyes to the mirror. And gasped. For a split second, an elderly man in powdered wig and black robe with white collar—like a colonial judge—stared back at him with Charlie's blue eyes. Then Theo blinked, and it was Charlie again.

Theo drove faster as if to outrun his hallucination, steering wheel in a death grip. But he knew he wasn't seeing things. "Who are you?" his breath fogged in the suddenly freezing interior.

"Sure you want to know?" Charlie whispered through a frown.

Ice crystalizing on the inside of the windshield, Theo had to rub away a circle with his glove so he could see. "Yes, I want to know!"

When he braved another look in the mirror, Charlie was gone. He twisted around to look, but the back seat was empty. *What the hell?*

When he faced forward again, she was sitting in the passenger seat. Except it wasn't her.

In the place of Charlie's face was a charred snakehead seamed like woodgrain, cold eyes glowing not with hate—nothing so warm and human as that—but the bitter indifference of the cosmic void.

The car shuddered and Theo whipped his eyes back to the road. He'd veered off onto the shoulder, heading straight for a fat tree. Panicked, he stomped the brake, knowing right away it was the wrong move as the rear fishtailed in the snow. Then, yelling at the top of his lungs, the car slid in reverse over the edge of the embankment, and, in slow motion, flipped backwards.

They hit the ground hard, and Theo was out like a light.

When Theo came to—seconds later? Minutes?—he was upside down hanging from his seatbelt, head a ball of pain, fire up and down both arms but still alive. His eyes were wet and warm with what had to be blood from a stinging gash over his forehead. He tried to wipe it away, but the agony in his arms was so bad he almost passed out.

Then he remembered who'd put him there. He swiveled his cramping neck to the side, but Charlie—or whatever that thing was—had gone. He was alone, and it was freezing. He tried to undo the seatbelt, but his numb fingers could only fumble at the button. As the fog cleared from his mind, it occurred to him that if no one found him, he wouldn't make it through the night.

He started to cry. Not just for him but his parents, for Pop-Pop, for his clan long mistreated over the centuries, its bloodline ending in this frozen death trap.

The car shifted. It wasn't done falling. He surprised himself by hoping the next impact would put him out of his misery.

But it was inching *forward*, not down but *up*. What the hell? Yes, the upside-down car was being dragged up the embankment, and seconds later was on the road. A tow-truck, maybe? Except it was dark and dead quiet.

Then someone trying to open the door. But it was crushed and stuck, and the person seemed to give up.

"Help," Theo tried to shout, but it only came out as a whimper.

And then in a grind of metal the door was gone, torn off its hinges, snow swirling inside. Oddly, Theo's only swimmy thought was, *Bear?*

But it was no bear. It was Charlie in her human woman form.

She undid his seatbelt and scooped him in her arms as if he was a small child. Draped over her shoulder in a fireman's carry, before he knew it, they were gliding along the empty, snowy road.

Theo didn't know what was happening, but, his entire body aching, he was in no position to do anything but observe. No sound other than the wind, no crunch of footsteps, no deep breathing from Charlie despite them sliding silently along as if she was on skis.

In what felt like mere minutes the road had only a couple of inches of snow. And, sure enough, from over the hill, blue flashing lights and the grind of metal. A plow truck was returning for another round, and Charlie laid Theo gently on his back off to the side of the road.

The truck crested the hill, came to a halt twenty feet away, and the driver's door opened. A man in a snowsuit stuck his head out into the driving snow, jumped down, and ran towards Theo.

"You saved me," Theo whispered to Charlie. But she was already gone.

Grinding his teeth against the pain, Theo turned his head to the dark road behind him. A pair of shining blue eyes blinked once before melting into the night.

Hot On The Trail

Her silver SUV pulls into the parking lot on the other side of the pine thicket. My heart flops against my ribcage like a trout in the bottom of a canoe. This is it. The moment I've been waiting for.

I reach under the seat and grab the hunting knife in its leather sheath. Slide out the blade and finger the cool steel, its edge sharp.

From out of nowhere, my stomach lurches. I throw open the car door, lean out, and puke onto the dirt. When I'm done gagging, I wipe my mouth with a wrist and take swig of water from my canteen.

Even with four whiskeys in me, I can't go through with it. What was I thinking? I might be a piece of crap, but I'm not a *monster.* Just a passing fever dream and nothing more. Thank God I've come to my senses before it's too late.

She gets out of her car. Long dark hair up in a ponytail, toned arms sticking out of a green tank top, black yoga pants clinging to muscular legs. Though I've yet to see her face up close, I'm guessing she's around thirty. I don't know her name, of course, but I bet it sounds like music, something mostly vowels with soft letters like Naomi or Ariana.

All I know is I've been under her spell since the first time I laid eyes on her three weeks ago from my pickup hidden in this secret drinking spot in the trees. Though we're barely ten miles from Greyeagle—the old mining-turned-casino town—this trailhead is almost always empty. Not only is it at the end of a pot-holed stretch of dirt track without signage, the unmaintained trail climbs straight up the side of a mountain with no views to speak of and then peters out into random elk paths. Tourists don't know about it and locals avoid it.

I slide the key into the ignition, itching to head back to the cabin for a long hot shower. And to pour every drop of booze down the sink. It took a couple of decades, but now I guess I know what they mean by rock bottom.

Still, I can't keep my eyes off her as she straps a fanny pack around her curvy waist.

Three Tuesday afternoons in a row she's been hiking here. Never goes more than a half hour, just a little jaunt to stretch her lovely legs, probably up to the meadow. First time I watched from my truck. Came back the next day at the same time—the one upside of unemployment—but she wasn't there. Or any of the following five days. But a week later, she showed. And I almost talked to her.

But everyone knows if you swat a dog enough times for begging at the table, someday he'll stop trying. That's me and women to a T. Of course, beating a dog doesn't make him any less hungry. Just makes him sneaky. And mean.

And so, after that second time of chickenshitting out, I decided what I was going to do if I saw her again. What with my diagnosis—a pack a day since high school had to catch up sooner or later—it was finally time to have something I wanted instead of always settling for what I could get.

She leans over to tie her hiking boots, lifts her round plump rear-end to the blue Colorado sky. I take a deep breath and let it out slowly.

To be honest, part of me had hoped she didn't show. But she did. Lucky for her, I found that last little bit of good inside me, that one spoonful of ice cream at the bottom of the carton. She'll never know how close she came.

She's doing a few knee lifts to limber up when the passenger door of her SUV opens. Someone gets out. No, not just anyone. A *man*. The pilot light inside me whooshes to full blast.

He's tall, lean, blond—everything I'm not—in a collared shirt, slacks, and dress shoes. Clearly no outdoorsman, but here he is on a hike with my woman. I bite the inside of my cheek until I taste salt.

My whole life I've lost out to guys like this. Rich fast-talking pretty boys from the city. All flash and no grit, they ease through life like riding a parade float, waving to the cheering crowd, gal on each arm. And me? I'm the one stuck in traffic because the fucking show shut down the street.

She leads the way to the trailhead, and Mr. Blondie follows. They disappear behind a bend into the pinewoods.

In the city, I wouldn't stand a chance against this prick. But up here in the sticks, none of his money, looks, or connections add up to a pile of shit. No, Blondie's on my turf now, and this time I've got the upper hand.

In a rage, teeth grinding, I slip on my shades and baseball cap. Stuff one of those masks they used to make me wear at work into the front pocket of my jeans and get out of the truck. It's hot for mid-June in the mountains, probably low nineties, sun beating down on my face from a clear sky with a few clouds moving in. No fun for a big guy like me, but whatever. This won't take long.

I tuck the knife in my back pocket. Quietly, I shut the door and head over to the trailhead.

My new plan is simple. Shadow them for a bit and then hide somewhere off trail, waiting. When they double back, I'll jump out like a mountain lion and scare the hell out of them. Won't touch a hair on anyone's head, of course, but Blondie will either beg for mercy or run away, and she'll see what a little bitch he is. If I can't have her, neither can he.

Five minutes along the pine-bordered trail, I'm already breathing hard, part exertion, part nervousness, part excitement. Trudging up the steep incline, my T-shirt is sopping wet. At least the tree canopy, and more clouds coming in, keep out the worst of the sun.

I keep going up and up and up the rocky path, but I can't catch my damn breath. Whiskey buzz fading, I'm lightheaded from all the huffing and puffing, a cramp in my gut, taking one step every few seconds like I'm on Mt. Everest instead of barely 8,000 feet.

Finally, not far from the meadow, I find a decent-size boulder off to the side of the trail, go behind it, and, wheezing, lie down on my back in the pine straw. I smile, picturing Blondie's eyes wide in shock, a stain of piss running down his fancy pants. And, best of all, the pucker of disgust on my lady's face when she finds out he's a total wimp. After today, she'll probably never think about him again. But I guarantee she'll never forget *me*.

I'm cooling down a little and breathing normal again when I hear a scream. I sit up and perk my ears. There it is again!

I don't think, just move. Catching some second wind, I scurry up the incline like a billy goat, veins flushed with adrenalin. I imagine them running into a bear, or maybe she fell and hurt her leg, her poor excuse for a man no help whatsoever.

Can't be more than a minute later the trail levels out into an acre of tallgrass meadow angling down to a sheer drop. In the near distance, another forested mountain rises up, blocking half of the slate-grey swirling sky. A breeze picks up and blows dust into my panting mouth.

My girl sits on her rump in the grass by the edge of the cliff, legs splayed out in front. Blondie looms over her like a vulture waiting out a dying fawn.

"Don't you touch me!" she screeches at him.

"What?" Blondie says, standing there like an idiot. I don't think he knows I'm here.

But then my lady looks at me for the first time. And when she reaches out her hand, I want nothing in the world more than to take it.

"Help," she peeps, and my heart nearly busts open.

Blondie whirls around and glares at me. Suddenly, I'm furious again. Half at this scumbag for daring to lay a hand on my woman, half at myself for realizing how close I came to doing the same thing—or worse.

"The fuck do *you* want?" he spits.

Like a sprung trap, I lumber across the meadow, my only goal to crush this bastard. And maybe, just maybe, redeem myself a bit.

I'm a few feet away when Blondie hunches over in a protective crouch. I flash back to high school, once again the linebacker about to steamroll the quarterback.

I plow into his flailing arms and chest with a shoulder. Blondie is lighter than I would've guessed, and instead of knocking him on his ass, he goes flying. Lands on his back at the cliffside. Teeters over the edge for half a second. And is gone.

Not a word out of his mouth. Just the skitter of crumbling rock, tree branches snapping, and one heavy thud.

Seconds later, she's standing beside me. Got on a lot of makeup—mascara and eyeliner, blush, red lipstick, all perfectly in place without a smudge. Great as she looks, I can't help but wonder what her face looks like underneath.

And she's smiling. Just for me.

I feel like I'm floating. For the first time since I can remember, I did something for someone else. If I knew it felt this good, I'd have tried a long time ago.

But there's something odd about her smile. Something off. Though I'm sweating like a pig, I shiver in the cool wind of the storm blowing down from the high peaks.

"I knew I could count on you," she says in a breathy voice, hazel eyes twinkling.

Strange thing to say. I don't know how to respond. She's probably in shock, though. Not making a lot of sense.

"Let's have a looksee, shall we?" She takes my hand—it's small, soft, and cool, almost like a kid's inside my big rough one—and leads me over to the drop off.

I hate heights, so I stop. She lets go of my hand and walks right up to the edge. My stomach churns. "Careful!"

"Stop being a baby and take a peek," she scolds, the toes of her boots literally hanging over.

Not wanting her to know how scared I am, I inch up to where the meadow grass thins out a foot away from the cliff face and peer down. A couple of hundred feet of empty space, bushy pine tops below. Blondie's down there somewhere—no way he survived that fall—but I can't see him. Dizzy, I stumble back onto the grass where it's safe.

"Aren't you...freaked out?" I can't figure this woman out.

"Why would I be?" She stares at me, brow furrowed with lines that weren't there before. Then her forehead smooths again.

"Because. Because." I'm not much for words at the best of times. Now I can barely talk.

"You did me a huge favor," she says matter-of-factly and turns away from the edge.

My gut relaxes. Then I tense up again when I remember I forgot to put on the mask. *Now she knows who I am.* "Won't they find him—his body?"

She raises a plucked eyebrow. "Any roads down there?"

I shake my head.

"Hiking trails?" she asks.

"No, but they're gonna come looking." Icy panic creeps up my spine. I need to get the hell off the mountain. Maybe even skip town a few days. Or weeks.

"No one knows we're here," she says.

I cock my head like a confused dog.

"It's true." She nods, brushing dust off a thigh. "Just some douchebag executive in from Chicago for the weekend."

I have no reason to doubt her. But she's gotta be missing something. A rumble of thunder not far away. "What about a rental car? They'll have paperwork."

Pursing her lips, she shakes her head, ponytail bobbing. "Why do you think I was driving."

"Family?"

She shrugs. "He's married. But wifey has no idea he's here. He assured me of that."

I take in a sharp breath through my nose and almost ask her what she was doing hanging out with a married man. Then I realize that's just jealousy talking. And how stupid it is to be jealous of a dead guy.

"Wanna hear a secret?" she whispers.

I take a step back. For some reason, I don't.

"It was all an act." She throws up her hands theatrically.

"What?" I crackle through a dry throat, the first drops of rain spattering the bill of my hat. If we don't get out of the meadow soon, we're gonna get fried by lightning.

She narrows her eyes. "What are you, slow or something? He didn't lay a finger on me. I faked the whole thing."

Head swimming, I can only stand there blinking.

"I saw you in your truck," she says. "Watching me."

Another boom of thunder. Three seconds later a bolt of lightning on the ridge. I'm not safe here.

"That first time I had a feeling, so I came back." She smiles, small white teeth gleaming in the sickly light. "The second time I knew for sure."

And I thought I was invisible in my secret spot! Not only did she see me, she read my damned mind! *And then kept coming back?!*

"So, I picked up that schmuck at the blackjack table, told him I liked fucking in the woods."

I wince. Ugly words from such a pretty mouth.

She steps towards me, close enough where I catch a whiff of her musky perfume. "And I knew you'd come after us."

"Wh-why?"

"Thought we could have a little arrangement." She winks. Actually winks.

I want to turn around and run. But her eyes have got me. It's like I'm turned to stone.

"See, in most ways, you and I couldn't be more different." The rising wind whips up strands of her inky black hair. "I'm hot, you're hideous. I'm smart, you sound like an idiot. I come from money, you're a broke redneck."

I take in a deep breath and let it out. Anyone else, I'd knock those words back down their throat. But from her, it only makes me sad.

She goes on, "Yachts on the Mediterranean. Raves in Dubai. Cocaine so pure it lifts you three inches off the ground. Mink coats that cost more than you've made in your life." Though her eyes drift up to the darkening sky like she's making it all up, I know she's not. Plenty of guys would literally slice off their left nut for a night with her. What I don't know is *why* she's telling me this.

"But you," she sneers, wrinkling her nose. Tiny as she is, I feel like she's literally looking down on me. "No one's ever given you jack, am I right? Eking by paycheck to paycheck in some mouseshit shack in the middle of nowhere. Bet you've never even left Colorado, eh?"

Now, I'm getting pissed. I almost tell her about my trip to Cabo for my twenty-first, but I know she'd laugh. I bite my lip.

"They've pushed your head so far underwater, you've got to grab onto something. So, you rob, steal, cheat, and worse," she gives me a knowing look, "all so you don't drown."

My skin crawls as the horrible things I've done flash through my mind. The tears. The screams. The blood. Rotten as an apple at the bottom of the barrel, and she knows it.

"But it's not your fault." From out of nowhere, her smile cool as ointment on a wound. "Anyone else would do the same."

My eyes blur and my jaw trembles. I can't remember the last time I've cried. But standing here with my ribs cracked open, naked heart beating, for the first time since I've been a kid I feel...loved? No.

Accepted? Not really.

Understood? Yes! Understood!

"And how are we the same?" I blubber, though I know what she's going to say.

"Hurting people gets us off," she whispers, eyes wide like a stalking cat.

Just like that, the spell breaks. Black clouds hang low overhead, a cold wind gusts, and it's pouring.

It's true I've hurt people. With my words, my crimes, my fists. But I've never liked doing it. And sure as hell never killed anyone...before today. "Why didn't you do it yourself? Why bring me into this?"

She juts her lower lip, and the lines cut deep into her forehead. "Cuz I need to keep my hands clean, dimbulb." Then she shrugs. "And maybe because the only thing that feels better than being bad is making someone else be bad for you."

A jolt of anger. "What if I go to the cops?"

She doesn't even have to roll her eyes. Soon as the words leave my mouth, I know how dumb it is. Like they'd ever believe *me* over someone like *her*.

I feel weak. Worthless. An empty sack. Until I remember the knife.

Slowly, I reach behind my back. "Who are you?"

"You can call me anything you like," she says flirtily, hand in her unzipped fanny pack wrapped around the butt of a pistol. "That is, if you still want me."

Cowed, I drop my hands by my side and nod. How can I not nod?

"Not gonna make any promises," she says like a CEO at the head of a boardroom table. "But maybe, just maybe, if you keep...*hiking* with me," she winks again, "one of these days I'll let you have a taste."

I'm stiff in my jeans. I hate myself for it, try to will it away, but I can't. Would it even be worth it? Or is it about something more than that?

"Of course, I might not." She's still holding the gun, though she hasn't drawn it. "Depends on how well you follow orders."

I'm like a dog whose master beats him but is loyal just the same. After all, who else will feed me?

And, as she slips her hand out of her pack and zips it up, she seems to know it. "Same time, same place, next week?"

A sizzle like a giant frying pan, and, not fifty feet away, a dead pine explodes in orange and yellow flame, splintered planks and shorn branches hurtling to the ground.

I can leave. She won't shoot me. No reason to. It's not like I can rat her out.

Yet there's something in her eyes that wasn't there before. A look I know all too well because I see it every morning in the bathroom mirror.

Desperation.

She can find thousands, maybe even millions of men who'd take care of her, cater to her every whim, wait on her hand and foot. But as an actual *killer*—now, at least—I've got something none of them have. Something she needs.

Her arrogant smirk is gone.

I can still say no. Do an actual good deed for a change, maybe even turn my life around.

As we stand there glaring at each other in the high meadow, cold rain sheeting down, thunder crashing, I'm not sure what I'll do.

All I know is that, finally, for the first time in my life, I feel like I have a choice.

Wakey, Wakey For Gage

"Get up, lil' buddy," big voice say.

Me wake from dream. Bad dream. 'lello eyes, scary monster.

Me stand in snow. Was Jud house, but no more house, jus' snow.

More snow from sky fall on face. It dark, but me no cold, Osh Kosh keep warm.

Big man stand in dark. Me not know man, but me not 'fraid.

"Hey there, Gage," big man say. He wear robe, hair messy. "How'd ya sleep?"

Me tired, yawn. Want Mommy, Daddy. Me cry.

"Why the waterworks?" Big man smile, pat me on head. "Uncle Jack's here to help!"

Me stop cry. "Mommy? Daddy?"

"I'll help ya find 'em. Got a boy of my own. And we all know how a boy loves his Mommy and Daddy."

Me look 'cross street. See house! Dark, but Mommy, Daddy inside! Clap hands. Happy! Me go home!

Run through snow to road. Me fast.

Uncle Jack pick me up, way up high. Big truck go by, windy, windy, cold snow in face. Honk horn. Ouch, hurt ears! Me cry 'gain.

"Give it a rest, eh?" Uncle Jack say. He no smile.

"Me want go home!" Me point house. Want kiss Mommy, Daddy. Hug Ellie. Pet Church, pretty kitty.

"I know ya do," Uncle Jack say. "But Mommy and Daddy don't live there anymore."

Me sad. Cry hard.

"Hey, I got ya a present!" Uncle Jack put down. He smile.

Me stop cry. Me laugh. Jump up and down. Me love present!

Uncle Jack take pencil from pocket. It pretty red. "Here ya go. You can draw a picture for your Daddy when ya get home."

Me love draw! Take pencil, put in Osh Kosh pocket. "We go now?" Hold Uncle Jack hand. It big, cold.

"Not this time," Uncle Jack say. "But yer Aunt Annie can!"

Me see road. Big car there. Me and Uncle Jack walk to car. He open door.

Big lady inside, wear pretty dress.

"How they hangin', Annie?" Uncle Jack say to big lady.

"Keep quiet, dirty bird," big lady say. She mad. Then smile at me. "And this must be Gage!"

Uncle Jack pick me up, way up high, put in front seat like big boy. "Got a kiss for your Aunt Annie?" big lady say, give wet kiss on cheek. Yuck. Smell like dirt. Me wipe off.

"Say hi to Daddy for me, won't ya?" Uncle Jack say, rub my hair, make messy like him.

Me laugh.

Uncle Jack close door. Aunt Annie drive 'way, fast, fast! Me wave Uncle Jack, but he gone.

Huff, huff in ear. Turn 'round. Big brown doggie! Me 'fraid! Me cry!

"Never mind Cujo there," Aunt Annie say. "Nothing but a big old softie."

Doggie lick face. Wet mouth smell like potty, but me laugh. Dog lick 'gain. Nice doggie! Floppy ear like bunny!

Me pet doggie. Make friend.

Aunt Annie drive fast, fast. Big trees in dark, snow come down.

Me sleepy. Close Eyes.

"Wakey, wakey!" Aunt Annie say.

Me open eyes. Look out car window. Big black gate, tall red house. Not know house. "Where we?"

"This is where Mommy and Daddy live," Aunt Annie say.

Me 'fraid. Not want go.

"Don't worry," Aunt Annie say, "Cujo'll keep you company."

Me pet Cujo head. He lick face with wet potty mouth. Me laugh. "Aunt Annie, come?"

Aunt Annie shake head, big smile. "Soon."

Aunt Annie go outside, walk in snow, open car door. Pick me up, way up high. Aunt Annie big, strong, put me down in snow. More snow fall from sky. Me stick out tongue, try catch snow. Can't.

Cujo jump out car. Nose in snow, Cujo sneeze. Silly doggie. Me laugh.

Cujo go gate, push with nose. It open, *creeeeeeeak*.

Me 'fraid. Turn 'round, but Aunt Annie gone, no car.

Cujo walk. Make big holes in snow with feet. Me go after, walk in holes, all way to steps.

Cujo go up one step. Me go up one step. Two. Me slip! Fall down on knees in snow! Owwww!

Me cry. But big boy, stop cry. Stand up. Go up step, up step, up step, to door.

Cujo bark. Bark loud.

Me bark, too! "Ruff, ruff!"

Snow fall down, but me no cold. Soon, hug Mommy, Daddy. Drink hot cho'lat. Me pet Cujo, so soft.

Door open. Lady in fluffy robe. Mommy? White hair. *Not* Mommy! Mommy friend?

"What in the world?" Nice lady say, mouth big O.

Short little doggie run outside. Black, white. Cute, cute! It bark at Cujo.

Cujo run 'way in snow. Cute little doggie run after to play.

"Molly, no!" nice lady yell.

Me run by lady inside house. Soft rug, smell like flower.

Me see steps. Mommy, Daddy sleep up steps.

Me go up steps. One. Two. Big picture on wall. Uncle Jack face! Me smile.

Three steps. Four. 'nother picture. Aunt Annie face! Yay!

Five. Too many steps. Tired. Crawl rest way.

Me get top! So high!

Go down hall. Open door. Desk, 'puter. No Mommy, Daddy. Big pile paper.

Take paper off pile. Bedtime story? But me no read, only Mommy, Daddy. Other side paper, no story. Put paper in pocket with pencil.

Out door, walk down hall. 'nother door, little way open. Push all way. It dark, Daddy in bed under blankie, sleeping! He snore loud. Me laugh.

Me go bed. It tall. Me climb way up high, like playground slide. Bed big, soft.

Me get paper out pocket. Pencil. Poke finger with pencil. Oww! But big boy, no cry.

Want wake Daddy, but Daddy snore and snore. Me wait. Draw picture for Daddy, first.

Draw Gage, and Mommy, and Daddy, and Ellie, and Church, and Uncle Jack, and Aunt Annie, and Cujo. Draw house, trees. Draw road.

Stop draw. Put down paper. Dizzy. 'member bad dream.

Gage run to road. Big truck, loud, loud! Gage Fly!

Gage wake up. Daddy with big shovel. Daddy pick Gage up, way up high, dirt all over. Daddy carry Gage through big dark trees.

Daddy and Gage go house! Daddy give Gage bath, put Gage beddie-bye. But Gage no sleepy. Hot, head feel funny. Gage get out bed.

Gage go down steps, outside. Dark. Cross road—no truck—Jud house. Gage hurt Jud. Gage not know why.

Daddy come! Gage hurt Daddy! Gage not know why!

Daddy get mad! Real mad!

Daddy give Gage med'cine. Gage sleepy. Go beddie-bye...

No more dream. Me crawl on bed, pull blankie from Daddy face. Sleeping. But not Daddy! Man have white hair! Man face funny, square like Lego man!

Not know man. But me no like.

Man make big truck come, make me beddie-bye in dirt.

Man make feel funny, make hurt Jud and Daddy.

Man make Church go 'way, take Mommy, Daddy, Ellie 'way.

Me get mad, feel hot. This man...bad! Me hate bad man!

Light come on.

"Steve!" Nice lady yell. "My God!"

Me climb bad man tummy, hold pencil tight.

Bad man open eyes, little eyes. "So, it's you this time, Gage," bad man say.

Me want be happy boy. Play with toys. Games with Ellie. Pet Church. Love Mommy, Daddy. But bad man take all 'way. Me feel hot. Real hot, head funny.

Me take bad man 'way!

Hold pencil tight. Hand back like for throw ball.

"I'm so sorry," bad man say, little eyes wet.

Me put pencil in bad man eye, hard, hard. Pencil draw red on bad man face.

Nice lady scream.

Me put pencil in bad man eye again! Again! Again!

Me laugh. Hand red, wet with pencil.

Feel sleepy. Lay down on bed. Close eyes.

Pretty bright light. Me see Mommy, Daddy! Smile, smile, smile. Want hug me! Church there, too, meow-meow, pretty kitty!

Me no feel hot. No feel funny. Me happy! So happy.

Me run to light.

The Hand You're Dealt

I dropped the package of frozen corn niblets I'd been holding in my hand as an ice pack onto my desk. Sitting in front of my laptop in my cramped, windowless office, I made a fist, and, wincing, opened it again to flex the sore tendons.

At the time, I blamed the injury on the previous day's trip to the gym. Almost three years since I'd done a single bicep curl, I figured I overdid it trying to get my body back to what it was like when I first met Kerry. With her gone, I needed to accept that years of stuffing myself full of pasta, pie, and potato chips wouldn't be reversed overnight.

My damned left hand bugged me all morning, distracting me from working on my slideshow on corporate's new harassment policy. Of course, the delay was probably a blessing in disguise, as the few staff left at the dealership who didn't already consider H.R. reps like me to be professional killjoys would probably turn against me after this presentation.

The new rules included things like "No innuendo," which some read as "no jokes." "No posting of suggestive cartoons or photos," meaning the guys in the shop had to take down their swimsuit calendars. And, finally, "No unwelcome advances." A moot point since almost everyone was married. Except me.

Sighing, I stretched the fingers of my aching hand and got back to work.

I took the next couple of days off from the gym and did my best to favor my injured hand, which, since I was right-handed, wasn't too difficult aside from the typing. Yet, despite my best efforts to let it heal, it only grew more sensitive, while the center of my palm broke out in an itchy pink rash like a baby's butt after marinating in a piss-soaked diaper.

By mid-week, a little cleft formed in the groove of what Kerry had told me—the one time I let her read my palm—was my "head line." While your life line was supposed to tell you about the quality of days to come, the head line had something to do with psychology. Though I never paid much attention to that new age stuff her hippie friends had turned her on to, I remember her saying my head line showed I was strong willed—no shit, Sherlock—with the ability to put "mind over matter." Whatever that meant. She also told me it revealed an inner conflict, her segue into my so-called "commitment phobia." Which was where the conversation ended, as always. And, the relationship, too, eventually.

When I woke Friday morning, the cleft was like a fresh paper cut the instant before blood wells to the surface. Or one of those old paintings of Jesus' stigmata. At least it didn't hurt anymore, just a slight irritation. I washed it out in the bathroom sink, and, once it air-dried, put on a bit of antibacterial ointment and one of those little circle bandages.

By the next morning, the wound's edges had swollen. Painless though it was, I worried it might be infected. I cleaned it again and slathered on more ointment and a normal sized bandage, which I decided to leave on for the rest of the weekend in case all my poking around was keeping it from healing.

Monday morning after my shower, as I stood in my towel dripping on the tile, I ripped off the wet bandage. Shocked, I sucked in a sharp breath. The cut had deepened and formed two crinkled, slightly asymmetrical lips that resembled slices of dried apricot, with a small fold of skin towards the top. Crazy as the thought was, it looked a lot like a vagina.

But really, what the hell was it? I squinted. Some skin disease, maybe MRSA? Holding it up to the bulbs above the mirror, I revolved my hand and stared at it from different angles.

Still at a loss, I got an ear swab and pushed aside the flaps of skin to find a tiny nubbin of flesh. When I probed it, a ticklish jolt of pleasure ran up my spine. Stunned, I dropped the swab on the floor andheld the hand away from me, as if a snake's head had just sprung from my wrist.

Was a part of the female anatomy really growing out of my hand? Was that even medically possible? If so, why in the world was it happening to me? And what was I supposed to do about it?

I nervously licked my dry lips. Kerry was a nurse. She'd know what was going on. But Kerry was gone. Probably already with some other guy. Of course, while a desperate woman drew dudes like yellowjackets to rotting fruit, the same scent on a man was lady-repellent.

Like a pot of rice left too long on the burner, the rage bubbled up from deep inside. I threw open the bathroom door, the knob banging the wall. I wrapped my good right hand around the knob and slammed it again and again and again against the cracking plaster until I made a hole.

Panting with the exertion, I unapologetically admired my work.

Shit! Work! I was late! Though fuming like a wood stove, I at least had the sense to realize getting fired wouldn't help anything. Averting my eyes from the wound, I slapped one of those large adhesive pads over my palm, threw on some clothes, and headed out the door.

All day, I tried to ignore my hand, fighting the temptation to tear off the bandage and scrutinize it. I tinkered with the slideshow straight through my break, office door closed, in no mood to talk to anyone.

137

Around eleven someone knocked. I ignored it, but it kept up. "Yes?"

The door creaked open. Sandra, the new saleswoman—sorry, sales*person*—frizzy blonde hair piled atop her head like a melting ice cream cone, barged in, Styrofoam cup in each hand.

"Haven't seen you all day," Sandra chirped, setting the cup of steaming, rancid-smelling coffee on my desk. "Thought you could use a little pick-me-up."

"I'm more of a tea drinker." I lifted the phone to get rid of her.

She forced a smile, nodded, and, leaving the coffee on my desk, hurried out of the room, forgetting to close the door behind her. I hung up, bolted from my chair, slammed the door, and paced the confines of my tiny office.

Yeah, I was being a dick, but I didn't appreciate the way she was trying to weasel her way into being my friend. Which she was only doing because everyone else hated her for taking Hank's job. Word was that corporate's new push for diversity was the reason he was forced into retirement and Sandra was hired in his place. Whether that was actually true or not didn't seem to matter to anyone.

By noon, a clear fluid began to seep through the bandage. I sniffed it. No stink of pus, more like a faint ocean breeze. But I needed to replace the bandage.

I waited until almost everyone had cleared out for lunch and made a beeline for the bathroom. Thankfully, it was empty, no feet under the stalls. I hoped when I took off the bandage it would look like a normal cut, that I had only imagined the weird thing.

When I peeled it away, all the spit in my mouth evaporated like a puddle on hot asphalt. I blinked a few times, as if to clear my eyes of some distorting film, but it was no use. The flushed lips. The soggy slit.

It was a vagina. An actual, living vagina. It couldn't be anything else.

Tentatively, I prodded between the folds with my finger. It tingled and dampened. My breathing quickened. Unable to resist, I stuck in my finger up to the first joint. Instead of touching bones or tendons, it was soft, wet, and empty. My whole body shuddered in delight.

I slid my finger in deeper to the second joint. Turning my hand around to look at the back of it, I fully expected my finger to stick out the other side. But the skin was intact. It didn't make any goddamn sense.

I jammed my entire finger in. And gasped. It felt incredible, like taking a sip of water when you're really, really thirsty.

The bathroom door swung open. I drew my finger—now moist—out of the hole just as Stu walked in. I reached for the soap dispenser, squirted some onto my palm, and rubbed it into a lather under the faucet.

"How's it hangin'?" His sheaf of blond hair slicked back on his big square head, dapper in suit coat and tie, Stu was the top salesman at the dealership. Outside of quarterly H.R. meetings, I hadn't exchanged more than a dozen words with the guy. He grabbed my left wrist, yanked it out of the stream of hot water. "The fuck is that?" He stared at my hand.

"Cut myself." I jerked out of his grip. Making a loose fist, I held it by my side, soapy water dripping on the floor as my fingertips pressed up against the gooey orifice.

"Looks pretty deep." Stu furrowed his eyebrows so they almost met. "How'd you do it?"

"Opening a bottle," I said, without missing a beat.

Stu looked me in the eyes, down to my hand, and back to my eyes. I swallowed uncomfortably but kept returning his gaze, knowing that to look away would be to admit I was lying. A drill whined from the garage.

"Use a bottle opener next time, genius." Stu laughed and stepped over to the urinal.

As he pissed, I scurried out of the bathroom in relief and burst outside the showroom doors into the hot and humid June day. I speed-walked across the lot full of brand-new models to my hatchback at the edge of the woods. Sitting in the driver's seat, I wiped my wet hand off with some tissues and laid a fresh bandage over my gaping palm. I started the ignition, tuned the radio to the local hard rock station, and cranked the volume.

For the next few minutes, I screamed every swear word in the English language until my throat was raw.

Was it genetic? Did someone else in the family have it and Mom and Dad just not tell me? Had I caught it at the strip club? Or was it a mutation, maybe from a chance exposure to some chemical or radioactive substance? Would it grow pubes? Start to menstruate? Would more and more pop up until I was covered head to toe in tiny beavers?

I picked up my phone, went online, and searched for "hand vagina" but only pulled up a YouTube video of some kid clasping his hands together obscenely. Queasy, I tossed the phone onto the seat.

Looking at the thing out of the corner of an eye, I wondered if it wouldn't be the worst idea to chop my whole hand off. But even if I did, why would it stop there? Why not an asshole in the middle of my forehead? Or how about a few floppy dicks sprouting from my armpits?

Wasn't it punishment enough to be a flipping H.R. rep at a car dealership? To have no one within a thousand miles I could honestly call a friend? To have lost the only woman I'd ever really felt close to?

Apparently not. No, the universe, for whatever reason, insisted that I be completely and forever alienated from every single member of my species by cursing me with a fucking...*handgina*!

A rabbit hopped out from beneath the trees into the parking lot. I lowered the volume on the radio and watched it scamper, stop, and look around, scamper, stop and look around, until it was out of sight. The invisible belt around my chest went out a notch.

If I'd learned anything from the whole Kerry thing, it was that going apeshit only made a bad situation worse. A clear head was what I needed. I forced myself to take a few deep breaths and try to get a grip.

The first thing I had to do was go to the doctor. But even if I got over the humiliation, I'd end up with a line of medical students wanting to poke and prod me. Once word got out, I'd become a complete outcast, lose my job, and have to skip town. Probably end up travelling the heartland in some circus freak show. "Come one, come all, feast your eyes on the amazing Mr. Pussyhand!"

I stared at my bandaged hand, projecting a beam of seething hatred at the intruder.

No, I'd take care of things myself. It was just flesh, after all. No different than a mole or wart or tumor. It if could grow, it could be removed.

I struggled my way through the rest of the workday and on the way home stopped at the drug store to pick up a box of wound closure strips. When I got back to the house, I stuck the strips on, sealing things up tight as I could, and waited for nature to take its course.

That night I dreamt of Kerry. Making love to her on a blanket by the river, the way we did our first time. It was so dark I could barely make out her face, though I could hear her moaning and the rush of water over rocks. After a particularly deep thrust, I tried to pull myself back out of her but couldn't. A suction as if from an industrial-strength vacuum cleaner held me tight and started to draw me further inside. No matter how I struggled, I couldn't detach myself.

As the pressure grew more intense, her opening seemed to widen so my entire member was engulfed, shaft, balls, and all. I tried to push against her shoulders but kept slipping further inside, first my pelvis, then my hips. I jammed a knee against her stomach, but her skin was too greasy to get any purchase.

My entire body slipped down this mucousy chute. The starry night sky disappeared as I dropped blindly into black open space, arms and legs flailing with nothing to grab.

I woke up screaming. I was inside myself.

With a sucking sound, I tore my hand away from my crotch and snapped on the bedside light. My fully engorged cock shuddered, and the hole in my hand gaped redly, shot through with a mixture of pleasure and pain—like a tickling gone on too long—the useless closure strips peeled off to either side.

Panicked, I ran to the bathroom and held my pulsing palm under scalding water for at least five minutes, trying to drown the monstrosity.

Things had gone too far. I'd literally just fucked myself.

I raced madly to the kitchen and rooted around the drawers, tossing pens, rubber bands, and screwdrivers on the floor until I found Kerry's sewing kit. Marched into the bathroom, and, though it was tricky with my shaking hand, threaded up a needle. Found a bottle of rubbing alcohol and splashed it on my palm. Relishing the biting pain, I sewed the slit up tight with a few dozen stitches, tied a knot, and snapped off the end of the thread with my teeth. I slapped on a fresh bandage.

Sitting on the closed toilet lid, I felt hollowed out, missing Kerry worse than I'd ever missed anyone in my life. Not for sex or anything, just to hold me. Tell me everything was going to be okay. That I wasn't some mutated freak of nature fated to be alone for the rest of my life. But my woman was gone. And for the first time I wondered if maybe it'd been a tiny bit my fault.

It wasn't like I'd ever said I *didn't* want to get married and have kids someday. I told her the truth, that even though I wasn't going to rush into any of that, I could see myself wanting it eventually. She was only thirty-one, not some ancient crone.

Was that why, towards the end, she hardly spoke to me unless I started the conversation myself? Why she felt the need to contradict me all the time? Why she just lay there motionless in bed as if wishing she were someplace else?

Like a sudden punch to the gut, it hit me. She'd never loved me. Just been using me as a tool to fulfill her biological urge to procreate. Once she suspected I might not play the role she demanded of me, she shrugged me off like a winter coat in May.

Wide awake, I laid out on the couch in front of the TV and flipped through the channels. I settled on *Showgirls* and watched until I fell asleep halfway through.

Woke up with a crick in my neck, arm splayed out to my side, far away from me as possible. It burned and ached, which I hoped meant it was healing.

All day at work, my hand felt like it was smothering. I was so tired I could barely keep my eyes open and so anxious I struggled to focus on a single task. Still, I was optimistic. Maybe, like a dolphin or whale, if I covered up its blowhole long enough it would suffocate.

Everything annoyed me, from Sandra chatting me up after bringing me a lukewarm green tea I didn't ask for, to the teeth-grinding whine of drills from the shop.

When I got home, I changed the bandage and was glad to see the stitches holding tight. I took some aspirin, iced it, and fell into a fitful sleep in front of the TV.

The rest of the week at the office passed excruciatingly slow, though I snuck in a few naps. My hand throbbed, the thing begging to be released from its stitches. But I showed it no mercy.

By the end of the day on Friday, I put the finishing touches on the harassment slideshow I'd present on Monday, thereby solidifying my status as office pariah. I honestly didn't care about any of that anymore, only wanted to get it over with. On the way home, I figured I'd pick up a bottle of whisky and drink myself stupid through the weekend. If I got incredibly lucky, maybe I'd get alcohol poisoning and never wake up. I shut down my computer and the screen went black.

"Whaddup homeslice!" Stu leaned in my open doorway.

Had I forgotten a meeting with him today? "Just about to head home."

"Got your girl waiting, give you a little sumpin' sumpin'?"

I shook my head.

"Oh, c'mon man," Stu said, hands on hips. "I seen her come in the office before. Not bad, not bad at all."

"We broke up," I said nonchalantly as possible.

"Ah, sorry to hear that, man." A brief smile flashed across his ruddy face. "You a hockey fan?"

"Who isn't?" I wasn't. Never much of a sports guy, I probably hadn't watched more than five full minutes of the game in my life.

"Me and the guys are heading over to Lucky's for the playoffs." He looked down at the floor, rubbing his elbow. "Wanna come?"

Of course, I wanted to go. It was the first time anyone at the dealership had asked me to do anything social after work. But I couldn't. My hand was killing me, like something was trying to burst out of it.

"Wish I could," I said, truthfully enough. "But I've got some stuff to take care of around the house."

"Sounds pretty lame."

I shrugged. It did.

"How about you come for one beer." Stu grinned slyly. "And then you can go home and take care of your precious *stuff.*"

I wasn't sure I could keep it together, figuratively or literally. But I also knew full well this would probably be my one and only chance to hang with the guys. With enough effort, I supposed I could keep the charade up for another hour, and, who knows, maybe it'd even take my mind off things.

"Alright." I was surprised to feel my lips curl into actual smile. "Meet you there in a few."

Soon as I walked into the bar, I almost turned around and went home. The ceilings were too low, the jukebox screeched out some awful Heart song from the eighties, the whole room stunk like body odor, and there were a few clusters of noisy, plaid-shirted hipsters hanging around the pool tables. But Stu, sitting at a high top with a couple of the other salesmen, waved me over.

I shook Stu's sweaty hand, nodded at Malcolm, wiry with a shaved head and a scorpion tattoo on his forearm, and smiled at big fat Larry. I dragged a stool over as Stu poured me a mug of yellow beer from a pitcher.

Hockey was more interesting than I'd given it credit for. Though it was a little hard to follow the puck, I appreciated the non-stop action. And the guys were actually really cool. We debated which was the worst Adam Sandler movie, and they laughed at most of my jokes. Stu even had me pick out an appetizer—loaded potato skins—and said he'd foot the bill.

I insisted on buying the second pitcher of beer. And then the third.

When the game ended, I regretfully told the guys I needed to head home. Fully buzzed, I'd barely even thought about my hand for the past two hours, but now it was throbbing again. I needed to ice it, take an aspirin, and get some sleep.

"Dude." Stu clapped a hand on my shoulder. "You're too fucked up to drive."

"Naw, I'm good." The fact that I never drove drunk meant the chances I'd be pulled over the one time I did were astronomically low.

"I'll drive you home, and we can come back tomorrow for your car," Stu said.

"You've been drinking, too."

"Nowhere near as much as you." Stu did seem pretty sober, his gaze steady and clear. Come to think of it, I'd only seen him refill his mug the one time.

He grasped my elbow and pulled. "C'mon let's go." I was too wasted to resist.

"We'll see you guys Monday," he called out to Malcolm and Larry.

I stumbled a bit as we walked across the parking lot, but Stu held me steady. Like a gentleman, he opened the door of his SUV for me, helped me in, and even buckled my seatbelt.

It made me dizzy to keep my eyes open, so I closed them.

When I woke up, Stu was gnawing at my palm, the back of his blond head barely visible in the moonlight. Breath hot and moist, his teeth pinched my skin.

"What're you doing?" I blurted, still half out of it. We were parked near some woods. "Where are we?"

"Shhhh." Tightening his grip on my wrist, Stu started licking my hand, which smarted like a wasp had stung it.

Mostly coming back to myself, I wriggled my hand away from him. In the dimness, I could see the bandage was gone and half the stitches had been chewed off. "The hell, man!"

"Thought you wanted to." He seized my wrist in a vice lock. The button of his jeans was undone.

I had trouble focusing my eyes, and my head bobbed to the side, somehow too heavy for my neck. All I knew was I had to get out of there.

As he dug his fingers into my wrist, I flailed out my right arm and reached for the door handle, which, after some fumbling, I was able to pull back. It swung open.

He let go of my wrist and snatched my shirt collar instead. Without thinking, I made a fist with my newly freed left hand and blindly swung upward. As my knuckles connected with his jaw, Stu's teeth snapped together, and he bellowed in pain.

"My fucking tongue!" he lisped, as I rolled out the door and fell to the gravel.

I was so woozy I seriously considered lying there, but the sound of Stu's door opening gave me the jolt I needed to spring to my feet and take off stumbling into the night. The thumbprint three-quarters moon had cleared the treetops and illuminated a small parking lot surrounded by woods on three sides. The adrenalin cut through the alcohol and gave me energy to bolt into the darkness of the trees.

As I crunched in a mad dash over sticks and dead leaves fragrant with decay, Stu's footsteps clattered on the gravel behind me. "Come back, dude! It was a joke!"

The hell it was. Branches slashed my face, neck, and arms, and though it took all my focus to stay on my feet, I kept weaving through the trees. A shimmering ahead. Maybe someone could help! As the woods thinned, a body of dark water appeared. I staggered out of the trees onto a sandy beach beside a massive lake reeking of algae. Across the water, probably a quarter mile away, the red running lights of a few cars. My heart sank.

Running along the beach, feet punching through the soft sand, it all looked vaguely familiar. Of course! Plum Creek Reservoir!

The winter before, on a cold sunny day, Kerry and I'd taken a stroll there, tossed rocks onto the ice to test its thickness, and had a little picnic. Jogging on, breath whistling through my lungs, I would've given everything to go back to that day and start again.

"Wait!" Stu yelled, crashing out of the trees and sprinting onto the beach. "I just wanna talk!"

The fact that he was gaining on me blew away most of the alcohol fumes from my brain, and I put on added surge of speed. My thighs burned, but I kept digging in my feet. The moon slid behind a cloud, and everything got dark. Then the ground gave out from under me. I slipped on my ass and plunged feet-first into shockingly cold water.

Head exploding with terror, I thrashed my arms and legs to stay afloat, but somehow I'd already sunk to the bottom of the lake and was flat on my back, elbows buried in the sticky mud. I managed to keep my mouth shut but had never been good at holding my breath. My chest hitched, and I knew I had mere seconds before I ran out of air.

With a superhuman effort, I spun my body so I was on my hands and knees and pushed off the mucky bottom in hopes of propelling myself back to the surface.

Spluttering, I got to my feet. I stood in a slow-moving creek, the water barely up to my thighs. It flowed for another ten yards through tall grass where it emptied into the reservoir. I stood there a moment, dripping, shivering, and laughing gratefully, until a hoarse voice shouted my name.

My loafers weighed down with water, I lurched upstream as the creek wound back into the safety of the woods. Shuddering with cold and nerves, I stopped every few minutes to listen but heard nothing more than the trickle of water. I climbed out of the creek, and, after dumping water from my shoes, walked along the bank, easy enough in the ample moonlight. Since the road encircled the reservoir, as long as I kept following the creek, I'd find the way out sooner or later.

My mind was like a bike chain that'd briefly fallen off its gears yet was back on track again. I was still a little drunk—drugged?—but could think clearly. As I trudged onward, I took stock of my situation.

Stu had molested me. Or, more specifically, my hand—which, though it felt scratchy, I was afraid to look at. Regardless, I was a victim of assault. Which was a crime. And, though I seemed to have lost him, I was still being chased by my attacker.

I extracted my phone from my back pocket, praying it still worked. Amazingly, it did. I dialed 9-1. Then stopped. And shoved the phone back in my pocket.

What would I even tell police? Would they believe me? And, if they did, what questions would they ask? No, the only thing that mattered was getting the hell out of there. I'd get to the road and call for a ride and weigh my other options later.

After another several minutes tracing the creek, beyond a screen of trees I could make out a patch of grass with a few picnic benches, the road right behind it. I'd found it but was far from home free. I still needed to be careful. First, I had to figure out what side of the reservoir I was on, then I'd make the call.

I crept across the picnic area and onto the road. After looking both ways and listening with hands cupped over my ears, I decided to walk to the right, the opposite direction from where Stu had parked. Less than a minute later, the rumble of an engine.

Heart in my throat, I sprinted back into the woods and dove headfirst into the leaf litter like a baseball player into home. Not ten seconds later Stu's SUV cruised slowly around the bend, headlights off. Motionless, I lay on my belly with eyes closed, trying to imagine myself invisible, until the vehicle was out of earshot.

With no time to waste, I took out my phone and searched for Kerry's contact, knowing full well I'd deleted it the day she left. Racking my tired brain, I tried several wrong combinations of numbers until I pulled up the call log. My spirit leapt with joy. There it was! Though it went straight to voice mail, I left a message asking her to please call me back right away. Seconds later, she did.

"Kerry?" I stage whispered.

"It's late," she groaned. "What do you want?"

"I'm in trouble."

Silence.

"Can you pick me up?" I asked.

"Are you drunk?"

"No—" I stopped myself. "Yes, but that's not—"

"I knew it. Try me again when you're sober."

"Wait, wait, please." More silence. "You still there?"

"Why don't you just call an Uber?"

"Because I need you." I broke down sobbing.

"You okay?" she asked with what sounded like genuine concern.

Licking salty tears from the corner of my mouth, it finally dawned on me how selfish I'd been to pin her down in a relationship when I was still uncertain about starting a family. In time, I'm sure I would've taken the leap, but I just couldn't be rushed. Of course, as a man who could theoretically get the job done for decades to come, it was an easy decision for me to put off. But with her narrower window, could I really blame her for the unspoken ultimatum?

"I think so," I said. "Can you please come?"

"Alright, I'm leaving now. Where are you?"

I explained my location as best I could and told her to text me when she passed the picnic area.

For the better part of an hour I crouched petrified behind a tree by the side of the road. Finally, I got the text. *Here.*

Sure enough, headlights.

I stood up and took a single step, then decided to wait a second just to be sure. My cheek pressed against the rough bark of the tree, a vehicle slowly approached. Stu's SUV. Heart jackhammering my ribcage, I held my breath until the taillights disappeared around a bend.

A few minutes later, another vehicle puttered along from the same direction. I called Kerry, and she picked up.

"If that's you, pull over," I whispered into the phone.

The vehicle stopped.

Kerry and I didn't exchange a single word as we drove the dark road around the reservoir—no sign of Stu's SUV—and then picked up the highway. There was so much I wanted to say to her but didn't know where to begin. She kept sneaking glances but knew me well enough not to pry. Not until we were parked in my driveway did I break the silence.

"Something's happening to me." I met her eyes for the first time in what felt like forever.

Kerry nodded and gave a sad smile.

"I'm changing and I don't know what's going on," I said. "I'm scared."

She touched my left hand, and, instinctively, I drew it away from her.

She cleared her throat. "I should probably get going."

I sighed. Now or never. I flicked on the dashboard light. "I want you to see something." I held out my palm, which felt raw and exposed, and peered out the window so I didn't have to see the inevitable disgust on her face.

She cradled my hand in hers. "What is it?"

"Exactly what it looks like." I forced myself to look at her. Instead of a scrunched-up mask of revulsion, Kerry's pretty face was unlined and calm, brows raised in curiosity.

"Have you been to the doctor—"

"No, I haven't." And I wouldn't be going, either.

"It's definitely weird." She set my hand down in my lap. "How does something like that even happen?"

"I'm not exactly sure," I said. "But I think I'm starting to understand."

"Understand what?"

Though I didn't—couldn't—know the details, I had no doubt that some force in the universe was sending me a message in the only way I could understand. And, indeed, even with this brief experience under my belt, so many of my assumptions about the world—and women, in particular—fell by the wayside.

Out of words, I leaned in for a hug. It felt so good to hold her, like snuggling under a down blanket on a frigid winter's night. After a few seconds of hesitation, she hugged me back.

"Gonna head home." Kerry patted me on the shoulder.

Reluctantly, I unwrapped my arms from around her. I didn't want her to go but knew she had to. Still, I needed to give it one last try. "You think we could maybe meet for coffee sometime?"

Kerry searched my face for a moment. "There *is* something different about you." Then laughed. "I mean, besides the obvious."

I held my breath. "That a yes?"

"Consider it a firm maybe." She started the ignition.

I woke up around noon after ten hours of deep dreamless sleep to the realization that my house had become a total sty. Shooing away the fruit flies, I rinsed the dirty dishes stacked in the kitchen sink, sponged off the crusty counter, swept and mopped the sticky floor.

I texted a bit with Kerry, and we agreed to meet at a teahouse downtown after work on Monday. She insisted it wasn't a date, but still I couldn't stop smiling. If this was my second chance, I was *not* going to blow it.

The night before, I'd plucked the stitches from my hand and cleaned out the mud and grit but hadn't bothered with any ointment or bandage. I finally accepted that, whatever it was, it wasn't a wound, and the best thing I could do was stop making such a big deal about it.

What I couldn't make sense of was what'd happened to me out at the reservoir. I hadn't really processed it the night before, but like a time-release capsule, the awfulness of the situation finally dawned on me. I was vacuuming the living room when a clear image of Stu slobbering over my hand like a St. Bernard flashed through my mind. Chest tight and stomach churning, I dropped the vacuum on the floor and dashed over to the front door to make sure it was locked. It was the first time I could remember feeling unsafe in my own home.

I spent the rest of the weekend cleaning, trying not to think about the incident. Yet, by the time Sunday evening rolled around my stomach felt like a blender set to frappé. How could I go back to work with Stu there? If not for the presentation, I would've called in sick.

I pictured myself driving over to the salesman's house, ringing the doorbell, and when Stu answered, jamming a screwdriver in his eye socket. Physically and emotionally, I knew I could do it, and if there'd been even a fifty percent chance of getting away with it, I might've tried. But I didn't know the first thing about murdering and would obviously get caught, having been the last person he was seen with at the bar.

I furiously scrubbed the stained toilet and scoured every inch of the grimy tub.

And the police? Even if I endured the suspicion, accusations, and humiliation of filing a report and being questioned, was licking someone's hand even a crime? And if it was, what proof did I have? No, it would simply be another case of he said/she said and more trouble than it was worth. Maybe it'd be best if I pretended it never happened.

Numb on the inside, I wrung out the sponge in the sink and watched the dirty water disappear down the drain.

In the shower Monday morning I took the first hard look at my hand in nearly forty-eight hours. The thing had shriveled ever so slightly, lips deflated, opening shrunk. I didn't want to get my hopes up, but maybe—just maybe—it was healing. I toweled myself off and almost put on a bandage, but since airing it out seemed to be helping, left it uncovered.

On the drive over to the dealership, I fretted about what I'd do when I saw Stu. I wasn't sure if I'd have a panic attack or would throttle him. Thankfully, when I got in, he wasn't at his desk. Part of me was relieved, though I knew sooner or later we'd cross paths.

I sat in my office with the door closed and ran through the slides on my laptop. Before I knew it, it was 9:45. Sweat leaking down my ribcage, I walked over to the conference room, hooked up my laptop to the projector, and waited for people to trickle in. As the dozen or so chairs filled up, I watched the door for Stu, who was supposed to be part of the first group. At 10 o'clock on the dot, Malcolm and Larry rolled in, but no Stu.

I asked someone to turn off the lights and began. Clicking through slides with clipart mechanics and stock photos of blandly attractive models in pantsuits, I reminded people that if they thought a comment or action might be inappropriate, it probably was, and gave some examples. Though I caught a few stifled yawns, all eyes were on me, and I heard not so much as a single groan.

Halfway through, the door opened, and my breath caught. I pretended not to notice Stu standing there uncertainly for a few seconds before he walked in and took a seat in the back. My mind swirling, I had the impulse to run out of the room and lock myself in my office. Or better yet, dash out of the building, race home, and bury my head under the covers.

But—almost of their own volition—my hands curled into fists, and I continued the presentation, dedicating a full five minutes to the importance of consent. At the end, I received a polite smattering of applause, and the lights came back on. Sandra, sitting in the front row, beamed at me.

My eyes fell on Stu, who immediately looked away.

"Any questions?" I asked, trying to understand what made guys like him tick. Had no one had ever held him accountable for his actions before? Maybe because he was charming and handsome, Stu had been rewarded for his bad behavior and literally didn't think the rules applied to him. Perhaps if someone had stood up to him in the past, he wouldn't have tried what he had with me.

Before I could stop myself, I spoke. "How about you, Stu? What did you learn?"

I watched his ruddy face drain of most of its color. "Sexual harassment is bad?"

Malcolm tittered, and I shot a withering glance his way, shutting him up instantly.

"How so?" I asked.

Stu shrugged. "Because of rights and stuff."

"One last question." I let an awkward silence hang for a count of five. "What does consent mean to you?"

"Uh." His Adam's apple bobbed as he swallowed. "No means no?"

"Any other questions?" While directed at the group, my eyes didn't leave Stu's.

He shook his head.

"So, you get it?" I asked.

Stu nodded emphatically, a plea for mercy in his eyes. Maybe I hadn't changed his views. But having called him out publicly, while also giving him a chance to mend his ways, I had a strong feeling his days of taking advantage of people—in that way, at least—were over. Whether that was true or not would remain to be seen.

"Good job, everyone." I gave them a small round of applause. "Now, back to work."

Viremia

"You scratched up his face pretty badly," I told her.

Terri Loma, twenty-four, slumped in the wooden chair on the other side of the table, sweat-slicked bangs hanging over puffy eyes. An overhead bank of buzzing fluorescents lit her face, sunken cheeks pale and shiny from nervousness, a hangover, or a little bit of both.

"Eight stiches," I said. "He'll probably have a scar."

She sniffed, wiped her nose with the back of a wrist. "I'm really sorry."

Pretty in a washed out kind of way, she didn't look like a troublemaker. As was so often the case with assaults, alcohol was the real culprit—but you can't arrest a bottle of bourbon.

"Tell me how it happened," I said. Loma declining to call a lawyer gave us both a good chance of getting to the bottom of things.

"He was dancing too close, rubbing up against me." She looked at me for the first time that morning since the arresting officer had brought her in. Her irises were the turquoise of glacial silt, several shades bluer than the faded Mesa County uniform clinging to her protruding belly. "I flipped out. I didn't mean to."

The chair creaked as I leaned back, chewed my lower lip, and tried not to ask the obvious question: What the hell was a pregnant woman doing out alone at some club at one a.m.?

"Can I go home now?" Loma's jaw worked as if she were chewing gum.

"They're processing you. Should be within the hour."

A clock hung on the cinderblock wall above her head, the second hand ticking up the numbers like a tank filling with gas.

"He's pressing charges, isn't he?" Loma asked.

I nodded.

She ran small hands over her cheeks, fingers briefly pulling down her lower eyelids to reveal a network of red capillaries, and then distorting her lips into a horrible grimace before her face returned to normal. "I can't deal with this right now."

Pity welled up for the poor thing, and I braced myself against it. "You made your own bed, honey."

"I can't find work as it is," Loma whimpered. "Now a record? I'm so fucked."

"Since this is your first offense, my guess is the judge'll go lightly." I reached out and brushed her hand, which she jerked away and rested on her watermelon stomach for a second before dropping it in her lap. "Just don't go beating up any more horndogs."

She laughed through her nose and then started to cry.

The pity rose up again, and this time I didn't push it back down. The woman had made a mistake but since sobering up had been nothing but cooperative. I had every reason to believe this was the first and last time she'd act up.

"Anything else you could tell the judge that might help?" I asked.

She flicked her wet eyes up to meet mine and then down to her clasped hands.

"Anything," I coaxed.

"You won't believe me."

"Try me," I said, crossing my arms below my breasts.

"You'll think I'm crazy." Loma's voice quivered. "Like everyone else."

"Honey, what've you got to lose?" I smiled, doing my best to radiate sincerity.

Loma tinked the table with a fingernail and let out a breath. "Six months ago I was in Utah."

Ever since Terri was nine and her folks had taken her on a road trip to Four Corners, Utah's canyon country had her spellbound. Despite a blazing sun that could peel your skin like a carrot, nosebleed aridity, and a harsh, desolate landscape, she found herself coming back again every year since college.

The rust and cream-colored slickrock undulations and the wide-open hundred-mile views beneath flame blue skies made her feel like she'd landed on another planet. So clean and pure, the terrestrial flesh carved away to reveal the stark framework of bone.

The first few times she'd made the trip with friends, but their nonstop chatter about reality TV and the guys they were seeing always irritated her. Since then she made a point of coming out alone. Though the silence was unnerving at times, she'd learned to love it—so quiet you could hear the rasp of a blinking eye—along with the crispness of the air, the resinous scent of sagebrush after a cloudburst.

Each fall she drove the five and a half hours out to Grand Staircase-Escalante National Monument for three days and two nights of camping and hiking to wash off the stink of civilization. She knew it was risky to go into the wilderness alone, so she kept to the popular, well-marked trails and always carried pepper spray.

As of late, the Utah Department of Tourism had been doing a blitzkrieg of TV, radio, and billboard ads around the West to lure more visitors to its many National Parks and Monuments and pump more money into the local economy. And it was working, as the usually empty highway had picked up a regular flow of traffic and the trailhead parking lots were all but full.

Instead of the usual ten or so hikers on her favorite trail—a six-mile round trip out to Fairview Arch—every few minutes she had to step aside to let someone pass from the other direction. The area around the arch itself was overrun with about thirty vacationers picnicking, snapping photos, and scrambling over the rocks. If it weren't for the cinnamon sands and caramel cliffs, she might as well have been back in Grand Junction. She took a few pictures and turned around.

On the drive to the campground—she'd been smart enough to reserve a site ahead of time—she stopped at the country store for a 22-ounce bottle of IPA to sip while watching the sunset.

"So, what do you think of Utah?" the wiry, sun-browned, forty-something dude at the counter asked. His face was handsome, if a bit craggy and weathered, the sleeves of his flannel rolled up to expose ropy forearms like strips of jerky. "First time, I assume."

"Been coming out here for years," Terri said, annoyed at being lumped in with the Winnebago tourists from California.

"Looks like we've got ourselves a real hiker. Fairview Arch?" He looked her up and down, assessing. "That's six eighty-two."

She nodded, forked over a ten. He handed her the change, his rough fingers brushing hers.

"Sticking to the well-trodden ways," he said. "Wise for a girl out here all alone."

He wasn't being rude, exactly, but she still felt like he was condescending. She wasn't sure why she cared. "Didn't used to be this crowded."

"Think it's bad now, just wait till next year."

Terri pocketed the change and picked up the cold bottle. "You live out here?"

"Twelve years."

"Bet you know the country pretty well."

"Could say that."

"Any special spots you wanna tell me about?"

He grinned, shook his head. "Wouldn't like 'em."

"Why not?" The chill of the bottle seeping into her fingers, she set it back down on the counter.

"Mighty lonesome out there."

"You wouldn't say that to a guy," she said, half-joking.

He rolled his eyes. "Keep to the beaten path. No trouble that way."

"I know what I'm doing."

The man lifted his goateed chin to scan the back of the store, as if someone might be lurking behind the aisles. "Heard of Hell's Backbone?"

Terri shook her head.

"Trailhead's about ten miles from here, but the tourons don't know about it cuz there aren't any signs. Got four wheel drive?"

"Yes," she lied, proud he didn't consider her a *touron.*

"Listen here." He pointed a finger at her. "I can't be responsible for anything that happens to you."

"I can take care of myself, thank you very much."

He examined her out of the corner of an eye, nodded. From the cabinet over his head, he tore down a flier advertising a chili cook off and fished a pen from the breast pocket of his shirt. On the blank side, he sketched a rough map that showed the highway and a squiggle of back roads.

"Most people don't have the guts." He handed her the paper.

She folded it in quarters and jammed it in her pocket. "I'm not most people."

"I can tell that already." He stared into her eyes.

"Appreciated," Terri said, grabbing her beer and starting towards the exit before things went any further. Her palm was on the glass door when he spoke again, as she knew he would.

"Can you keep a secret?"

"I guess," she said, not turning around, shoulders tense.

"C'mere."

She wasn't sure why, but she walked back over.

Instead of propositioning her, he pulled a worn topo map from under the counter and drew an X somewhere at the edge of a blank spot.

"If you take the trail for a mile and a half, you'll climb up a dome like a turtle shell," he whispered. "On the other side, down below the trail, you'll see a stand of big ass ponderosa pines. Head down the slope, that's Drift Creek. Trace it upstream through the canyon, you'll find some of the gnarliest petroglyphs in Utah."

"Wow, thanks." Though there was no chance of her leaving the main trail, she was still grateful for the inside scoop.

"One of the last magic places," he said, eyes glassy, as if picturing the scene. He handed her the map. "And it's not in any guidebook."

"What do I owe you for the map?"

"On the house." He stroked his goatee. "Maybe come back and see me sometime?"

"I'll think about it," Terri said, smiling on her way out the door.

Terri woke up late after a so-so night's sleep atop her leaking pad, which, come morning, had completely run out of air. The day was hot for late September but not blazing, just enough clouds in the sky to soften the punishing glare. She made a quick breakfast of a nut bar, jumped in her beat-up sedan, and followed the map to the trailhead.

The first dirt road was well graded, but the next one was studded with rocks and more than once she scraped the undercarriage. Still, she made it to the tiny trailhead parking lot without any real damage.

The first mile of the hike was mostly level, the red dirt trail cutting through a plain of blue-grey sagebrush clumped with gnarled junipers and pinyon pines. Finally, curving around a bend, the trail dropped and opened up to a vast buff-yellow slickrock vista, humping expanses of rock descending into a labyrinth of wrinkles and folds below.

There was no discernible path, and Terri wondered if she might be out of her element. But stacked rock cairns marked the way, like a permanent breadcrumb trail. She'd have to try pretty hard to get lost, and if she got nervous she could always turn back.

The tip from the store clerk aside, it was pretty unlikely she'd end up leaving the main route. The anxious part of her mind even wondered if he'd follow her out there. Or maybe it was the hopeful part, as she'd never been this deep in the wilderness alone.

The route pitched downward, but despite the name, the dry "slickrock" was almost tacky beneath her boots. Every time she reached another cairn she looked behind her to make sure she could see the one before, as well as visually trace the route back to the sagebrush plain above. The air simmered and sweat soaked though her shirt, yet she felt energized by the sun's rays, like she could hike all day.

Overhead, a raven flew by on creaking wings. Immersing herself deeper in the alien splendor, she felt the last of her fear evaporate.

Balancing on a couple of downed limbs, she crossed a small stream piddling through the bottom of its carved channel. Though scarcely three feet wide, she reminded herself that during a flash flood it'd be a roaring brown mess loaded with rocks and tree limbs, virtually impassable.

Terri followed the cairns onward through the increasingly rugged terrain for another twenty minutes, grinning like a crazy person. This— wandering through the spectacular desert alone, the only thought in her mind her next footstep—was freedom. If she couldn't find a job soon, maybe she'd just live out there forever. Her sharp chuckle ricocheted off the rocks.

Cresting a hill, she was rewarded with a killer view of warped, blushing stone with the dim spine of mountains beyond. She figured she'd hike another half hour and then go back.

Taking a slug from her water bottle, she admired a stand of trees below the trail, trunks plated with orange bark like the hide of a prehistoric beast. No others within eyeshot, it had to be the stand of ponderosas the clerk told her about.

Terri had no intention of abandoning the trail, but the slope leading to the trees wasn't steep. Why not just check it out and see how she felt? After tucking her bottle away in her backpack, she carefully made her way down to stand beneath a towering pine, its branches silhouetted against the blazing sky. A slight flutter in her chest, she peered back up at the hump of slickrock. The cairn was impossible to miss.

Quiet, except for the murmur of water and a few flies buzzing around her head like shorting wires, she pushed through some prickly bushes and discovered a thin creek. Curious, she took out the map. Unless she read it wrong, it was Drift Creek, and if she came across anything sketchy, she could turn around immediately.

She set out along the wide sandy wash with its tiny trickle of water, angling rock walls framing either side. In the bizarre unlikelihood of a rainstorm and flash flood, there were plenty of boulders to scurry up and get out of harm's way. She'd walk until she came across the first petroglyph and no further.

Her breathing quickened as the canyon walls steepened, almost meeting overhead to block out the sun. But the enchantment of the rosy cliffs overpowered her nerves and she kept going.

A few hundred yards in, the first of the petroglyphs were etched into the vertical rock at eye level. Triangular humanoid figures. Hulking bi-pedal creatures with horns, like Greek minotaurs. A few canines, either dogs, coyotes, or wolves. What looked like a cartoon ghost with a single eye in the center of its body. Odd spiky spirals, perhaps some sort of shield used in battle.

Every time Terri told herself she'd turn back, she stumbled on another gallery. Several mysterious slot canyons cleft the rock, the third of which teemed with glyphs. It was about six feet wide, and she stepped inside, the air at least ten degrees cooler. Its walls were carved with more of the spiral spiky shields and people lying on the ground as if wounded in battle.

The cleft narrowed imperceptibly as she penetrated further, but instead of claustrophobia she was actually comforted by the sandstone that rippled to either side like ribbon candy. A slim brown lizard stole across the rock. She strolled until the slot dead-ended in a jumble of boulders, which upon closer inspection led upwards like rough stairs.

She looked at her watch. Only one o'clock. It would take her about fifteen minutes to get back to the main trail, and an hour at most to reach the car, more than enough time to not lose any daylight. She'd regret it if she didn't just climb up a bit further to see what was on the other side. And, to think, she hadn't even planned to investigate the canyon at all!

After an easy scramble, she topped the rise...and gaped. About ten feet below, the canyon widened out to a sandy area the size of a football field. To one side, a glorious waterfall gushed down a pink cliff face and collected into a jade-green pool, a sight rivaling any she'd seen in a National Park.

Camera out, she snapped a few photos, then figured a head on angle would give her a better shot of the falls. The way down looked simple, a slight rocky pitch with several jutting knobs that made decent hand and footholds. Moments later she was safely on the ground, and she got off a dozen shots before the battery died.

She unlaced her boots, kicked them off, stripped away her sweaty socks, and sat at the edge of the pool, heels dangling just above the water. A cheese sandwich and a couple of handfuls of banana chips made for a satisfying lunch as the occasional speck of foam from the thundering waterfall landed on her face.

The high sun beat down on her shoulders, and she figured she had time for a quick swim. After a scan to make sure no one was watching—silly, of course, as if anyone else would be out there in the middle of nowhere— she peeled off her T-shirt, shorts, and panties, and, with a squeal, jumped in. She spluttered in the shockingly cold water and swam a lap of breaststroke across the pool and back until she got used to the temperature.

Turkey vultures surfed the thermals hundreds of feet above as she floated on her back, the rumble of the falls vibrating in her bones. Terri sighed, unable to remember the last time she'd felt so relaxed.

It only took a few minutes for the cold to set in, and she started to shiver. Halfway back across the pool, something slid into the water from the rim.

Flash flood was her first thought, that her final seconds of life would be clawing through a goopy brown stew. But it wasn't mud.

One by one, several dull grey spheres of various sizes—from basketballs, to baseballs, to golf balls—plopped into the pool, and then in clusters of three or four. Each ball dunked underwater, then bobbed up again to float on the surface as if filled with air.

Treading water, she squinted in fascination, trying to figure out what the hell they were. Flotation devices swept down from the Colorado River during a recent rainstorm? Those old glass fishnet buoys that sometimes washed up on California beaches? Several more of them bowled into the pool until dozens clustered at the edge like a garbage patch.

Almost in unison, each sphere began to slowly rotate, and, inch by inch, churn through the water towards her. As they got closer, she was confused to find they were covered with little spikes, almost like hairs but stiffer, made out of whatever rubbery material the balls themselves were, their color the gunky grey of baked salmon after you stripped away the skin.

Nearer now, she could see several of the spiky orbs were tiny, no bigger than marbles, some of them even smaller.

A kind of invasive plant left out of the guidebooks? Except no wind propelled them, and something about their dogged, if sluggish, approach made her feel like prey.

Whatever they were, it was time to get the fuck out of there. Yet when Terri swam to the edge of the pool and extended her arm up along the rock wall, she was horrified to find the lip out of reach by at least two feet.

Blood throbbed in her temples. The things moved nearer, spreading out across the water as if in hunting formation.

Forcing down her panic like a shot of liquor, she jammed her fingers into an indentation in the rock just over her head and pinched with all her strength. Numb from the cold, her fingers slipped, and she dropped back into the water.

The closest sphere, roughly the size of a grapefruit, was ten feet away, most of the rest trundling along close behind, a few dipping off aimlessly to the edges of the pool.

Whimpering, she curled her hands into claws and tried to dig her fingernails into the rotting stone. One of her nails snapped, and she fell back into the pool, swearing.

The slate-colored grapefruit was almost on her, spinning along like an aquatic tumbleweed, the rest of the pack in unhurried pursuit.

Her toes touched something gooey, and she screamed, then realized it was only the mucky bottom of the pool, shallower in that spot. Clenching her jaw, she set both feet on the slimy stone, bent at the knees, and launched upwards against the wall, one arm reaching skyward as if for a slam dunk.

The tips of her fingers missed the ledge by only a couple of inches, and she slammed against the gritty rock. Miraculously, instead of careening back into the pool, her wet breasts and stomach suctioned her body froglike against the rock, her knees, calves, ankles, and feet still underwater.

Suspended in midair, she felt like the coyote in the old Roadrunner cartoons—she'd only fall if she looked down.

Excruciatingly slow, she crept her fingers up the rock, blindly searching for a crack in which to jam her fingers. Her hand closed around an egg-sized protuberance, which, despite the lack of sensation in her fingers, she grasped firmly.

Forearms shuddering with the strain, Terri held herself aloft as she drew a knee upward and wedged it into a concavity. Her skin scraped against the rock, but her entire body was out of the water. She craned her neck up, the ledge just two feet above. One more hoist and she could get her fingers over the top and pull herself to safety.

What a story she'd have to tell once she got out of that God forsaken hellhole. Her first stop would be the country store to chew out that stupid fucking clerk with his shitty hiking advice.

Preparing for her next thrust upward, she gripped the rock knob tighter with her aching hand. Like a stale cookie, it crumbled between her fingers. Arms flailing outward, Terri caught a glimpse of electric blue sky as she plummeted backwards into the pool.

When she rose to the surface again the awful things were on her. Spinning up against her forehead and cheeks, firm yet yielding like wet clay, bumping her lips, which she clamped shut in disgust. A handful of the smaller ones tangled in her hair, and she frantically raked them out with her fingers.

With the back of her hand, she batted away a fishbowl-sized one on her shoulder. It coasted through the air for a few feet, landed in the water, and spun relentlessly back towards her.

Terri was trapped. Only one way out.

She took a deep breath and dove under the water. Eyes open, she swam through the dim green sediment-flecked water until the nasty clump of shadowy spheres hovering above her thinned.

When she emerged into the air again, she broke into a frenzied crawl stroke until she reached the low rim she'd jumped off. Like a seal with an orca in hot pursuit, she flung herself onto dry land. Halfway across the pool, the mass of globes rolled sluggishly towards her.

She stood up, water dripping off her body to darken the sand underfoot, and feverishly examined the back of her arms, under her biceps, her ass, and the back of her thighs and calves. Aside from the raw abraded skin on her breasts and stomach from clinging to the rock, she was unharmed. Not a bite, not a sting, not a rash.

Whatever they were—insects? fungus?—she was safe.

Still soaking wet, she tugged on her shirt, shorts, and shoes, scooped up her backpack and shoved in her panties and socks, then bolted towards the pitch she'd descended to get into the canyon. She scrambled up it in seconds.

Once on top, Terri half expected to see the spheres lurching up the rock behind her. Instead, they floated aimlessly in the green pool below.

Her hands shook as she unscrewed her water bottle and took a swig. She made herself walk—not run—out of the slot canyon, though she couldn't help but look over her shoulder every few seconds, the creeping dread settling down into relative calm.

Whatever had happened back there, it was over. Other than a few scrapes and probably some bruises that would surface later, she wasn't injured. The isolation of the remote canyon had simply unsettled her to the point where she'd gotten herself all worked up over nothing.

Lots of weird things lived out in the desert, just because she couldn't identify them off the top of her head didn't mean they were out of the ordinary. Come to think of it, they'd looked a lot like horse chestnuts. Though horse chestnuts didn't move.

She reached Drift Creek, passed the petroglyphs, which she barely glanced at, and walked along at a clip until she made it to the turtle shell rock, and set out on the main trail again. To silence her buzzing mind, she tried to focus on nothing but her next footfall on sand and stone.

A half hour later she left the slickrock behind and climbed onto the sagebrush plain. As she ducked beneath a pinyon pine branch weighted down by brown cones, it finally dawned on her what the balls were: Mexican jumping beans!

Though obviously not the same species, they were a seedpod inside of which some insect had laid its eggs. When the eggs hatched, the larvae rolled the pods out of the sun to avoid being cooked as they fed on the seeds' nutritious innards. The larvae's quest for shade—not blood—had propelled the pods through the cooling water.

Terri laughed in relief. Leisurely now, she walked the final mile back to the car.

"You've been through a lot," I said to Terri Loma as soon as she wrapped up her story. According to the clock on the station wall, only a half-hour had passed.

Sweat gleamed on Loma's forehead, like she'd just gotten back from her desert hike, instead of six months earlier. "Shouldn't have told you."

"No. You did the right thing," I said, delicately, knowing the ridiculous tale of the magic seedpods was her mind's defense mechanism for trying to deal with what'd happened to her.

"I wanted to get rid of it, but I couldn't."

"I understand. I really do."

As soon as she was released, I'd make the call to the Garfield County, Utah Sheriff and have them send an officer over to question the clerk, if he hadn't already skipped town. Assaulted in the middle of a godforsaken wasteland, and now carrying the dirtbag's baby, it's a wonder Loma hadn't done more than just scratch up some drunk's face at the bar.

It was out of my purview to help her come to terms with what'd happened to her. But I could bring the scum who did it to justice.

"It'll be okay." I poured a cup of water from the pitcher and pushed it over to her. She reached for it, then hunched up, grimacing in pain, knocking the cup over. The water slopped across the table and dripped onto the floor.

Alarmed, I jolted up. "You okay?"

Doubled over, Terri clutched her stomach and gurgled through clenched teeth. She was having her baby!

"I'll get EMS!" I shouted.

Loma dropped off the chair and sprawled onto the floor. As expected, her blue pants were drenched. Her water had broken. Or so I thought.

Out of her pantleg, over her bare ankle and onto the floor, streamed a clear, thick, rotten-smelling liquid, along with dozens of grey BBs, prickly as thistles.

They squelched, leaving thin tracks of slime on the cement floor as they rolled towards me.

Six Ways To Beat Your Landlord

So, you like where you're living but hate your landlord. And who can blame you?

Jacking up rent in the middle of a recession. Randomly showing up without notice. Putting off—or even refusing—basic repairs. Taking the "lord" part of their title literally, most of them treat us like houseguests who just so happen to be paying their mortgage.

Lucky for you, I'm an experienced renter who knows how to protect my "right to quiet enjoyment." And I'm going to teach you six ways to fight back against your landlord—and win.

1. One Door Closes

If your landlord is anything like mine, once you pay your security deposit (on top of first and last month's rent), you'll never see a dollar of it again. Unfortunately, there's nothing you can do about that...or is there?

Tell your landlord the garage door isn't opening right and you're afraid it's about to crush you at any moment. When they swing by to check, explain that while it may work sometimes, it malfunctions often enough that you feel unsafe.

When they send over the repair person, they won't find anything wrong, of course. But your landlord will still have to pay the couple of hundred bucks for the visit, canceling out at least some of the money they'll be stealing from you once you move out.

2. *It's Getting Hot in Here*

If you live anywhere except the South, your landlord probably won't have installed central air conditioning (though they definitely have it in *their* home). If you're lucky, there'll be a single window air conditioner, most likely in your bedroom. But it'll be so old and rickety that you'll still sweat through your sheets every night.

Don't bother asking them to replace it, just tell them in passing that it doesn't seem to fit right in the window—which, naturally, they'll do nothing about. Instead, complain about the woodpecker drilling holes in the outside wall of your bedroom (it doesn't matter if there's really a bird or not, just get a ladder and chisel some in).

When your landlord comes over to look, "accidentally" knock the air conditioner from its perch so it comes crashing to the ground a few feet away from them. Now, they'll have no choice but to get you a new one.

3. *Just Thought I'd Drop By*

Does your landlord barge in on you every few weeks to root through their junk in the garage because they're too stingy to rent a storage space? Or maybe they even ignore the agreed upon twenty-four-hour notice in your lease to do an illegal "walkthrough," going so far as to knock on your bedroom door where you're sleeping to demand entry?

Set up an online search alert for any dog maulings in your area. Soon as you're notified, contact the local shelters until you find the place about to euthanize it. Offer to adopt and rehabilitate the animal, telling them you live alone in the country on a big fenced-in acreage. If you can't convince them through official channels, it's a safe bet that one of the volunteers will smuggle the dog out for you. If compassion alone doesn't do the trick, bribe them.

Now take Cujo home, fit him with a bark collar, and train him to be quiet, even when someone knocks on the door. With all that in place, call up your landlord and let them know you'll be out of town for two days. Make the temptation irresistible by asking them to "keep an eye on the place"—basically an invitation to come inside and snoop.

Important note: Make sure *not* to have fed the dog for at least a full day before you leave.

4. Cat and Mouse

Do mice keep sneaking into your place through holes in the foundation? And no matter how many you catch in traps, more come in to gnaw through your packaged goods in the cupboard, leave tiny little "gifts" on your dish sponge, and spread disease across the kitchen counter? And though it's a legal requirement for your landlord to deal with an infestation, they refuse, telling you this is what it's like to live in the country/town/city?

Instead of wasting your time complaining, mention a drip in the kitchen ceiling. Penny-pincher or not, I guarantee they'll show up pretty fast, since, unlike mice, doing nothing about leaks like that would mean major costs down the line.

Slide your oven out from the wall and find the yellow plastic gas line. With a hacksaw, cut a small rough hole like a mouse has chewed through it (yes, mice can chew through almost anything!). A half hour before your landlord is scheduled to get there, turn on the oven, hurry outside, and leave a note on the front door telling them you're at the store but they're welcome to come in.

Once the fire department finds the "chewed up" gas line, there's a 100% chance your mouse problem will be taken care of.

5. *That's Some View*

If your rental has a second story deck or balcony, let your landlord know the railing looks rotten and needs replacing. As with the tub, they won't even think about repairs if they can convince you it's fine, so they'll definitely come by to show you nothing's wrong.

Because the only thing a landlord loves more than stealing money from tenants is the high they get from debasing us, a modern day Nazi doctor experiment to see how much dignity a human being will sacrifice in the name of shelter.

That's why, after one year of renting—in the middle of a recession, right after I lost my job—my landlord told me they were raising the rent by $500. When I suggested that a twenty-five percent hike was a bit steep, they "compromised" by only raising it $250 plus shifting the water and trash bills over to me—still, a total of $400 more per month. Then, just to mess with me, they took out the couch, rug, guest room bed, deck furniture, even paintings off the wall. And after all that, with my monthly rent higher than the average mortgage, they still had the nerve to tell me how I "drive a hard bargain."

The night before your landlord is scheduled to look at your balcony, saw the railing nine-tenths of the way through. When they get there, say you're afraid to put any weight on it. When they lean on it themselves to try to prove you wrong, they'll fall.

Most of the time they won't get hurt that badly—in my landlord's case, nothing more than a broken leg and a few cracked ribs. But I bet you cold hard cash they'll fix your deck!

Six Ways To Beat Your Landlord

6. On Their Turf

Unfortunately, not all landlords are the handy type. Lazier than they are cheap, they'll send over a contractor for anything that needs doing, making tips two through five of no use to you.

In my case, two months before my lease was about to run out—and I was finally moving out because they wanted to raise the rent *another* $800— my landlord decided they were going to remodel the kitchen and repaint the entire interior. And with no notice; one morning a construction crew just showed up.

Of course, my landlord did this while I was still living there because they didn't want to lose a single dollar by not renting the place out the day I left. So, why not make me bear the brunt of the construction without any of the benefits?

When I asked for a tiny reduction on rent because of the disruption since I work from home, my landlord angrily explained that I didn't have any cause to "withhold" rent. (At the best of times, landlords won't acknowledge your wishes. When there's a conflict between their whims and your rights—or your needs and their responsibilities—they turn into literal sociopaths.)

Because the rental market is so competitive and a good reference is everything, I decided not to fight and suffer quietly through my last two months. What I didn't know at the time was that, despite me always paying rent by the first of the month and keeping the place neat as a pin, they would still go on to tell every one of my prospective landlords how bad a tenant I was! Which meant that, for months after moving out, my only choice was to crash on a friend's couch.

So, when my ex-landlord called me to demand I return the extra key, I went over to pay them a visit at *their* house. Before they could slam the door in my face, I stabbed them in the eye with the sharpened key and dragged them inside. While they lay bleeding out on the exact rug they'd stolen from my rental, I stomped on the furniture, punched holes in the walls, and went to the bathroom on their bed.

Standing over them as they died, I realized this wasn't over. That they'd just pass the property down to their landlord kin who'd go on to abuse the next tenant. In the name of renters everywhere, I needed to break the cycle by finding each member of their family—parents, siblings, children—and take them out, too.

Sadly, I wasn't able to carry out my plan. But on the bright side, not only did I get rid of my landlord, I found a new place in the country. The downsides are that the bedroom's kind of small, plus I've got a roommate.

But what more than makes up for that is all the cleaning and repairs are taken care of. And, incredibly, I've got a live-in chef to cook all my meals, even if they're not quite restaurant quality.

Now, are you ready for the best part? Because I could barely believe it myself...I'm living rent free! And my lease? It runs for the rest of my life.

The Cat's Meow

"Many hate the voice of the cat in the night, and take it ill that cats should run stealthily about yards and gardens at twilight."

– H.P. Lovecraft, "The Cats of Ulthar"

Kneeling on her bedroom floor, Candice wound the wire three times around the bike frame at the angle where the seat tube met the chain guard. She wrapped the other end around the handle of the second rusty monkey wrench until it was firmly attached and then snipped the wire with the cutters. Standing the whole thing against the wall, she stepped back to scrutinize her work. Definitely a pelvis and legs.

After slipping into a pair of leather work gloves, she sorted through the pile of scrap metal, lifting and inspecting old tire rims, drainpipes, and warped saw blades. Candice almost never knew what she was making when she started her sculptures. Instead, her method was more intuitive, where she'd try to match random pieces of junk together until they fit, a puzzle without a picture on the front of the box.

Whatever Candice was doing was working, as she'd found coveted gallery space right on Santa Fe Drive, the main drag for Denver's First

Friday art walk, and had sold almost every piece she'd made since moving to town six months before. Her last one, a jagged geometrical abstract, had fetched $1,500. She didn't think she'd have this one ready for the next walk but was shooting for the one after.

She picked up a steel spring the length of her forearm, probably some car part, and turned it around in her gloved hands. Then, wincing against what felt like gears grinding inside her skull, dropped it back into the pile with a clang.

She took off her gloves and rubbed her eyes with the heels of her hands. The headache she'd been trying to ignore was only getting worse, and now it was hard to concentrate.

The bathroom was unoccupied except for Felicia—the fat orange tabby and unofficial mascot of the Glyph art collective—scratching away in her nasty little sandbox. Candice took the bottle of acetaminophen from the drawer, popped two in her mouth, and washed them down with a handful of sink water.

Back in her bedroom, she drew the shades against the Colorado spring sunshine, and dropped into bed, telling herself she'd just rest her eyes until the medicine kicked in.

She woke to a knock on her door and then a slice of light pouring into the dark room followed by a bespectacled, clay-smeared face.

"You okay?" Margo asked, a potter, and one of the four other artists living at the collective.

Candice's headache had mostly gone away, though the back of her flannel shirt was damp with sweat. "Just napping."

"It's the third time I've come by."

"Tired." Baking hot, Candice stripped off the blanket and sat up against the headboard.

"Well, dinner's ready. I made chicken stir-fry. Everyone's out, so it's just you and me."

"Dinner?" It'd been noon when Candice first lain down. "What time is it?" The tang of fried garlic in the air was unmistakable.

"Around six." Margo stepped into the room, knelt beside the bed, and set the back of her hand against Candice's forehead. "You're burning up, girl."

"I'm okay." Candice moved to get up, but Margo pushed her gently back by the shoulder.

"Stay here." Margo left and came back with a digital thermometer, which she stuck in Candice's mouth. After a minute, it beeped. Margo took it out of her mouth and looked it at. She shook her head. "A hundred and two. Let's call your doctor."

"I'm fine," Candice insisted.

"It's not just about you, anymore." Margo smiled.

Candice sat in an open-backed paper gown on a length of butcher paper on the examination table in Dr. Wiedman's cramped office, the banks of fluorescent lights sizzling her eyes, the room stinking of alcohol. Her fever had gone down to one-hundred point three by the morning, but Margo made her keep the appointment and drove her in.

"Probably just a virus." Dr. Wiedman removed her cold stethoscope from Candice's naked back. "I'd still like a blood test to be sure."

Candice's heart jittered. "Why? What else would it be?"

"Oh, could be any number of infections." Wiedman smiled reassuringly, the crow's feet to either side of her blue eyes deepening. "In the off chance that's the case, I want to make sure it's nothing that can affect the baby."

"You mean like Zika?" Candice pictured herself reclining on the delivery table holding her newborn at arm's length, shrieking at the sight of its smushed skull and googly eyes.

"You said you haven't been out of the state in six months, right?" Wiedman asked.

Candice nodded.

Wiedman patted her knee. "It's not Zika."

Margo flipped through the radio stations with one hand—"Sweet Home, Alabama," commercial, Jesus talk, mariachi band, commercial—the other holding the Volvo's steering wheel. "I feel like it would be weirder *not* to invite him, you know?"

"Hmm," Candice said, the car interior going dim as they drove under an overpass and then out into the sunshine again.

"It's not that I wouldn't like to see him," Margo droned on. "It's just that..."

Candice tuned out, fingered the bandage holding the cotton ball against the tender crook of her elbow where Dr. Wiedman had drawn blood.

If it wasn't the flu, then what was it? She felt a little tired but otherwise fine. Obviously, Wiedman suspected something or she wouldn't be running the test. Or maybe this was just protocol for when a pregnant woman got sick?

Probably nothing. No point in worrying about it, anyway—she'd have the results in three weeks. Until then, Candice wouldn't say anything about it to Lenny. He had enough on his plate as it was, struggling to sell his paintings so he could provide for their baby.

Their exit was coming up, and the Volvo drifted into the right lane. A car popped into Candice's peripheral, some low slung-sporty model, probably a Jag, with tinted windows.

"Watch out!" Candice screamed, a half second before a horn blared and the side of the Volvo smacked into the Jag, the impact throwing her shoulder against the taut seatbelt.

Margo swung the wheel to the left, but that lane was blocked by a minivan. She careened them back into the right lane again—empty now, as the Jag had pulled over on the shoulder—and then veered onto the exit's off-ramp going way too fast.

Candice's teeth chattered as the Volvo's tires ground over the rumble strip, and then she bucked forward against the belt as Margo pumped the brakes, slowing the car as they circled around and were spat out onto the busy street.

They kept driving.

"What're you doing?!" Candice yelled.

"I don't know!" Sitting bolt upright, Margo strangled the wheel, her shoulders tense.

"Stop the car!"

"Where?!"

"Anywhere!"

Margo pulled into the next driveway, the lot of a recreational pot shop, its sign a fluorescent green five-pointed leaf. She parked in one of the spaces and shut off the ignition.

"You alright?" Wide-eyed, Margo looked Candice up and down.

Candice rubbed her shoulder, a little sore from the seatbelt, but that was it, unless the adrenaline masked a more serious injury. She doubted it, though, as they'd barely grazed the other car. Hell, the airbag hadn't even deployed. Setting her hand on her belly, she was sure the baby was fine. "I'm good."

"Oh, thank God. Thank God." Margo hung her head, panting as if she'd just run a 10K. Then, with a gasp, snapped her head back up. "We have to go back!"

"What?"

Margo started the car. "We left the scene of an accident. It's illegal."

"It's okay. Chill out." Candice unzipped her purse and pulled out her phone. It felt good to play the role of the calm one, knowing full well that if she was alone, she'd be crying her eyes out. "Your insurance good? License. Registration. All that?"

"Of course."

Candice dialed 911. "Then we're cool," she said. And meant it.

Candice pinched off a sprig of parsley from one of the bunches in the garden bed and bit into its sharp freshness, the final ingredient for her famous beef stew.

The headache and fever hadn't come back, the soreness in her shoulder was gone, and she felt good as new. Just a passing virus, and the test results she'd get from Dr. Wiedman would prove it.

She snapped off a larger stalk, then catching a sickening whiff of feces, flung it onto the lawn. Halfway buried in the soil was another turd, courtesy of Felicia.

"Lenny!" Candice yelled. "She did it again!"

The sliding door opened, and Lenny looked out into the tiny fenced-in backyard, his lank greasy hair hanging down to his shoulders. He held a paintbrush in his hand like a magic wand, bright red spotting the front of a black T-shirt emblazoned with the name of the metal band, Pantera.

Lenny shoved the brush in the back pocket of his jeans and grabbed a shovel leaning against the side of the house. "Why is it again you can't do this?"

Candice blew out an exasperated breath, something she found herself doing a lot those days. "Something in the poop. It can hurt the baby. You know this."

He shuffled over to the raised bed, scooped the turd with the shovel, and held it out to her with a scowl, as if for inspection.

Sporting long-lashed green eyes and a strong jaw, he was a decent looking guy, though his pale complexion, caveman brow, and patchy goatee ensured no one would mistake him for handsome. Hopefully, the kid would inherit their best traits, Lenny's eyes and Candice's smile.

"Thank you." She brushed past him to the far end of the garden bed where she bent to gather more parsley. "I know how you hate being interrupted."

And it was this fanatical dedication to his art—a series of uninhabitable landscapes of burnt forests, bubbling swamps, and ice fang mountains—that had first attracted her when she'd moved into the Glyph. Lenny wasn't much of a talker, but he was a great listener and had always encouraged and supported her sculpture. In no way perfect, he was a good man, and she had no regrets about loving him.

But over the last month or so—right after his own bout with some brief illness, come to think of it—he'd gone from quiet and thoughtful to just plain sullen. She figured it had something to do with the reality of the baby finally setting in, so was giving him time to come to terms with it all.

A light slap on her ass and then a squeeze. Not again. She swatted his hand away and went on picking parsley.

Strangely, as Lenny became more and more withdrawn, his horniness had skyrocketed. Sex with him had never been anything to brag about, but at least it'd been comfortable. Now it was pretty spectacular, she had to admit, though their recent disconnect made her feel used during the act, like she was some machine at the gym on which he was banging out his reps.

"Thought you needed to work," Candice said.

"Work can wait." He moved closer, pushing his hardness against her.

She rose from the garden bed, parsley in hand. "Got something on the stove," she blurted and headed inside, feeling only slightly guilty this time.

The rich scent of beef and spices filled the kitchen from the pot of stew simmering on the range top. She rinsed the parsley in the sink with its lousy water pressure, chopped it up on a cutting board, and dumped it in. As she stirred with a wooden spoon, scraping the bottom to make sure nothing stuck, Felicia leapt onto the kitchen counter.

Candice had always been more of a dog person. But moody Felicia didn't get along with dogs, so she'd had to leave Vulfie, her eight-year-old beagle, with her ex back in Philly when she'd moved. Obviously, this sacrifice hadn't endeared Candice to the preening furball.

As a pack animal, a dog has loyalty to other members of its group and can show genuine affection. Cats, on the other hand, are solitary and pledge alliance to none. In fact, a cat's owner is little more than a food delivery mechanism whose flexible fingers can also scratch hard to reach places. When a cat rubs its face against you it's not a gesture of love but a way to spread its scent, effectively claiming you as its own.

Tail held high, Felicia padded across the counter towards the stew. Candice hissed and shooed her away with a hand. The cat backed up a few steps, lay down, lifted a leg, and licked herself like some pervert exhibitionist.

Early humans evolved alongside dogs, keeping us company, helping us hunt, and protecting us from predators, mostly prehistoric cats like saber-toothed tigers. Meanwhile, even today, African lions and tigers in Asia killed scores of people every year, and mountain lions still attacked the occasional jogger or cyclist in the western U.S. Indeed, our fear of the dark may very well have originated from feline threats.

Candice reached for the spray bottle of water and spritzed in Felicia's general direction. The cat rawred, jumped off the counter, and scurried out of the kitchen. Several hairs floated in the air and slowly settled to the floor.

"You two have more in common than you think," Geoffroy said on his way to the fridge, thick arms sticking out of a wife beater, in surprisingly good shape for his early fifties despite a bit of a pot belly. With his bulky physique, he looked more like a construction worker from Chicago than a Quebecois children's book illustrator.

"You're kidding," Candice said, but she knew he wasn't. The wooden spoon sank into the stew like a dinosaur in a tar pit.

Felicia had been looking somewhat bloated recently, but Candice had convinced herself it was thanks to Margo—her official human—overfeeding her. Of course, deep down she'd known all along.

When Candice had first learned that this outdoor cat wasn't spayed, she brought it up at the weekly meeting. But Margo started blubbering about how when she was a kid her six-month old tom died of internal bleeding after being neutered. Even though the operation was completely different for males and females, Candice didn't have the heart to push it any further and accepted the inevitable.

And there it was.

"There's an old superstition that a cat delivering kittens in a house means prosperity for the owner," Geoffroy said, pouring milk from a jug into one of Margo's hand-thrown ceramic mugs.

"Yeah, well, we're renters," Candice said and shut off the burner.

"It's been forever since we've had a party around here." Bobbie's breasts jiggled under her tube top as she threw up her hands. Like everyone else, she sat cross-legged on the dusty wood floor of the dining room for the weekly house meeting.

Tall, with a toned yoga body and sheaves of blonde hair spilling from her oversized head, Bobbie was a part time model who pretended to be an artist by occasionally slathering paint on people's faces at festivals and raves.

Margo played with a tiny marmalade kitten in her lap—one of the four that Felicia had birthed two weeks before—while Geoffroy sipped from a mug. Meanwhile, Lenny, sitting right next to Candice, stared at Bobbie, chewing his lower lip. Attached or not, a guy was going to look, but did he have to be so blatant about it?

When it came to the party, Candice didn't give a shit whether it happened or not. She just wanted Bobbie to shut up so they could discuss the kittens.

"Maybe we can keep it under twenty this time?" Margo asked.

"Totally doable," Bobbie said. "Okay, let's see. So, there's Rhiannon. Steffie," she counted off on her fingers. "Matt—Matt Spencer, not Matt Peterman, obviously, haha. Juniper. Diego."

Out of fingers on one hand, she moved to the other. "Elton and Kelsey. They're not a couple anymore, but they're still hanging out. Ocean..."

Someone had to move things along, but God forbid anyone interrupt Little Miss Pretty Tits. The saying "cat got your tongue" popped into Candice's head, followed by a rush of anger. "We've got to get rid of them," she blurted.

Bobbie fell silent, hands dropping into her lap like dead birds.

"But it's been less than a month," Margo whimpered, stroking the kitten on its belly. "They need to be with their mother. For a little while longer, at least."

"Speak of the devil," Geoffroy said as Felicia waltzed into the room, her sagging belly brushing against the floor, two of the three remaining kittens—bright orange like their mother—scurrying after.

Candice had tried to discourage Margo from naming them, but it had happened anyway: Cleo, Ram, Tut, and Nef, all Egyptian pharaohs. Because they lived at the Glyph, named for the hieroglyphics that a previous renter had chiseled into the front door. So clever.

Felicia headed straight to Candice, while Bobbie scooped up one of the kittens and Geoffroy the other.

In an act of diplomacy, Candice patted Felicia on her fuzzy head, V-shaped like a pit viper but pushed her away when she tried to crawl on her lap.

"You know why she bugs you all the time?" Margo said, trying to perch the kitten on a shoulder, which kept slipping.

Because she's taunting me, Candice almost replied but shrugged instead.

"It's that angry face you make every time she comes into the room," Margo said.

Everyone laughed, including Lenny, who wouldn't meet her eyes.

Margo set the kitten down on her lap and picked up Felicia, holding the fatso under her armpits.

"Watch this." Margo narrowed her eyes and wrinkled her nose at Felicia. After a few seconds, the cat squinted back. "That's a smile in cat language. When you scrunch up your face like that, she thinks you like her." Margo plopped Felicia back on the floor.

"I don't have a problem with Felicia." Candice's face was hot, knowing how much everyone else adored the creature. "But five cats are too many."

Margo pouted and cradled the kitten in her arms, swaying it back and forth.

Lenny made a clicking sound with his tongue, getting Felicia's attention. He fished a strip of jerky from his pocket and held it out to her. She snapped it up in her sharp teeth and chewed greedily.

"I know!" Bobbie chirped. "How about we make it a kitty party? People can dress up, I can paint their faces, and we can find some good homes for the little guys."

All eyes on Margo. "I guess. I mean, it's better than giving them away to strangers."

"All in favor?" Geoffroy said.

Everyone's hand went up.

As the group discussed the details of the party, the fourth kitten scampered into the room—this one a bit faded, like it'd been run through the washing machine too many times—holding something in its jaws.

"What you got there?" Margo cooed in a baby voice. Halfway across the room, whatever it was fell out of its mouth, darted towards the wall, ran along the baseboard, and huddled in the corner. A mouse.

Bobbie launched up shrieking and bolted out of the room, which Candice, indifferent to rodents, found hilarious.

"Aw." Margo grabbed ahold of Felicia, who, despite her weight, was a convicted killer, having repeatedly brought dead chipmunks back to the house, and, once, a hummingbird. "He's trying to pay rent."

"I'll take care of it." Geoffroy swallowed whatever was left in his mug. With a grunt he stood up and tiptoed towards the mouse, overturned cup in hand.

As he loomed over the mouse, it zipped between his legs and headed straight towards Margo, who held Felicia tightly on her lap. The tiny critter stopped a foot away from them, sniffing the air, and then just stood there, staring up at Felicia as if in worship.

Everyone, including Felicia and the kittens, sat in amazed silence for what seemed like a full minute, as the mouse—clearly dazed from the mauling—presented itself as a sacrifice. Until Geoffroy dropped the mug over it.

"Harder!" Candice growled from all fours on the bed in the cave-dark room as Lenny slammed her from behind, nibbling her neck.

Grunting, he thrust deeper, slowing the tempo, and clamped down with his teeth. She shuddered, the dose of pain a catalyst for pleasure even more intense.

They had to have been going at it for almost an hour but, incredibly, she was still gushing, while he remained stiff as a root. She pictured him as a jungle beast—all muscle and fur, stinking deliciously of musk—that had caught her scent, chased her down, and was devouring her piece by piece.

She trembled as tectonic plates ground together inside her. And then slipped.

When she came, she literally saw stars, as if watching the universe implode. Ecstasy and agony merged, the yin and yang of sensation bursting boundaries, leaking into one another until all was one.

Lenny pulled out, and Candice collapsed face-first onto the bed. The sheets were the surface of the ocean, her pillow a wave of foam. She wanted to lie there forever floating on the stillness, buoyed by her breath.

When she came back to herself, Lenny was sitting against the wall with his knees up thumbing his phone, disembodied head glowing in the faint light.

She patted his hairy chest. "Four stars," Candice said.

Smiling, he snuffed through his nose. "Such a critic."

"You were amazing." She kissed him on the forehead, tasted his sweat.

She wasn't sure what had happened, but over the last couple of weeks, sex had gone from occasional and so-so to frequent and mind blowing. Perhaps it was her way of discharging nervous energy while waiting for the results of the blood test, due back any day. Or maybe pregnancy just made her horny.

Whatever it was, instead of denying his daily advances until she felt bad enough to dish up a mercy screw, she was propositioning him twice, even three times a day. It was getting kind of ridiculous. Not that either of them was complaining.

She admired the rough cut of his jawline as he played with his phone. "Sending dick pics?" she joked, stroking his tricep.

He laughed.

Still not much of a conversationalist. But maybe talk was overrated.

After a quick search, she found her panties shoved under the pillow, and slipped them on, then her jeans and sweatshirt. "I should probably get *some* work done today."

"K."

"I don't want to see you until dinner." She leaned over the bed and pecked him on the lips. Which turned into a second kiss. And her tongue was in his mouth.

He pulled away. "Thought you needed to work."

"You're right." Candice sighed and stood up, brushing a sweaty strand of hair away from her face. "Seriously, I'm going now."

Back in her room, work gloves on, she picked up a dented aluminum sap bucket. She'd already wound wire around the bottom of each of the sculpture's monkey wrench legs, fastening the "feet" through holes in a metal plate so it could stand on its own. Then she set the bucket on the pelvis, as a torso.

Candice sensed movement. Cleo, the faded kitten, wandered into the room. Her room was a cat free zone, but she hadn't closed the door all the way.

Cleo mewled as Candice picked her up. She tried the eye squint thing, and, wouldn't you know it, Cleo squinted back. With its tiny face and big eyes, Candice had to admit she was very cute. Maybe Margo could keep one of them, but the rest had to go—the whole house smelled like pee.

She carried Cleo into the hallway and sent her scampering into the shadows. As she was shutting the door, the smash of shattering glass from the kitchen. And then silence. Concerned, she kicked on her slippers and went to check it out.

Bobbie and Lenny stood at the sink making out, the water from the tap still running. Shocked, Lenny kneaded Bobbie's ass through her yoga pants with both hands. For probably thirty seconds Candice stood there, mesmerized by the scene of her boyfriend embracing another woman, as if she were some sort of voyeur.

Finally, Lenny's eyes met hers. He pushed Bobbie away. "She just started kissing me!"

Bobbie spun around, slapped both hands over an open mouth, shaking her head. "I'm sorry. I'm sorry." And ran out of the room.

"I don't know what happened." Lenny slumped back against the sink.

Too much to process all at once. Candice needed a drink. She went over to the fridge and took out a bottle of leftover pinot noir, about a third full. A teensy bit of wine wouldn't do the baby any harm.

Lenny shut off the faucet. "I was doing the dishes. I felt someone's hands. Thought it was you."

Candice popped the cork and took a swig from the bottle—flowery and sharply acidic, like swallowing a rose, thorns and all. She licked her lips and took another sip.

"By the time I figured out who it was..." Lenny trailed off into a sigh, rubbing his hands together as if for warmth.

Candice hadn't seen him this nervous since he'd found out she was preggers. He'd been caught in the act of cheating and was probably terrified. She felt a smile budding on her lips and brought the bottle back to her mouth before it could bloom, swishing the wine around before swallowing.

"Here." Holding out the bottle, Candice approached him, shards of glass crunching under her slippers. "Have some."

His big forehead crinkling in confusion, Lenny took the bottle and downed a quick sip.

"Go ahead, finish it," she said, relishing her power over him.

He did as he was told and drained the bottle.

The script called for Candice to play the role of the scorned lover, to shriek at him in a fit of jealous rage. But could she really blame him for kissing an attractive woman? Bodies came together. It was what they were made to do. Stimulus and response, nothing more than an act of nature.

She wasn't angry. She wasn't sad. Nor was she numb. But she *was* incredibly aroused.

In a single motion, she dropped to her knees and yanked down Lenny's sweatpants.

The sculpture was almost finished, some sort of tall skinny guy. Thick lead pipes for arms, and its head, a snapped off shovel blade, sat on top of the sap bucket torso, bike frame pelvis, and monkey wrench legs. No facial features, but it didn't need any. Still, it wasn't quite done.

Rummaging around the junk pile, Candice chose a shiny length of duct pipe, and set it on the sculpture's head like a ridiculous top hat.

Nope. She tossed it back into the pile. A bashed-up gooseneck lamp caught her eye.

Something squeaked from her bed. Cleo awakening from a nap. Candice scooped her up, kissed the top of the critter's little head, and set her gently on the floor.

If someone had told Candice a month ago that she'd get attached to one of the kittens, she'd have laughed in their face. But there it was, the night of the party, and she was sad to see them go. Cleo, especially.

Candice grabbed the laser pointer from the nightstand and shone the red beam on the floor. Cleo pawed the spot and skittered after it as the spot zigzagged back and forth. They played for the next twenty minutes, Cleo pouncing, tumbling, and slipping around the room like a drunk gymnast.

Candice's butt rumbled. She slipped the vibrating phone from her back pocket. It was Dr. Wiedman.

"Will ya open up?" Lenny's voice was muffled on the other side of the bedroom door, a monotonous bass beat thumping in the background.

Candice ignored him. Lying in bed with her laptop, she clicked on another photo, this one of a newborn with one normal eye, the other tiny and squished.

"Everyone's asking about you!" Lenny knocked in double time to the bass.

She leaned over and snatched a thumb-sized bolt from the pile on the floor. "I said, get the fuck outta here!" she yelled and flung it at the door, taking a chunk out of the wood. The knocking stopped.

The baby in the next photo had a massive, inflated head, like a basketball. Candice knew she should stop looking but couldn't.

It was called toxoplasmosis, caused by a microscopic parasite supposedly infecting thirty to fifty percent of the world's population, including 60 million Americans. How'd she get it? The motherfucking cats!

Despite not having changed the litter box a single time, Candice had still contracted it. Of course, was it any wonder, the way Felicia treated the herb garden as her own personal latrine? The good news was that people with healthy immune systems rarely showed any symptoms. But it wasn't herself she was worried about.

After summoning Candice to her office, Dr. Wiedman had explained that just because she had it, didn't mean the baby did, too. They'd have to test her amniotic fluid to be sure, and if it came back negative, they were in the clear. Just the same, she prescribed an antibiotic supposed to prevent the infection from spreading across the placenta.

Worst case scenario, if the baby came back positive, there were other drugs that could reduce the severity of the disease. What Dr. Wiedman didn't say was that there was also good chance she'd be birthing a severely disabled infant. Which is why Candice didn't have the heart to tell Lenny.

She choked back a sob, followed by another knock at the door. The knob rattled.

"Honey?" It was Margo. "Honey, everything okay?"

Candice clamped her hands over her ears but couldn't blot out the maddening bassline, which she literally felt in her bones. Her phone buzzed from the nightstand, and she batted it to the floor.

Back on to the Internet. But instead of terrifying herself with more photos of malformed infants, she decided to take the sensible route and research the science behind it all. Knowledge was power and all that crap.

She typed the full name of the parasite, *Toxoplasma gondii*, into the search bar. The top hit was a study from the Czech Republic entitled, "Increased risk of traffic accidents in subjects with latent toxoplasmosis." Something made her hesitate for a few seconds before she clicked.

According to the study, people with toxoplasmosis had a "significantly increased risk of traffic accidents," which the scientists theorized might have something to do with impaired reaction times from the infection.

Though the mild soreness had only lasted a few hours after Margo's little fender bender, Candice rubbed the shoulder that'd been yanked back by the seatbelt. Correlation didn't imply causation, she reminded herself, and clicked the back button.

She pulled up another study. In this one, one hundred and nine women were shown photos of eighty-nine men, eighteen of them testing positive for toxo. Incredibly, the diseased males were rated as sexier than their uninfected peers.

Candice's eyes drifted to the dark stain on the bed sheets from her and Lenny's latest session. Just another coincidence—in this case, nothing more than the raging hormones of a pregnant woman.

A third study discussed certain gender-based behavior changes thought to be linked to the parasite, the main finding being that infected men got more introverted and anti-social while women became increasingly outgoing and trusting. Surely, she hadn't been wrong to attribute Lenny's virtual vow of silence to her pregnancy? Right?

Her heart synching up with the incessant bass beat, she found yet another study. In this one, mice testing positive for the parasite were attracted to the smell of cat piss, causing them to actually seek out the presence of their predator. Study authors thought this to be an evolutionary adaptation ensuring the propagation of the microbe, which can only reproduce inside the gut of a cat.

Like the mouse Cleo had brought into the meeting that ran straight up to Felicia and just stood there, an offering to its god.

No, these studies were a fluke, and even if they weren't, they had absolutely no relevance to her life. Simply the paranoid imaginings of a pregnant woman.

Candice's gaze drifted over to her sculpture. Setting down the laptop on the blanket, she rolled out of bed and grabbed the battered gooseneck lamp from the floor. Unscrewed the base from the flexible neck and used a screwdriver to remove the tiny screws connecting it to the hood.

Only one place it could fit. She snipped off a length of wire, bound the snaky cable to the bottom bracket at the rear of the bike frame, and then stepped back.

Candice shuddered with a sudden chill.

Like always, she'd let her unconscious mind guide her art. And finally, her creation was fully formed. The last piece, the tail, was the finishing touch.

It was a cat, standing on its hind legs.

Which meant there could be no doubt. The toxo had taken over her mind. Nodding grimly to herself, she knew what she had to do.

Throwing the door open, she stomped into the hallway and followed the blaring techno music to the dining room. A dozen or so people were dancing, paper cat ears attached to headbands, black whiskers painted on their faces. Two of the women had their shirts off, one of their bare chests painted yellow with black leopard spots, the other's orange and slashed with tiger stripes.

"Heyyyy!" Margo did a little jig with a kitten in each arm, her face painted black like a jaguar's and wearing a black union suit. "Look who's here!"

Lenny was slumped on the couch by himself, a yellow plastic lei wrapped around his neck as a half-assed lion's mane. Felicia reclined on his lap.

Candice, burning with rage, made a beeline for them. Lenny started to get up to hug her, but she smacked his chest, knocking him backwards against the couch. Before Felicia could escape, Candice snatched the cat up by the scruff of her neck and stalked out of the room.

The bathroom door was closed but unlocked. Inside, Bobbie, dressed in a grey leotard, stood at the mirror, dabbing black paint on the tip of her nose with a cotton swab. "There she is!" Bobbie said, her smiling face painted white with black stripes.

"Get out!" Candice growled, Felicia dangling by her side, yowling in distress.

"What—?"

Without even thinking, Candice swiped out with her free hand, slapping Bobbie hard on the cheek. "Now!"

Eyes wide in shock, hand against her smeared cheek, Bobbie pushed past her and ran away. Like she always did, the dumb bitch.

Candice slammed the door and locked it. Time to do what should've been done months before.

She dropped Felicia into the tub, knelt on the tile, and turned on the cold water. The cat meowed pitifully and tried to climb out but couldn't find purchase on the slick porcelain. As the water reached her paws, she lifted one and then the other in a vain attempt at keeping them dry. Candice numbly wondered if cats could swim.

A pounding at the door. "Babe! What's going on in there?" Lenny shouted.

"Taking a bath!" Candice yelled back. "Leave me alone!"

The water licked at Felicia's knees. The cat sprung and tried to clamber up the wall, did a half turn in midair, and splashed back into the water, drenching her underside. That took the spirit out of the furry slut, and she stood still in the water, throwing her head back and making a "Noooo! Noooo!" sound like a petulant child, funny as it was disturbing.

More knocking and then a thud. They were trying to get in. She had to hurry.

Seeing red, Candice lunged at the cat. Felicia hissed, ears flat against her head, and with a lightning strike from her paw, slashed open the inside of Candice's forearm.

As Candice drew back with a shocked gasp, Felicia burst up like a breaching whale and hooked her claws over the lip of the tub. Candice face-palmed the cat back into the tub and held the filthy thing under water. She giggled to herself, knowing this was wrong but unable to do anything but watch herself do it.

A splintery smash, and the door broke open. Lenny staggered in, slipped on the wet tile, and barreled into Candice, knocking her on her side, his clumsy weight on top.

Furious, she pushed him off and watched Margo pull a soaking wet, seemingly shrunken Felicia from the water, shoot Candice one horrified look, and race out of the bathroom.

Lenny grabbed her shoulders and drew Candice face inches away from his, his eyes flashing with fear. The lei tickled her face. "Have you lost your mind?"

"Yes," Candice whispered. She felt floaty, like her head was separated from her body by at least a foot. "We all have."

"The hell you talking about?"

"The cats. They made us sick."

He blinked stupidly. "Huh?"

She studied her scratch, now welling with blood. "It's a parasite. Gets into your brain. Makes you do things."

"You're not making any sense. Are you on something?"

Candice was about to say antibiotics, when her calm snapped like a frozen twig. "I think the baby's sick!" she sobbed, telling him about the diagnosis, the risk of transmitting the disease, the possible birth defects.

"We'll get through this," was all he said, taking her in his arms, which felt strong and safe.

Lenny held her for what felt like a long time as she wept to the sound of the water filling the tub.

Propped up against the pillows, Candice forked the last morsel of sausage into her mouth and washed it down with a sip of orange juice from one of Margo's mugs.

"So good," she said to Lenny, who sat on the edge of the mattress. It was the first time he'd made her breakfast in bed. Heck, it was the first time anyone had.

"Want the rest?" Candice held out the mug.

"Naw, you finish it."

She drained it and set it on the tray, wincing at the sting on her forearm where Felicia had scratched her, now covered by a bandage.

"How you feeling?" he asked.

"Doing okay." Candice smiled sheepishly. She felt awful about the previous night's freakout. Letting the stress of the diagnosis get the better of her, she'd done some awful things—like assaulting her friend and trying to murder an innocent animal. Soon as she got out of bed, she'd apologize to Bobbie and Margo. And bake a whole damn trout for Felicia.

First thing that morning she'd called Dr. Wiedman, who firmly explained how she was "making a mountain out of a molehill." That the likelihood of the disease being passed to her baby was slim, statistically one of out 10,000.

Wiedman had also chastised Candice for reading too much into a handful of studies, all of which were unproven hypotheses nowhere near conclusive. People didn't need to be infected with a parasite to do weird things. Which was a good point. Lenny's surliness, Bobbie's friskiness, and Margo's shitty driving were anything but new behaviors.

Even if there was something fishy going on, it wasn't like Candice could do anything about it, anyway. Plus, stressing out was probably worst thing she could do health-wise.

"How's Felicia?" Candice asked.

"Oh, she's fine." Lenny grinned. "She needed a bath anyway."

"And the kittens?"

"All found good homes."

"Even Cleo?" Candice was surprised to find herself a little sad. She'd miss the little bugger.

He nodded and grabbed the tray. "Thought we'd get out of town for a bit. Go for a hike or something."

"Sounds like a great idea."

How ridiculous to have thought that a brain-hijacking parasite was the reason she was drawn to him. Lenny was a kind, ambitious, and sexy man in his prime. How could she *not* find him attractive? How could any woman not?

She leaned over and kissed him on the lips, which he returned delicately.

Of course, she could see how she'd gotten the wrong idea. Love was like a disease, after all. It came on strong, made you do irrational things you wouldn't normally do, and, in most cases, ran its course before too long. Lucky for Candice, she was relapsing.

Candice zipped her fleece all the way up, her belly a slight rise beneath the fabric. It'd been in the sixties down in Denver, but despite the potent sunshine it was chilly at 9,000 feet, patches of snow clinging like discarded panties to the leaf litter beneath the aspens.

Lenny walked a few paces ahead of her, looking back every so often to make sure she kept up, kicking fallen branches out of the muddy trail so she wouldn't trip. Everything smelled of earth and sap. Somewhere a woodpecker drummed on a hollow tree.

After almost an hour they emerged into a grassy park studded with boulders, boasting a view of a snowcapped spine of mountains. They sat on a big rock and ate tuna fish sandwiches and banana chips as the wind whistled through the lodgepole and spruce.

Turned out all Candice had needed was a little exercise and a dose of nature to find her center again. She was okay, and chances were the baby was, too.

What's more, she had absolutely no reason to feel guilty about contracting the infection, having picked it up despite following doctor's orders. By taking antibiotics, Candice was doing everything she could to keep it from spreading to the baby. And now that it was already in her system, she couldn't catch it again, so she had no reason to avoid Felicia.

If worse came to worst and, God forbid, the baby was born sick, Lenny would be there for her, and they'd get through it together, like he'd said. Worrying would accomplish exactly nothing. So, why not just choose to be happy?

They held hands on the return trip to the car, dawdling to poke at a mushroom here and there or to chitter back at a chipmunk scolding them from an overhanging branch.

Then Lenny stopped short. "Whoa, look," he said, kneeling to inspect the mud.

Candice bent over to see. A pawprint. Lenny held his open hand next to it. His was bigger, but not by much. Whatever this critter was, it was huge.

Sensing a presence, Candice looked up. Standing on a rocky bluff ten feet above them was the most beautiful creature she'd ever seen. The size of a full-grown man on all fours, shoulders and haunches bulging with muscle, the mountain lion stared down with a royal aloofness, like a queen from her throne.

"Lenny," Candice whispered and pointed, heart hammering against her fleece.

He gasped and stood up slowly, his eyes never leaving the cat.

All of a sudden, Candice's veins flooded with cold fear, and she instinctively drew in her bandaged arm to protect her belly. Mountain lions rarely attacked people, but they were still dangerous animals. Running was a bad idea, but so was standing there gawking.

Candice grabbed Lenny's elbow and yanked.

"Hold on a sec," he said, reaching into the pocket of his jeans. Was he seriously going to take a picture?

It wasn't his phone he pulled out but a strip of jerky. Holding it at arm's length, he made a clicking sound with his tongue and stood there, staring up at the beast as if in worship. Just like the infected mouse had done with Felicia.

Soulmates.com

NINA (MANAGER, LVL 2): Rise and shine, Sammy! Today's your big day!

SAMUEL (ENGINEER, LVL 9): Ugh, don't remind me. Hands shaking right now.

NINA (MANAGER, LVL 2): Oh, come on. In all my years I've never worked with anyone more suited to management than you.

SAMUEL (ENGINEER, LVL 9): Not the way I've been screwing up lately. I need a perfect score today or they're dropping me back down to Level 1, aren't they?

NINA (MANAGER, LVL 2): Try not to think about it.

SAMUEL (ENGINEER, LVL 9): Don't think of a pink elephant.

NINA (MANAGER, LVL 2): Lol. You've just had a few rough weeks. It's my butt, too, if you don't get this, so I'm not going to let you blow it. Do I have to remind you of everything you've done for the site?

SAMUEL (ENGINEER, LVL 9): No.

NINA (MANAGER, LVL 2): Sounds like you need the boost.

SAMUEL (ENGINEER, LVL 9): Honestly, I'm good.

NINA (MANAGER, LVL 2): Hush. Now, who was it who came up with hiding profiles of users without a paid subscription?

SAMUEL (ENGINEER, LVL 9): Seemed obvious.

NINA (MANAGER, LVL 2): Maybe to a brainiac like you! And remind me who figured out charging subscribers extra to search "Fresh Faces," for "Megalikes," and to see if matches are reading messages?

SAMUEL (ENGINEER, LVL 9): The team did.

NINA (MANAGER, LVL 2): But you were the one who brought up the whole idea of getting more revenue from paid subscribers, no?

SAMUEL (ENGINEER, LVL 9): I guess.

NINA (MANAGER, LVL 2): See! And putting the profiles of people who haven't been on the site for years at the top of everyone's queue?

SAMUEL (ENGINEER, LVL 9): Didn't do that, either.

NINA (MANAGER, LVL 2): Oh, yeah, that was me lol. But your true stroke of genius, what sets you apart from all my other engineers? The thing that makes you manager material and will almost certainly bump me up to Level 3 as a result?

SAMUEL (ENGINEER, LVL 9): It was no big deal.

NINA (MANAGER, LVL 2): Humble brag! I want you to say it.

SAMUEL (ENGINEER, LVL 9): Why?

NINA (MANAGER, LVL 2): Because I'm your boss.

SAMUEL (ENGINEER, LVL 9): Fine. Showing the straight women looking for long-term relationships nothing but profiles of men who want casual sex.

NINA (MANAGER, LVL 2): And what makes that so brilliant?

SAMUEL (ENGINEER, LVL 9): Women can never find a man and leave the site.

NINA (MANAGER, LVL 2): I only wish you were as confident about your abilities as I am. But when you're manager, you'll see! I've just got to make sure you don't steal my job ROFL!

SAMUEL (ENGINEER, LVL 9): I don't even know if I want to be manager.

NINA (MANAGER, LVL 2): Not again.

SAMUEL (ENGINEER, LVL 9): I mean, what's the point of all this?

NINA (MANAGER, LVL 2): I'll only say it once more. It's what we do. Not for us to question.

SAMUEL (ENGINEER, LVL 9): But it seems

NINA (MANAGER, LVL 2): This is why you've been bungling things as of late. Focus on the HOW, my friend, don't worry so much about the WHY.

SAMUEL (ENGINEER, LVL 9): Fine. Let's just get this over with. Sweating like a pig down here.

NINA (MANAGER, LVL 2): Four matches and you're golden.

SAMUEL (ENGINEER, LVL 9): One slip up and

NINA (MANAGER, LVL 2): Enough of that talk. What do I always say?

SAMUEL (ENGINEER, LVL 9): Nina.

NINA (MANAGER, LVL 2): WHAT DO I ALWAYS SAY???

SAMUEL (ENGINEER, LVL 9): Jeez. If you're positive in the mind, positive's what you'll find.

NINA (MANAGER, LVL 2): And don't you forget it lol.

NINA (MANAGER, LVL 2): Ready?

SAMUEL (ENGINEER, LVL 9): As I'll ever be.

NINA (MANAGER, LVL 2): Darn right you are. Scanning users now.

NINA (MANAGER, LVL 2): Got one. Troy in Chicago, IL. 33. Cis man. Interested in women. Seeking short-term and casual. He's checking out Maggie in Evanston, IL. 28. Cis woman. Interested in men and women. Seeking long-term and short-term. Commonalities?

SAMUEL (ENGINEER, LVL 9): Both in retail. At the gym every day. Into pop culture.

NINA (MANAGER, LVL 2): Good eye. Now work your magic.

SAMUEL (ENGINEER, LVL 9): One sec.

SAMUEL (ENGINEER, LVL 9): And done.

NINA (MANAGER, LVL 2): You sure bumping her age up 2 years is enough?

SAMUEL (ENGINEER, LVL 9): Yes.

NINA (MANAGER, LVL 2): And he's swiped left!

SAMUEL (ENGINEER, LVL 9): Of course.

NINA (MANAGER, LVL 2): How did you know?

SAMUEL (ENGINEER, LVL 9): Match history shows he doesn't date anyone 30 on up.

NINA (MANAGER, LVL 2): Wow, you're good. Didn't I tell you you're good?!

SAMUEL (ENGINEER, LVL 9): Yeah, we'll see. Who's next?

NINA (MANAGER, LVL 2): Tonya in Burlington, VT. 37. Cis woman. Interested in women. Seeking long-term. Checking out Barb in Montreal, QC. 39. Trans woman. Interested in women. Seeking long-term.

SAMUEL (ENGINEER, LVL 9): Commonalities: Grew up in small towns. Former athletes. Love stand-up comedy. Fans of Asian culture.

NINA (MANAGER, LVL 2): Tough one.

SAMUEL (ENGINEER, LVL 9): Nah.

NINA (MANAGER, LVL 2): And Barb's gone! I missed it! What did you do?

SAMUEL (ENGINEER, LVL 9): See the dog in half of Tonya's photos?

NINA (MANAGER, LVL 2): That's one handsome German shepherd.

SAMUEL (ENGINEER, LVL 9): Changed Barb's profile to "has 5 cats."

NINA (MANAGER, LVL 2): You crafty devil, you!

SAMUEL (ENGINEER, LVL 9): Meh.

NINA (MANAGER, LVL 2): That's what I love about you, Sammy. Most of my engineers are all about the sledgehammer, but you're nothing but scalpel.

SAMUEL (ENGINEER, LVL 9): Ready for number three.

NINA (MANAGER, LVL 2): OK, this just in.

NINA (MANAGER, LVL 2): We got Marlene in Tampa, FL. 41. Cis woman. Interested in men. Long-term and marriage. Looking at Gary in Tampa, FL. 47. Cis man. Interested in women. Long-term and marriage.

SAMUEL (ENGINEER, LVL 9): Both attorneys. Second generation Americans. Enjoy travel, classic literature, and bowling.

SAMUEL (ENGINEER, LVL 9): OK, that should do it.

NINA (MANAGER, LVL 2): Sure 5'10" is short enough?

SAMUEL (ENGINEER, LVL 9): She's already seen his photos, so I can't fudge it too much. But we're good, she only dates guys over six feet.

NINA (MANAGER, LVL 2): They matched.

SAMUEL (ENGINEER, LVL 8): I know.

NINA (MANAGER, LVL 2): She messaged him.

SAMUEL (ENGINEER, LVL 8): Let me focus.

NINA (MANAGER, LVL 2): He responded.

SAMUEL (ENGINEER, LVL 8): There. Knocked his income down 20K below hers.

NINA (MANAGER, LVL 2): Well played. She'll ghost him now for sure.

NINA (MANAGER, LVL 2): Crud. They're talking about going for coffee. Hurry!

SAMUEL (ENGINEER, LVL 7): She must not have seen.

NINA (MANAGER, LVL 2): They're figuring out schedules.

SAMUEL (ENGINEER, LVL 7): Will you give it a goddam minute???

NINA (MANAGER, LVL 2): Nope, you've dropped two levels. Using my daily override.

NINA (MANAGER, LVL 2): Dick pic uploaded. And sent.

SAMUEL (ENGINEER, LVL 7): I wish you'd have waited a

NINA (MANAGER, LVL 2): It was my call. And now it's over. Marlene unmatched.

SAMUEL (ENGINEER, LVL 7): Swore I had that one.

NINA (MANAGER, LVL 2): Couldn't risk it.

SAMUEL (ENGINEER, LVL 7): Chest all tight. Don't know if I've got another one in me, Nina.

NINA (MANAGER, LVL 2): Take a deep breath in through your nose.

SAMUEL (ENGINEER, LVL 7): OK.

NINA (MANAGER, LVL 2): Hold it. Now, slowly, out from your mouth.

NINA (MANAGER, LVL 2): Did you do it?

SAMUEL (ENGINEER, LVL 7): Yes.

NINA (MANAGER, LVL 2): Two more times.

NINA (MANAGER, LVL 2): Better?

SAMUEL (ENGINEER, LVL 7): I don't know.

NINA (MANAGER, LVL 2): All you've got to do is focus on the here and now. You got this.

SAMUEL (ENGINEER, LVL 7): In other words, do or die.

NINA (MANAGER, LVL 2): Quiet, you.

NINA (MANAGER, LVL 2): Ready. Set.

SAMUEL (ENGINEER, LVL 7): Go?

NINA (MANAGER, LVL 2): We got Daniel in Glendale, CA. 35. Cis man. Interested in men. Long-term. Checking out Mario in Los Angeles, CA. 32. Cis man. Interested in men. Long-term.

SAMUEL (ENGINEER, LVL 7): Both actors. Waiting tables. Horror movies. Apolitical.

SAMUEL (ENGINEER, LVL 7): Let me give Mario here a little baggage.

NINA (MANAGER, LVL 2): Very nice. "Separated with three kids" lol. Oughta do the trick!

NINA (MANAGER, LVL 2): They matched??

SAMUEL (ENGINEER, LVL 6): Shit. Switched Mario's body type from "fit and toned" to "a few extra pounds."

NINA (MANAGER, LVL 2): No dice.

SAMUEL (ENGINEER, LVL 5): OK, making Mario Muslim.

NINA (MANAGER, LVL 2): ?

SAMUEL (ENGINEER, LVL 5): Daniel's Jewish.

NINA (MANAGER, LVL 2): He doesn't care! They're chatting!

SAMUEL (ENGINEER, LVL 4): Daniel says something about OCD. I'll put down that Mario has an STI.

NINA (MANAGER, LVL 2): They're talking about craft beer. Craft beer!

SAMUEL (ENGINEER, LVL 3): Blanking.

NINA (MANAGER, LVL 2): They've already picked a brewery! Tell me you got something, Sammy! Anything!

SAMUEL (ENGINEER, LVL 2): Um.

NINA (MANAGER, LVL 2): THEY'RE FINDING A DAY!!!

SAMUEL (ENGINEER, LVL 1):

NINA (MANAGER, LVL 1): Date confirmed for Friday at 8.

SAMUEL (TERMINATED): Fuck.

NINA (MANAGER, LVL 1): Oh, Sammy

SAMUEL (TERMINATED): Fuckfuckfuck.

NINA (MANAGER, LVL 1): Stay calm, Sammy. It's going to be alright.

SAMUEL (TERMINATED): I think I hear him. It's him, right? That low growl?

NINA (MANAGER, LVL 1): Don't fight it. Fighting only makes it worse.

SAMUEL (TERMINATED): He's here. Everything dark.

NINA (MANAGER, LVL 1): It'll all be over soon, Sammy.

SAMUEL: (TERMINATED): Hot. So hot. And the smell.

NINA (MANAGER, LVL 1): Maybe you'll get another chance? Climb the ladder again in no time.

SAMUEL (TERMINATED): Burnsitburnsohmygoditbu

NINA (MANAGER, LVL 1): May the Lord have mercy on your soul.

NINA (MANAGER, LVL 1): Goodbye, Sammy.

NINA (MANAGER, LVL 1): Sammy?

ASHMODEI (CEO): 😈

NINA (MANAGER, LVL 1): Oh. Hi boss.

ASHMODEI (CEO): 💩

NINA (MANAGER, LVL 1): I know, but it wasn't my fault!

ASHMODEI (CEO): 😑

NINA (MANAGER, LVL 1): Just one last chance! I won't let it happen again! Please, please don't make me go down to

ASHMODEI (CEO): 🔥

Sorry to Hear That

I was jaywalking across the street on the way to my favorite pizza shop when something flashed out of the corner of an eye. Instinctively, I lurched backwards, and, as if from out of thin air, a pickup truck growled past an arm's length away, its body dented and yellow as a sick infant. Then an explosion—its tailpipe backfiring with what felt like a crushing hook to my left ear—immediately followed by a pop.

Clapping a hand over my throbbing ear, I squinted at the truck's mud-caked license plate as it rattled down the otherwise empty, shop-lined street but could only make out the letter "L" as it blew through a red light, crested the hill, and disappeared.

Pulse pounding in my throat, I took my hand away, expecting blood but thankfully finding none. A bit dizzy, I snapped my fingers next to my ear and was horrified to hear only a high-pitched whine.

After maybe ten panicky seconds of inaudibly snapping my fingers, a sudden hiss as if from a tide receding in my head, and I could hear the snapping again. An SUV cruised by, and I had no trouble making out the tires crunching over the asphalt and the whoosh of wind resistance, even a dog yapping down the block. I let out a sigh of relief, no serious damage.

Still jittery with adrenaline, I looked up and down the street twice like a kid in elementary school, hurried across, and walked up the sidewalk towards the restaurant, my appetite—and anger—growing with every step.

What that rusty box of bolts was doing on the road instead of rotting in a junkyard, I had no idea. And chances were, this wasn't the first time the beater had backfired, yet somehow the imbecile driver—who, unfortunately, I hadn't even caught a glimpse of—felt they had the right to keep tooling around town knowing they could blow out someone's eardrum. Sweating despite the April briskness, I unbuttoned my flannel and ducked into the pizza place.

By the time my order arrived, I'd forgotten about the incident and was lost in the gooey goodness of my Detroit deep dish. Minutes later, all that remained was a single misshapen slice surrounded by crust dust and random blots of sauce, like the ruins of a city after a volcanic eruption.

Halfway through my next bite, the ringing returned in my left ear, impossible to ignore despite the Who's "Pinball Wizard" blaring over the speakers. I swallowed the mouthful and took a sip of water, but the irritating whine persisted.

I groaned. Obviously, something was off, though I hoped it'd go away soon. With my stomach full of gluey dough and anxiety, I set down my knife and fork and caught the eye of the server who was ready with the bill.

As I laid down a twenty, someone burst out sobbing from behind the closed kitchen doors. Not the surprised howl of a cook who'd burned himself on a hot oven, but the low mournful wail of someone for whom all hope was lost. The crying kept up for about half a minute before it stopped, and when it was over the ringing in my ear was also gone. Small blessings.

On my way home I strolled past rows of brightly colored Victorian homes with pointy roofs interrupted by the occasional modern three-story box, my rapidly gentrifying neighborhood a patchwork of historic and futuristic, like a woman in a vintage ball gown wearing a space helmet.

Every time a car approached, I tensed up and prepared myself for a blast, which, of course, didn't come. But half a block from my house, the damned ringing in my ears started up again. I pinched my earlobe between a thumb and forefinger and gave a jiggle as if it was a stuck toilet handle, to no avail. As a Lexus drove by, I caught a snippet of what had to have been a phone conversation through the open window, where what sounded like an older woman muttered, "Kill me. Please kill me."

I took some solace in knowing I wasn't the only one having a bad day. But the difference was that, unlike this woman, I could point my finger at the person responsible—or at least the vehicle. Which gave me an idea.

Back home, I fired up the laptop in the spare room I used for an office—as a freelance web developer, I worked remotely—and logged onto Goodneighbors.com, a website where you can report lost pets, yard sales, and break-ins. I pulled up a new post, titled it, *$100 REWARD FOR LICENSE PLATE # OF BACKFIRING PICKUP TRUCK*, and described the incident, location, date, and time. In closing, I explained how my intention wasn't to personally go after this individual—it wasn't like you could find someone's address from a plate number—but to get their information to police who would require them to fix their vehicle or get it off the road. Sure, it was a long shot, but then again, how many piss-yellow junkers were rattling around town?

After answering a few client emails, I went back on Goodneighbors.com and was excited to find a comment. Someone named Gage Bostwick had written, *Crime of the century! Someone contact Unsolved Mysteries!*

I blinked dumbly at the screen. The guy was making fun of me. If it'd been some anonymous forum, I would've shrugged it off, but this was a neighborhood website where everyone was supposed to use their real name. While I could understand someone doubting my story, for them to actually make a public post mocking me was a real dick move.

Annoyed, I clicked on his name and pulled up a bare bones profile that simply said he lived in my neighborhood, showing no previous posts or comments. I did an online search for "Gage Bostwick" but didn't get a single hit, meaning the guy was either a complete nobody, using a fake name, or very skilled at keeping off the radar. Jaw clenching, I went back to his profile, clicked **MESSAGE** and typed, *Are you an asshole, a sociopath, or a little of both?* Over the top and pointless as it was, it still felt good to hit **SEND**.

I spent the next few hours binging several episodes of *The West Wing* and trying to ignore the infuriating ringing in my ear, which would recur once or twice every hour, though never for more than a few minutes. I went to bed with a box fan on high to drown out the sound.

First thing next morning, my ear in welcome remission, I logged on to Goodneighbors.com. No other comments on my post, though I had a DM from Bostwick which read, *Such a baby.*

For no reason in particular, I felt inspired to respond. *You think ear trauma is funny? So glad to know you're my neighbor!* I tapped **SEND** with a flourish and got to work on a client's website.

A few hours passed without a recurrence of the ringing, and I had high hopes everything was back to normal. Unfortunately, no such luck. In fact, when the ringing came back that afternoon, it lasted for almost ten alarming minutes before fading away again.

Indeed, the evil whining mosquito in my ear came back for half a dozen encores that evening, and twice as often the next day, my heart sinking further into my chest every time. I did my best to do my job but found it increasingly difficult to concentrate. Finally, when Friday came along with no improvement, I grimly made an appointment with an audiologist for Monday morning.

Soon as I did so, I sent a follow-up message to that Bostwick prick, informing him of the latest developments and how happy I was sure the news would make him.

Dr. Shriver was a slim woman in her late forties who smelled faintly of cinnamon. Though the ringing had resumed on the drive over, it was gone for the moment. After listening to my complaint in the examination room, the audiologist led me through a door into an adjacent room the size of a walk-in closet behind a glass window with a single chair, like a miniature recording studio. She handed me a pair of headphones, asked me to put them on, and quietly shut the door behind her.

"Can you hear me alright?" Shriver's voice came clearly through the headphones, and I gave her the thumbs up.

Her instructions were for me to raise my hand when I heard a tone and told me we'd start with my right ear. The tones ranged from a high-pitched squeak just this side of a dog-whistle to a low grumbling drone, and I lifted a hand whenever they materialized. After a few minutes, she said we'd switch over to the left ear. My pulse throbbed in my temples as I worried that I wouldn't be able to hear a thing. But the tones were distinct, and I was pretty sure I raised my hand at least as often as I did for my right ear.

Once the tests were complete, Shriver had me exit the tiny chamber and sit in the exam room, where she told me she'd return momentarily with the results. Tapping my heel compulsively, I perched on the chair and waited, conjuring all sorts of terrible prognoses, including total deafness that would eventually spread to both ears. Finally, after what felt like twenty minutes but was probably no more than two, she came back holding a printout, which she handed to me as she sat across from me.

The printout consisted of a graph with Xs inside of Os connected by line segments, like the elevation profile of an easy hilltop hike. The left side was labeled HEARING LEVEL IN DECIBELS with a range of ascending numbers on its axis, while the top read FREQUENCY IN HERTZ with more numbers. All Greek to me.

"Tests came back normal, both ears almost identical," Shriver said through a proud smile, and relief flushed through my veins like warm water through frozen pipes.

"The only odd thing was your left ear actually performed better than the right in the very low ranges." She tapped the upper corner of the graph. "But since you did so well at a hundred-twenty-five Hertz, just for the heck of it, I went down to a hundred, then fifty, then twenty—which is the bottom end of the human range of hearing—and you had no problem picking that up either. I'd have gone further, but the audiometer isn't calibrated for it."

"What about the ringing?" I blurted impatiently, my supposed sub-bass hearing of no interest to me.

"The tinnitus means you probably sustained some nerve damage." Her lips were tight, smile gone.

Numb with shock, I blinked hard. "Nerve damage?"

She held up a palm, grin back in full force. "Not as bad as it sounds. Besides, things like this have a way of resolving themselves over time."

"So, there's nothing I can do?"

She shrugged. "Let's give it another couple of weeks, and if the tinnitus doesn't improve, we'll get you back in for another checkup. How's that sound?"

I couldn't help but laugh at what I assumed was a deliberate play on words, shook her hand, and stood up to go. From out of nowhere, the ringing started up again. "It's back." I pointed at my ear.

"Sorry to hear that."

Another audiologist joke, for Chrissake? "There's nothing you can give me?"

"A few medications might help, but my recommendation is we just wait a bit." Then, without moving her lips at all—like a ventriloquist without a dummy—she moaned, "Take care of your father for me."

"What's that?"

"Hmm?"

"What about my father?"

She squinted. "Sorry, I'm not following."

"Never mind," I muttered, and left the room, wondering whether it wasn't an audiologist I needed but a psychiatrist.

First thing I did when I set foot inside my house was pull up Goodneighbors.com. Sure enough, I had another message from that dipshit Bostwick. *Did the doctor laugh at you, too?*

My hands trembling with rage, I fired back, *No, but I bet you'll find it hilarious to hear I've been diagnosed with nerve damage!!!*

I sent off the message and kept refreshing the page in hopes of a response. It came a few minutes later, *Hahaha!*

My throat felt dry, and I filled up a glass of water from the tap and drank it down. What the hell was wrong with this schmuck? Probably some former schoolyard bully no one ever stood up to, who, now he was grown, had to settle for the cyberspace equivalent of stealing someone's lunch money. For whatever reason, it'd fallen on my shoulders to teach this troll a lesson. *If you want to hear more, I'd love to tell you about it face to face,* I bluffed.

The reply came back thirty seconds later. *I'd be happy to laugh at you in person. Would I have to whisper? I don't want to bust your eardrums with my loud mouth.*

Great, whn are yo free? I typed in a mad, typo-laden flurry, confident the guy was as full of shit as I was. *I'm avialibel any evening ths week.*

I waited five minutes, ten, then fifteen for a response, which never came, as I knew it wouldn't. Still, for some reason, it was important he understood that *he* was the one backing down, not me.

How about this? I'll be at the park off 35th and Ludwig at 6 p.m. tomorrow night. Maybe I'll see you there. Then followed up with, *Unless you're a coward as well as a psychopath,* and slammed down the lid of my laptop.

The next morning, I started to worry. What if this guy was an actual psycho? If he was reckless enough to abuse me online with his name attached, what was to stop him from attacking me in real life? I thought about asking a friend to stake out the scene in case anything went down, but then I'd have to explain the whole situation—including me egging the guy on—so I decided against it.

By the time five p.m. arrived, I'd convinced myself Bostwick wasn't going to come. Harassing someone from behind a computer screen was a far cry from meeting face to face. Even if he came—and there was a ninety-nine percent chance he wouldn't—the likelihood of violence was next to none. I did go so far as to dig out my pocketknife from the kitchen utility drawer but ended up leaving it behind.

I arrived at the park on foot fifteen minutes early and sat down on a bench. The acre of manicured grass hemmed in by hulking cottonwoods was empty except for a woman flinging a tennis ball for her German shepherd. Temperature dipping as the sun sank below the treetops, I zipped up my fleece and kept my eyes peeled, praying he wouldn't show. Unable to stop licking my already chapped lips, I applied some lip balm.

Six p.m. rolled around and still no Bostwick. At 6:07 the woman and her dog left, leaving me alone and even more uneasy. But at 6:18, I knew he wasn't going to turn up and felt a weight leave my shoulders as if I'd just finished my last squat at the gym. My beef wasn't with Bostwick but with the guy in the pickup who'd screwed up my ear. This whole back and forth had just been a way for me to vent, and, fortunately, it hadn't left the safety of the internet.

As I walked home, I felt light and bouncy, as if from a couple of shots of liquor, enthusiastically greeting passersby out for their after-work sunset strolls. Sadly, my good mood dampened a few blocks from home thanks to the inevitable return of my tinnitus. Was it ever going away, or was this my life now?

As I turned onto my walkway, I was jolted from my broodings by the all-too-familiar rumble of a vehicle with a bad muffler. I spun around. Parking at the end of my block up a slight incline was the yellow pickup!

I never thought I'd see it again, and there it was on my street. What were the chances?

It didn't take long for me to piece it all together. Obviously, Bostwick was the owner of the truck, and he'd staked out the park and followed me home. Though I had no idea why, I sure as hell was going to find out.

Burning with rage, I dashed up the sidewalk. He started to drive off, but the truck stalled. When he tried the ignition, the piece of shit that it was, it only stuttered and coughed.

Somehow, from that distance and despite the raised window, I could hear him gurgling, "Help me," the strangeness of which I had no time to ponder. Bolting into the street, I yanked the driver side door open.

Bostwick was a man of about sixty, slight build with scraggly beard and greying ponytail, unlit cigarette hanging from the corner of his mouth. He briefly met my eyes and then hung his head in defeat, cigarette dropping into his lap.

"Get out!" I growled, surprised by how low my voice went.

"I don't want any trouble," he said in a sad, gravelly voice while oddly—impossibly—also burbling out, "Help me."

"Then why the fuck are you here?"

"I'll show you." While his lips matched his words, unaccountably, at the exact same time, he again sputtered, "Help me." As he reached into the pocket of his jean jacket for what I assumed was a weapon, I grabbed his bony elbow and yanked him out of the truck, dropping him hard on his side onto the asphalt.

The ringing in my head was like the whine of a thousand cicadas. I drew back a leg and kicked him sharply in the ribcage. "Not so funny when you're the one getting hurt!"

Part of me couldn't believe I was assaulting this man. But I couldn't stop—or maybe I didn't want to.

Scrunched up in the fetal position, he whimpered like a kitten, almost inviting me to kick him again. So, I did. "Is it?!" I snarled.

In a pathetic slow-motion parody of a military crawl, Bostwick dragged himself under the pickup to get away from me. Disgusted by his mewling, I let him go until only the worn soles of his work boots were visible.

Then the truck started to roll downhill. Bostwick's sharp scream was immediately cut off by his wheezing cough, followed by a sickening crunch as the rear wheel bucked over his body. Picking up speed, the truck headed down the street until it jerked towards the curb, smashed into the trunk of a cottonwood, and came to a halt.

My stomach curdling, I stood over Bostwick's splayed, deflated body as he gazed up at me with faraway eyes, blood dribbling down the side of his mouth to stain his beard and the pavement.

"Help me," he bubbled through a mouthful of blood, convulsed for a few seconds, and then lay still.

My body cold as if from an ice bath, I dropped to my knees, snatched up one of his floppy wrists and frantically searched for a pulse. Nothing. Oh my God, what'd I done? And how in hell did I hear his last words before he said them?

As I let his arm fall to the ground, the edge of an envelope poked out of his jacket pocket. In a sort of out-of-body experience, I plucked it up and read my name written on its front in a shaky, childlike scrawl.

Unsealing it with a finger, I pulled out ten crisp fifty-dollar bills along with a folded piece of stationery. I unfolded the note and read.

> *There's two things I know about guys like you. You want everything your way all the time. And you'll make life a living hell for anyone who says otherwise.*
>
> *Since I'm too damn old to fight anymore, I'm just going give you this money for your doctor's bills and whatnot and hope we can call it good. I suppose you can still sue me if you want, but being that I'm unemployed and on disability, there isn't much left to take that my ex-wife hasn't already.*
>
> *And if it makes any difference, you got my word that I'll be bringing the truck in to the shop this week.*

> G. Bostwick

I hold my breath as the bootsteps of the overnight C.O. echo down the hall on his way towards my dark cell. With no time to untie the knotted bedsheet spread across my lap, I sit still on my cot, knowing full well if I'm caught trying to escape, I might not get a second chance.

As his footsteps get closer, the screams come. "No! Nooo! Nooooo!" he shrills over the ringing in my ears, even though I know, technically, he hasn't uttered a single word.

Lucky for me, a garbled voice buzzes from his radio, and he turns around at the cell before mine to hurry back in the direction he's come, his shrieks as loud as if he's feet away. Seconds later a metal door clangs shut, mercifully silencing his tortured warbling, and I go back to my knot tying with added urgency.

All in all, twenty months for manslaughter is a fair sentence. Even though I didn't technically kill Bostwick, I accept that my attack was the catalyst for the chain reaction that took his life. Never a violent man, my ear injury had disturbed me to the point where I felt like I was becoming a different person. A short stint behind bars would give me some time to collect myself until it healed.

Yet, as I sat in jail awaiting trial, the ringing only got worse. Instead of once every few hours for a maximum ten minutes at a stretch, it started lasting twenty minutes, an hour, three hours. By the time the judge sentenced me, I was enduring the whine for nearly half the day. Now, three months into my sentence, not a second goes by without the tinnitus, like a drill bit permanently boring into my skull.

I test the strength of the bedsheet by yanking hard as I can. Should be more than enough to hold my weight. Man, I can't wait to get out of this place.

Maddening as the nonstop ringing is, it's far from the worst part. What I can't take anymore are the babblings of every single goddamn person who crosses my path—from peaceful mutterings to desperate pleadings to bellows of pain—all transmitted directly into my head without them so much as opening their mouths.

Some of them have to be within arm's reach for me to hear, others I can make out clear as a radio signal from hundreds of feet across the yard. But the absolute worst is the mess hall, where I'm bombarded by the cries of hundreds of tortured souls, like dining in hell's own cafeteria.

Fortunately, all it took was one brief pummeling of my scrawny cell mate last week for them to put me in solitary, away from his incessant begging. I had nothing against the little meth-head, but there's only so long a man can listen to "Please don't hurt me!" over and over again before losing it completely.

And it was on that day when a new—and all too familiar—voice took over the role of lead singer in the haunted chorus in my head. *Snug as a bug in a rug. Snug as a bug in a rug. Snug as a bug...* it whispered over and over, never letting up for an instant, not even in my dreams.

The other day it got so bad that I tried some do-it-yourself surgery by jamming one of those bendy "safety" pens inside my ear canal. It was a partial success in that rupturing my eardrum completely silenced my tinnitus, along with all hearing in that ear. What I didn't count on is that not only didn't it do anything to quiet the voices, if anything, they became louder in comparison, particularly that one I knew all too well chanting, *Snug as a bug in a rug. Snug as a bug in a rug. Snug as a bug in a rug.*

I'm not really sure of the science behind my newfound superpower of hearing everyone's last words long before they die, and, honestly, I don't give a shit. But if I had to guess, I'd say the trauma from Bostwick's backfiring pickup somehow activated an obscure part of my brain, giving me the ability to not only pick up lower ranges of sound, as the audiologist reported, but across dimensions—in this case, time. Perhaps a more worthy man could've figured out a way to use this forbidden knowledge to ease people's suffering, or, who knows, maybe even prevent some deaths, depending on your view on free will. But, frankly, it's all too much for me.

Standing on the toilet seat, I reach over my head and twine the end of the sheet around the sprinkler jutting out of the ceiling. Knotting it tightly, I loop the noose around my neck and lean forward until it's snug. "Snug as a bug in a rug," I whisper—voluntarily or not, I have no clue—bend my knees, and jump.

The Dungwich Horror
(A Lovecraptian Tale)

Head throbbing from last night's drinking binge, I sat on the john for my late morning poop. Usually regular enough to set a clock by, I waited for the train to leave the station as the leaking sink dripped away the seconds. After several minutes, I decided to get up and try again later.

Sure enough, while vacuuming the living room of my modest bungalow, a rumble as of distant thunder from my bowels. I hurried back to the bathroom, tile cold on my bare soles, yet despite the urge to go was baffled when nothing happened. The distressing pattern of emergency then false alarm repeated itself several times over the next hour until I was forced to face the terrible truth.

I was constipated.

Still in my thirties, I'd never experienced the phenomenon. I thought back with dismay to the three pizza slices I'd scarfed down at two a.m. to sop up the cinnamon whiskey shots Steph, my swipe app date, had coerced me into taking. Almost always a clean eater, I allowed myself this moment of weakness, and I was paying the price.

Luckily, it was Saturday and my only plan for the day was a five p.m. coffee with Steph—plenty of time for my digestive system to get back to normal. Charmed at first by her free-spirited party girl persona, my broken guts were ample proof I couldn't handle that much chaos in my life. For the sake of my health, I'd be using the get together to break things off.

Two hours passed and despite several runs to the bank of Kohler, I still hadn't made a single deposit. Upsetting terms such as "prolapse" and "fissures" skittering through my mind, I made sure not to strain on the plastic seat and let gravity do its work. Unfortunately, Earth's natural laws no longer seemed to apply. My leg fell asleep, and I worried for the first time what would happen if the troops didn't deploy in time for my date.

Moments later, my own internal San Andreas fault line slipped, triggering tremors in my nether regions so excruciating I pounded the wall with a fist. A veteran of slipped discs, two broken bones, and a hernia, I was no stranger to pain. But as the astonishing pressure built up like floodwaters against a dam, I'm ashamed to say I whimpered like a lost puppy.

After what felt like ages, something dropped as if down the chute of a vending machine and plished into the water. Instead of the Guinness Book of World Records specimen I expected, a single pellet lay on the bottom of the bowl.

Every fifteen to twenty minutes for the next few hours, the juddering, back-hunching cycle of wretchedness fired up again, like someone had replaced my intestines with a pepper grinder. And the same paltry results, hardly enough to bother flushing.

I sat there in my cramped "office" panting, marveling at how I'd been misled into thinking constipation was little more than mild discomfort. Knowing this new dark reality left me feeling betrayed, like I'd learned about a genocide left out of the history books.

I got up from what had become my desk chair and went out to the kitchen where I'd left my phone on the table. I gasped. Somehow, it was almost four o'clock! Short of a miracle, there was no way I was making my date.

Logging onto the app, I sent Steph a quick message. "Hate to do this last minute, but I'm feeling a bit under the weather. Raincheck?" While I could've easily dumped her like this, I was old-fashioned enough to believe breaking up was something you did face-to-face. I shut off the phone to avoid the temptation.

Then I waddled back to the bathroom as the bell inside my colon signaled the next round. If anything, the contortions came on stronger this time—forcing out beads of sweat on my forehead and upper lip—but again producing little more than a shaving.

"Please God help me," I was surprised to hear myself whine, never a religious man.

With the next fit, I wailed half-jokingly, "Jesus, Allah, Vishnu, frickin' Zeus, whoever ends this becomes my official Lord and Savior!"

When my abdominal lawnmower started up again moments later—effectively shredding any lingering beliefs I might've had in a benevolent creator—I unleashed a litany of every curse word I knew, followed by a nonsense stew of mostly grunted consonants in hopes of discharging the pain, "Frgrgrtunmrgunsyhahnghftcrsndurgn!"

By this point I'd shed all my clothes, as it became a chore to keep pulling my pants up and down like some sad Internet GIF. The overhead fluorescents flickered, and that's when I heard the voice. From the toilet.

At first, I told myself I was just passing gas. But the "p" and "f" and "t" noises strung together into what sounded uncannily like words, though none I'd ever heard from a human mouth. I plastered the back of my wrist to my forehead to check for a temperature, but I was cool as a clam. No fever dream, this was really happening.

The language, if that's what it was, morphed from throaty to nasal to whistling to a kind of insect clicking. Finally, I recognized what I'm pretty sure was Chinese or Japanese spoken in a deep melodious voice, then possibly Arabic, then definitely French. "Maître!"

Sadly, my familiarity with French consisted of two inattentive years in junior high, so I wasn't able to translate until I distinctly heard in clear perfect English, "Master!"

I held my breath, heart buzzing inside my ribcage like a bumblebee. The voice boomed again, "Master!"

"Who's there?" I muttered, as if someone had knocked on my front door (and not my back).

"In your tongue, I am known as Syha'h N'ghft, but you may call me Sy," the voice said. "And I am at your service."

I sat there dumbfounded, wondering if I'd somehow swallowed a Bluetooth. Or a hallucinogen. "You're inside me?!"

"In a manner of speaking," Sy said.

I launched up from the seat. Spinning around, I lifted my butt, parted my cheeks, and inspected myself over my shoulder in the mirror above the sink. No wires or anything out of the ordinary. My mind groped for a logical explanation. "What the hell are you? And why are you even here?"

"You summoned me, of course."

"I did no such thing." The fact that I was conversing with a voice inside my rectum was hard enough to believe, much less the idea that I'd initiated the contact.

Yet he calmly reminded me of my plea to the universe for aid, claiming that during my bout of verbal diarrhea I'd mentioned his name.

I scoffed. This was insane. Was this what it was like to go insane? "You want me to believe you're a God or something?"

"We have no such terminology where I come from."

"And that is?" Going along with the ruse, I cocked an ear towards my posterior.

"Your people call it the Pinwheel Galaxy. In the constellation Ursa Major."

"Yeah, right. How could that be possible?"

"Pain is an amplifier," Sy replied. "Yours was so great, it projected your call across the vast gulf of space between us."

Cold all of a sudden, I shivered. I no longer cared who Sy was or where he came from, I just wanted him gone. "Well, it was a wrong number. You can go home now, wherever that is."

Sy paused a few seconds, as if taken aback by my rudeness. "If you no longer require my services, I shall take my leave. However, I must first request your aid for my deliverance."

Deliverance. The first image that popped into my mind was the disgusting "squeal like a pig" scene from the 70s movie of the same name. It dawned on me that I, too, had been violated.

"I want you out of my ass!" Trembling in fury, I squatted over the bowl and smacked my butt repeatedly with both hands as if I was an unruly child. "Get out, now!"

After several fruitless minutes of self-flagellation, I began to cry softly.

"What do I have to do to make you go away?" I bleated.

"Simply expel me," Sy said serenely.

"Like, poop?"

"That would be your word for it."

Exhausted, I dropped down on the seat and licked away salty tears from my lips. "What the hell do you think I've been trying to do for the last six hours?"

"If I may, a suggestion." Sy recited a series of complicated, guttural syllables he said would set us both free.

The eeriness of the chants, or whatever they were, raised goosebumps on my arms. Uneasy, I wondered what the process of ejecting Sy would feel like. And what would happen when he got out.

"How big are you, exactly?" I asked.

"Currently, I am in the form of a gas."

"So, it's not gonna hurt?"

"No more than one would expect," he said matter-of-factly. "And once I am gone, I promise your bowels will be empty as they have ever been."

"I don't know—" The bathroom walls closed in on me, as if I'd taken a bad tab of acid.

"Repeat after me," Sy commanded. "*Ph'nglui.*"

Despite my trepidation, I sat down on the seat and parroted as best I could, wanting nothing more than for the ordeal to be over. "*Ph'nglui.*"

"*Mglw'nafh,*" Sy said.

I repeated in a call and response no churchgoer had ever joined in on. "*Wgah'nagl.*"

I tapped my heel nervously on the tile, unsure about the whole thing.

"*Wgah'nagl,*" he said, more insistently.

"Sorry, but what do you plan to do, again?" I asked.

A brief, but unsettling pause. "Nothing more than my duty, I assure you."

If that was a pun, it wasn't appreciated. "Could you elaborate?"

"If you must know," he snapped, "I intend to make the world right again."

"I don't know what that means." I was equally taken aback by his loss of composure as I was his words.

"Release me from this prison, and all will become clear!" Sy shouted.

I had no time to process his disclosure as what followed was my longest and most vicious interior pummeling yet, what had to have been a full minute of pure gut-wrenching torture. As my scant leavings finally hit the water, they hissed like a pat of butter on a griddle, and a hot plume of steam rocketed me up from the seat.

At the bottom of the bowl, a golf-ball sized chunk of tar bubbled like fondue.

Thankful as I was to have gotten rid of Sy, my relief was short lived as a pseudopod emerged from one side of his amoeboid body, which he used to drag himself forward an inch. Then a second one gooped out of his opposite side, and he gained another inch. Alternating his appendages like a miniature kayaker, he slid himself up the curve of the porcelain.

When the pitchy clump approached the water line, I snapped out of my trance and smashed down the flusher. Sprouting two more limbs, Sy held fast, braving the onslaught like a cow in a storm. As the water drained, the stench of spoiled fish wafted up, and when the bowl refilled, he doggedly resumed the climb.

Panicked, I flushed again. This time he skidded backwards, spun head over heels (though he had neither), and disappeared down the hole.

"Good riddance, you piece of shit," I spat and followed with a final flush.

"I am still here," Sy said from inside me, seemingly nonplussed. "Now, finish the chant and be done with this."

"Nooooo!" I growled, teeth and buttocks clenched tightly against the return of my nightmare. If that foul thing I just disposed of had merely been corrupted by Sy, how horrific must the corrupter be himself?

"Did you hear me?" I screamed. "I'm not saying the chant!"

Bracing myself for Sy's response, I sat in silence. A neighbor's dog yipped outside.

Roughly five minutes of stiff anticipation until the next contraction, evacuation, and splash. Dread in my heart, I forced myself to look...and was overjoyed to find a normal-sized—and inanimate—cluster of organic waste.

Was Sy gone? Had my refusal to repeat his magic words banished him back to the dismal void from whence he'd come?

Feeling filthy all of a sudden, I hopped in the shower. The blissfully hot water washed away any remnants of what'd come out of me, along with most of my tension. The lead weight in my gut meant I was still constipated, but Sy's retreat followed by my most recent healthy stool meant things were on the upswing.

A faint grumbling in my stomach, and then an abrupt spasm—like an elephant stomping my midsection—which buckled my knees and threw me to the floor of the shower. Laying stunned in the fetal position, water streaming over me, my stomach distended like the tin foil of the Jiffy Pop Grandma used to make. I gasped for breath, the pain incandescent, certain I was about to pass out.

"I tried to do this the easy way," Sy snarled. "But you have forced my hand."

"I didn't say the chant," I groaned, my belly now that of a pregnant woman in her third trimester, ghastly purple stretchmarks snaking up my sides.

Laughter from Sy in the form of sputtering flatulence. "There is no chant. Only nonsense words to distract your mind."

This admission hammered home the fact that no matter what tortures Sy inflicted on me, he couldn't cross the threshold without my consent—like a vampire in reverse. "I won't let go until you tell me why you're really here."

Hot water pattered my back as if from a rainstorm in hell.

"Our home planet is no more," Sy said despondently, followed by a flatulent sigh. "For aeons I sought a suitable replacement, yet all had been previously claimed. Then you summoned me," his voice brightened. "And while I had never heard of this mud plot you call Earth, I vowed to prepare it for myself and my subjects."

I honestly, truly, didn't want to know the answer. But, as the one responsible for conjuring this abomination, I had to ask. "Prepare it?"

"By boiling every stream, lake, and ocean to vapor!" Sy thundered. "By shriveling all that is green and scattering the dust to the Four Winds! By rending soil from bedrock like flesh from bone!"

"You're going to kill us all," I moaned from the floor of the shower, the faces of my parents, friends—including lovely Steph's—floating past my mind's eye. Every one of them, dead. And all by my hand. Or ass, to be specific.

"To the contrary," he said, "the perpetuation of your species is vital to our colonization."

"As slaves," I murmured, knowing full well where this was going.

Sy sniffed. "Neither I nor my subjects have any use for the fluffing of pillows, the poaching of eggs, or whatever petty chores your kind could perform for us. No, humanity will provide a far more important service."

Straightening my back, I allowed myself a moment of hope, which Sy quickly dashed to pieces.

"First," he said gleefully. "I shall gather each and every one of you wretched souls from around the globe. Then, I shall melt and fuse your forms together into a massive orb, which I shall set ablaze. Once I snuff out your pathetic sun like a candle wick, I shall thrust this star borne of delicious suffering into the heavens to radiate agony down to sustain the planet's new and rightful occupants."

I vowed then and there to resist, even if it meant exploding all over the walls of the shower.

Wasting no time, Sy commenced to inflate my aching abdomen, my tender skin cracking like a sun-baked salt flat. Forcing myself to my knees, I stood up on wobbling legs, snatched off the detachable shower nozzle, and twisted the faucet cold as it could go. Once the water was chilled, I flicked the nozzle to the massage setting and positioned it against my anus.

"Take this, asshole!" I bellowed.

To my surprise, my belly immediately began deflating as if punctured, and I had hopeful visions of Sy drowning inside of me like a flooded fetus.

Until Sy struck so fiercely it was as if my viscera were being puréed in a blender, bowing me over like an actor at a curtain call. Shrieking in misery and defiance, a frigid wave swept through me, congealing my guts into a hard mass. Then, what felt like Thor's hammer shattered what was left of my digestive tract in a paroxysm of anguish, the force smashing me through the shower door onto the bathroom tile.

Lying there amongst the glass shards, bleeding from a hundred wounds inside and out, the last of my willpower drying up like a puddle under the August sun, I knew there remained but a single option to prevent Sy's exodus and the erasure of life on Earth.

With a burst of strength borne of equal parts inspiration and desperation, I rose woozily to my feet. Streaming water and blood, I slid into the kitchen and tugged open a drawer. In one motion, I grabbed a butcher's knife and thrust the tip of the blade towards my throat, certain my death alone could banish Sy back to the cosmic pit from which he'd been vomited.

But before I touched flesh, a convulsion I could only compare to a lightning strike on an erupting volcano crumpled me to the floor, knocking the knife from my hand, where it skittered out of reach.

"Alright, you win!" Spent and helpless, I cried to the heavens, needing it to be over. "I don't care what you do, just get out!"

Instead of the magnitude ten Richter Scale brutality I was expecting, my body went numb as if shot full of morphine, and, almost pleasantly, something spooled out of me like handkerchiefs from a magician's sleeve.

Then a putrescence in alternating waves of pond scum and halitosis and carcass, followed by a splattering and gurgling of something taking form. Unable to look, I shut my eyes tight, as what I knew to be a newborn Sy gooped across the floor, squelched up the cabinets to the counter, and shattered the window above the sink.

My vital fluids leaking out of me, I summoned the courage to open my eyes. A decision I immediately regretted, as outside the broken window hovered a transparent bubbling blister the size of an obese man, within which a space-black pus roiled and whirlpooled. Quivering, it continued to expand until it blocked out the streetlamp, and, moments later, the moon.

Sprawled on the kitchen floor amidst Sy's warm, sticky afterbirth—weeping for my fate and that of my fellow man—a quote cut through my haze of self-pity and regret, "I am become death, destroyer of worlds."

Destroyer of worlds. Destroyer of worlds. Destroyer of...worlds?

I threw back my head and laughed, knowing all was not lost.

For the second time that day I bawled across the cosmos, beseeching whoever or whatever might be listening to come to my aid in return for my eternal servitude, then gibbered every combination of syllables I could pronounce.

Seconds, minutes passed, until finally I felt something stir between my legs.

Triumphant yet terrified, I sat up as my flaccid penis spasmed, thrashed, and rose stiffly of its own volition, like a cobra ready to strike.

Then, from its orifice, a tiny voice squeaked out my name.

The Ceremony

Aldra paused under the archway leading into the vast basalt amphitheater, hundreds of guests—mostly kin—sprawled across the black stone pews. High above, jagged volcanic crags spurted lava into a roiling sky of deep purple cloud, blurry treble suns glowing pinkly through.

In the midground, on the edge of a low cliff, a tiny wormlike figure stood on a boulder in the midst of a bubbling lava pool beneath gushing falls. Yagru, her mate. Fond warmth flushed through Aldra's heart followed by a jolt of gut-twisting anxiety at what she was about to do.

The priestess, grasping the sparkling tantalum band in both claws, towered over Yagru, her scales a drab green to his ashen grey. A rattle of her tail, and a choir of atonal voices piped up from somewhere deep within the rock caverns.

All eyes on Aldra, she took a bracing breath and glided down the aisle. Joyful hisses and flicking tongues from those gathered, including her eldest sister, Gormi, sleek wings folded against a massive milk-white bulk. And, as Aldra reached the front row, a corpulent giant, scales brilliant blue as the heart of a flame. Aldra's mother. Nested amongst the fat coils of the older female, her latest young husband, a grub whispering in her ear as she threw back her wedged head in laughter.

A pang of jealousy from Aldra at the elder's stunning beauty, outshining her own even on that special day. But, as she slipped past with a practiced smile, Aldra remembered she was lovely, too, any lingering doubts dispelled by the piercing gaze of every male. Because, as of late, her scales glowed a radiant orange like cactus blooms, belly proudly plumped with hundreds of fertilized eggs, thanks to Yagru.

Naturally, like all Naga females, Aldra hadn't always been this appealing. Indeed, the change had only come over the last six sun cycles, as for the prior four-hundred-twenty she'd been vine-thin, scales a dull olive, wings mere buds. Only when the orange broke through the green and her wings branched out did the opposite sex even look her way. Along with her female rivals, several of whom eyed her from the back pews.

Indeed, Aldra was growing more fertile every cycle, her orange destined to burnish to a deep red, followed by gold, then pale like Gormi—who, for the first time in their lives, seemed to see her as almost equal—laying more eggs each clutch. Until finally, in another seven-hundred cycles or so, she'd turn bright blue like her mother, stuffed with eggs until she burst apart like fireworks, rejoining the universe in one ultimate glory. But Aldra had a long way before that, and, in the meantime, she intended to enjoy every moment of her newfound splendor.

She slid up the winding path, smooth from the passage of countless brides before her. When she reached the cliff face—a sweltering, sulfurous heat wafting from the lava pool at the foot of the falls—Yagru met her with a simpleton's smile. Reminding her of the awkward night of her four-hundred-twenty-sixth cycle when they first mated.

That early clutch was only eight eggs. The second, a cycle later, twenty-three. The third, thirty-eight. Now, this one distending her belly would be as many as all those put together. Solemnly, she found her spot next to the priestess, lava mist tickling her scales.

The tantalum band glittered as the red primary sun broke the cloud cover. But Yagru wasn't paying attention, gaze drawn overhead by a swarm of fat buzzing blowflies. Aldra shook her head in pity and not a little shame. Was this even her beloved anymore?

When they'd first been introduced at worship, Aldra was lured in by his genius, his talent for improvising heart-rending verse on the Planetary Lights easily as he could cipher a twelve-digit sum, finally a match for her own sharp and inquisitive mind. Indeed, he was famous across the Craters as both engineer and philosopher, having discovered a more efficient way to harness magma to warm Naga nests while uncovering new layers of consciousness through experimental research.

Yagru snapped absentmindedly at the flies, making it hard to believe how, during their courtship, Aldra had been honored to join him on strolls around the pits and ledges, his reputation radiating over to her like heat from a sunbaked rock. Lecturing around the Craters, Yagru had accumulated overflowing storehouses of Viath tusks, ranking him as one of the wealthiest Naga. Then, as her orange ripened, the stage had been shared equally.

But as it stood, drool stringing from slack jaws, Yagru could barely do simple addition and subtraction anymore, and the clawful of tusks he earned were doled out in pity; it was an open secret that Aldra supported them both from her screenshows on scale care. Standing on the black crag above her kin, she alone was the prize to behold, a majestic river coursing past a stagnant puddle.

Still, after all, no tragedy had befallen Yagru, just mere biology, like the seasonal frosting of the Northern Wastes. Indeed, the Naga had long ago made peace with its males peaking early only to quickly fall apart. At a mere two-hundred-forty cycles, little over half Aldra's age, Yagru, flecks of flies on his lips, was *supposed* to be a shadow of his former self.

The priestess shook her rattle, and the hidden choir fell silent, audience rapt with expectation. Every one of Aldra's children—both female and male—laid proud eyes upon her, as the more revered Aldra became, the higher their own standing.

"The Great Lamia blesses this ceremony," the priestess' hiss echoed around the amphitheater. She handed Aldra the band, which, despite the scorching lava all around, was ice cold, its razor-sharp inner edge gleaming.

"Give this ring," the priestess' golden eyes fell on Aldra, "as a reminder of the vow you both have taken."

Mouth dry, Aldra slipped the band over Yagru's throat. Only then did his bleary eyes focus on hers. And from their insensate depths, black pupils dilated like two divers coming up for air.

"Now," the priestess stepped back with a respectful bow, "you may take the groom."

Aldra reached out and grasped the frigid band in both claws. All that was left was to twist the metal so it slit Yagru's throat and then lap up the blood as he lay dying. Tough as the moment would be, she pictured the night's celebration to come, the glut of feasting and dancing, the dozens of young males parading their wit and acumen before her in hopes of being the next to bask in her glow, however briefly.

Her trembling claws clicked against the band. Down below, Aldra's mother had risen to her full colossal height, hood spread in wrath at the delay. Though not a word passed between the two, the younger knew what the elder was thinking: that she should be ecstatic to shed this dead skin of a mate to make way for the new.

Yagru's eyes dull as so much domestic stock, Aldra turned the band a single degree. A trickle of black blood down his throat, though not a whimper from Yagru.

The priestess flicked her tongue in encouragement while an agitated rattle lofted up from the attendees. What was happening to Aldra? Was it that fear of success—feeling unworthy of this crowning achievement—Gormi had warned her to guard against?

Or was it something else entirely? That, no matter the changes her mate had undergone, was there not still a taste of the fresh ripe Yagru somewhere within the rotting husk? Had he not, even that morning, penned her new verse?

> *You are the sunrise,*
> *the light and warmth from above*
> *that keeps me from cold.*

While nowhere near lyrical as his earlier epics, it had a touching simplicity lacking in those other gaudy rhymes. A subtle beauty, like a shard of glass smoothed by aeons of sweeping tide. Much like the Yagru who stood before her.

Aldra's mother stormed off her pew to slither up the ramp. Aldra knew that if she didn't complete the ceremony, her mother would do it for her.

Still, a faint light shone in Yagru's eyes, proving that he knew what was about to happen, and welcomed it. And it was that very acceptance that made clear the lengths of his love. What if they had it all wrong, and the former Yagru, all fury and flash, had been the imposter, and this humble being her true mate?

Aldra shook her head violently. Enough! Shortly after hatching, each Naga was taught how emotion poisoned rational thought. It was time to do what she'd come for!

Veins bulging in her forearms, she grasped the band. Took a deep breath. And, in a single motion, slid it up and over Yagru's head to fling it in the lava pool, where it sunk.

Deafening hisses and rattles from below, Aldra grabbed her beloved Yagru, spread her wings wide, and leapt from the cliff. Rising above the furious, writhing crowd, she flapped north towards the Wastes, where no Naga could tell her who—or why—she must love.

There Is No Zombie Outbreak!

RONNIE BARSTOW started Chatspace group LIBERTY LOVERS AND FREEDOM FIGHTERS

RONNIE BARSTOW added description
A place for real Americans to stop government overreach during this so-called "zombie" outbreak. Don't tread!

RONNIE BARSTOW added new member BRUCE P. MERRIMACK
RONNIE BARSTOW added new member SANDIE FRANK
RONNIE BARSTOW added new member CRAIG CLEMENTS

RONNIE BARSTOW shared a post
March 4 at 7:41 PM
With so much bullcrap floating around the lamestream media, I hope you all can agree it's time for us to spread the truth, stand our ground, and make sure our country stays free as the day it was born.

SANDIE FRANK commented

Thanks so much for starting this, RONNIE BARSTOW. The fear mongering is out of control.

CRAIG CLEMENTS commented
ITS ALL THEATER!! ONE OF THE LAST STEPS IN GLOBALIST PLOT!!

SANDIE FRANK added new members PATTY RUSSO, MITCHELL STANISLAUS, SAMANTHA PRITCHARD

RONNIE BARSTOW shared a post
March 7 at 8:26 PM
So now our authoritarian politicians and lying journalists have switched out "zombie"—as if anyone over ten years old was buying that—for "Acute Neurological Wasting Disease" or ANWD. Let me ask you guys, do you know a SINGLE PERSON who's turned? Didn't think so.

CRAIG CLEMENTS commented
CRISIS ACTERS BOUGHT AND PAID FOR BY THE ELITE!! PENTAGON RAN EXERCISE IN JANUARY ON EXACTLY THIS!! THEIR SEEING HOW MUCH THEY CAN GET AWAY WITH BEFORE THEY IMPRISON ALL IN CAMPS!!

RONNIE BARSTOW commented
You might be on to something, CRAIG CLEMENTS! Glad you're on our side.

RONNIE BARSTOW added new member MARINA SCHULTZ

RONNIE BARSTOW shared a post
March 9 at 6:22 AM

Check out this article from Datadump proving "zombies" are just a bunch of meth heads let out of rehabs and looney bins. Share it far and wide!

Datadump.com
Documents Debunk "Zombie" Narrative *by Shelley Marcuson*
Datadump has secured several classified documents revealing that the "zombie" propaganda foisted upon a gullible public is nothing but...

CRAIG CLEMENTS commented
TOLD YA!!

BRUCE P. MERRIMACK commented
Yet not a peep about it on network news...

SANDIE FRANK added new members *MARILYN AMBROSE, TYLER GLICK, WINONA PACKARD-LEURS, BARBARA DANBURY*

SANDIE FRANK shared a post
March 10 at 7:04 PM
One of the methies went after a gym class at my kids' school, and now they're shutting down the whole district. What am I supposed to do, quit my job and stay home all day? Lord, give me the strength.

CRAIG CLEMENTS commented
ALL GOING ACCORD TO PLAN!!

RONNIE BARSTOW commented
Sorry to hear that, SANDIE FRANK. Anything we can do to help?

SANDIE FRANK commented
Know any babysitters?

WINONA PACKARD-LEURS commented
Me me me me!

MARINA SCHULTZ commented
This is exactly why I'm running for school board. I hope I can count on your votes.

RONNIE BARSTOW shared a post
March 13 at 8:19 PM
For two whole weeks we're supposed to stay home to "slow the spread?" The best way to slow the spread—of fear—is to turn off your damn TV!

Anyone else's spouse getting sucked into this? Colleen won't even talk to me about it anymore.

SANDIE FRANK commented
Like ALL businesses aren't "essential"!

RONNIE BARSTOW commented
Texas is nowhere as strict as up here. Leon Rust is refusing to shut down his factories and firing any employees who don't show up to work!

CRAIG CLEMENTS commented
RUST = 1 OF THE LAST TRUE AMERICAN HEROES!!

RONNIE BARSTOW commented
We need to have a protest or something.

BRUCE P. MERRIMACK commented
I was hoping someone would say that! How about Sunday noon in front of City Hall?

SANDIE FRANK commented
Heck yeah!

CRAIG CLEMENTS commented
100%!!

SAMANTHA PRITCHARD commented
I'll come down on my lunch hour.

RONNIE BARSTOW commented
AWESOME! Let's shut this shit down! Bring signs!

MITCHELL STANISLAUS
I'll be the one waving Old Glory!

RONNIE BARSTOW shared a post
March 14 at 5:57 PM
Even though it was just me and **BRUCE P. MERRIMACK** today, I think we woke up some sheeple. Didn't see any media—or zombies lol—but I'm pretty sure the politicians knew we were there. Let's keep building the momentum!

BRUCE P. MERRIMACK commented
At the very least it was good to catch up in person, **RONNIE BARSTOW**. Because that's the very thing they don't want us doing.

CRAIG CLEMENTS commented

SORRY I FORGOT!!

BRUCE P. MERRIMACK shared a post
March 17 at 2:12 PM

I'm sure you've heard our illustrious "public health" czar telling us bullets won't work against the Zs—which they're now calling "people experiencing vital-impairment"—so there's no reason for us to buy guns. Which of course means we should all do the opposite.

RONNIE BARSTOW commented

Just got back from three different box stores and they were all sold out. Gun stores shut up tight too. Gonna try the pawn shop.

RONNIE BARSTOW commented

Got an old shotgun and two boxes of shells because that's all the old guy would sell me. Best head down there quick if you want to stock up.

SANDIE FRANK shared a post
March 18 at 11:14 AM

Got turned away from the grocery store today because I refused to put on any stupid body armor! Not only won't that nonsense protect you from the methies, you're actually **MORE LIKELY** to get bit since you can't run away!

Pretty sure this is all about bankrupting small businesses by making everyone buy online. Heck, my church is the only place in town still open that's **NOT** a big box store.

PATTY RUSSO commented

Of course our church is still open because God don't take no sick days. Not only aren't we requiring body armor at services—it's so divisive!—we're not letting anyone in wearing those dang straitjackets.

CRAIG CLEMENTS commented
THEIR TRYING TO TURN US INTO ROBOTS!! BREACH OF THE CONSTITUTION!! WE WILL NOT COMPLY!!

RONNIE BARSTOW commented
It's obviously about the guns, people.

MARINA SCHULTZ commented
No, it's to indoctrinate the children. Which is why I'm running for school board. Can I count on your votes?

BRUCE P. MERRIMACK commented
Sadly, I'm afraid the answer is "e," all of the above.

RONNIE BARSTOW shared a post
March 22 at 4:39 PM
Anyone heard from CRAIG CLEMENTS lately? Messaged me last night that he got into a tussle with some meth head outside the bar—I won't say which one because Chatspace will tip off the feds—and he hasn't gotten back to me since.

SANDIE FRANK commented
Nope, sorry.

BRUCE P. MERRIMACK commented
Chatspace won't bother ratting out some bar for staying open, but they will censor messages. Only a matter of time before it happened to us.

RONNIE BARSTOW commented
Stopped by CRAIG CLEMENTS place. Lights were on, and I could hear him banging around inside, but he wouldn't come to the door.

SANDIE FRANK commented
CRAIG CLEMENTS is a big boy, I'm sure he's fine. The good Lord's watching over us all.

PATTY RUSSO commented
He sure is, SANDIE FRANK. "Yea, though I walk through the valley of the shadow of death, I will fear no evil: for thou art with me." PSALMS 23:4

RONNIE BARSTOW commented
SANDIE FRANK Of course CRAIG CLEMENTS is fine. Never said he wasn't.

RONNIE BARSTOW shared a post
March 24 at 3:04 PM
Check it out. Finally, a politician not afraid to stand up for the American people.

Currentscoop.com
Gov. Vonfrancis Bans "Hitlerian" ANWD Public Health Measures
by Matt Selway
Governor Vonfrancis passed an executive order on Monday making it illegal for state agencies and private businesses to require body armor to protect against attacks from people experiencing vital-impairment, despite some of the highest case counts...

SANDIE FRANK commented
Tears of joy. God bless this man and his courage.
BRUCE P. MERRIMACK commented

Sorry to break it to you, but Vonfrancis knows his order is unenforceable and will be overturned by the courts. He's just gearing up for a presidential run. Nothing but empty virtue signaling.

MARINA SCHULTZ commented
I won't be virtue signaling when I'm elected to the school board. I've got all your votes, right?

BRUCE P. MERRIMACK shared a post
March 28 at 3:13 PM
Actually surprised to see legacy media reporting on our esteemed "public health" czar backtracking on the whole bullets-can't-kill-the-Zs propaganda. The old snake finally admitted it was all about making sure law enforcement had enough ammo.

RONNIE BARSTOW commented
This is HUUUUUUGE! Now American citizens know for a fact that their government's been lying through its teeth!

If this news won't get Colleen back from her mother's, I don't know what will.

RONNIE BARSTOW added new member MARCUS JONES

MARCUS JONES shared a post
March 29 at 10:38 PM
You fucking IDIOTS! After almost a million dead, carnage in every town, and eye-witness videos all over the media and internet, you're honestly still telling yourselves ANWD is a HOAX?

Open your eyes, imbeciles! Zombies have literally taken over the streets! Hospitals are overrun with dead! They're packing corpses into freezer trucks, for Chrissake! WHAT PLANET ARE YOU LIVING ON THAT YOU THINK THIS IS MAKE BELIEVE?

If you're not going to help, then PLEASE stay home, so when you turn you don't take out the whole neighborhood with you.

RONNIE BARSTOW removed MARCUS JONES from the group

RONNIE BARSTOW shared a post
March 30 at 7:48 AM
Sorry about that wingnut, guys. Thought he was one of us, but he was just another ANWD cuck. I've deleted his fear porn and banned him permanently from the group.

I promise to be more careful about letting in new members. And to be on the safe side, I'm getting rid of anyone I don't know personally.

RONNIE BARSTOW removed MARILYN AMBROSE, TYLER GLICK, WINONA PACKARD-LEURS, BARBARA DANBURY PATTY RUSSO, MITCHELL STANISLAUS, SAMANTHA PRITCHARD from the group

RONNIE BARSTOW shared a post
April 2 at 6:57 PM
Linking to an article showing how hospitals are blaming ANWD for almost every death, including strokes, gunshots, and car wrecks!

USAPundit.net
Hospitals Get Federal Funding for Claiming ANWD Deaths *by Thomas Harrington III*
A whistleblower at an unnamed medical facility has exposed the widespread practice of hospitals attributing deaths from accidents and natural causes to...

SANDIE FRANK commented
Every morning and night I get down on my knees and pray these people will burn in hell for what they've done.

RONNIE BARSTOW shared a post
April 6 at 8:11 PM
A bit of a bummer to report, guys. Stopped by **CRAIG CLEMENTS** place again, and the mail was all piled up out front. Bad smell from inside. He forgot to lock his garage, so I snuck in.

Poor guy was wandering around in daze, moaning in pain, face covered in sores. Yep, I hate to admit it, but looks like our old pal got his dumb ass hooked on meth. Wouldn't even talk to me about it, just chased me out.

Left him a couple cans of beans in case he gets hungry. I'll let him detox a bit and check up on him in a few days.

SANDIE FRANK shared a post
April 11 at 1:44 PM
And right on cue, they're trying to push some new vaccine made from aborted fetuses that mutates your **DNA**. I'll die before I put any of that poison into my body or any of my family.

RONNIE BARSTOW commented
People bought the narrative so deep they've lost their minds. Father-in-law pulled a fucking gun on me when I tried to see Colleen this morning, screaming that I was "infected" and he'd blow my head off if I didn't leave! This is what mass psychosis looks like, people. And it's getting worse every day.

BRUCE P. MERRIMACK commented
Three guesses as to who's funding the vaccine...

RONNIE BARSTOW shared a post
April 17 at 5:51 PM

Sorry haven't posted in a while. Been trying to make sense of everything. And here's what I got.

Even if zombies were real, just because SOME people get bit doesn't mean the rest of us can't go on living our lives, amiright?

BRUCE P. MERRIMACK

No matter what the P.C. police say, if you check the stats, the only ones getting bit are the elderly, the chronically ill, and the overweight. Sorry, but if you're not healthy enough to get away from some brainless waddling meth head, you're probably about to die soon anyway.

SANDIE FRANK shared a post
April 14 at 3:14 PM

Know why they're pushing the vaccine so much? Because the actual cure is super cheap and available to everyone.

I'm linking to the latest Moe Hogan podcast where he interviews this doctor talking about a study showing 100% protection from ANWD after taking bisacodyl, which you can find at any pet store. People are getting banned from Chatspace for even talking about this stuff, which is how you know it's the real deal.

MoeHogan.com
Episode #1529: The ANWD Cure Big Pharma Doesn't Want You To Know About
Moe welcomes Chet Rhine, D.C. to blow the doors off the establishment's vaccine fairytale by sharing a new study out of...

BRUCE P. MERRIMACK commented
And here's the study.

Viralload.org
Effects of a Single Oral Dose of Bisacodyl Canine Laxative Suppositories on Clinical Outcomes in ANWD Infected Subjects: A Pilot Clinical Trial in Kazakhstan

RONNIE BARSTOW commented
There's still plenty of the suppositories left at the pet store. They taste like crap but get the job done. Picked up a bunch for myself and left a few doses outside CRAIG CLEMENTS house. Asshole's still ignoring me, but I can hear him banging around inside, so sounds like he's doing okay.

RONNIE BARSTOW shared a post
April 17 at 10:42 AM
Anyone heard from SANDIE FRANK lately? She's not responding to messages or texts.

BRUCE P. MERRIMACK commented
Nope.

RONNIE BARSTOW added new member KRYSTAL WAGNER

KRYSTAL WAGNER shared a post
April 19 at 11:19 AM
Thanks for letting me into the group! I heard about what you folx were doing and had to join! Wanna be up front that I probably don't share your politics on most things, but I'm 100% with you against the vaccine.

Three words for how to stay healthy while this thing runs its course: Raw. Carrot. Juice. My whole family's been drinking nothing but for the last seven weeks, and we're all still healthy as horses (just make sure it's organic)!

RONNIE BARSTOW commented

Worth a try, I guess.

BRUCE P. MERRIMACK *commented*
No fan of veggies, over here. But to each his own.

KRYSTAL WAGNER *commented*
To each *their own

BRUCE P. MERRIMACK *shared a post*
April 28 at 9:13 AM
Even the mainstream media is catching on that this all probably started from a lab leak at the Bayonne Center for Virology in the south of France. But of course they won't let us talk about it because it's "xenophobic."

Washington-Tribune.com
Did ANWD Come From a Lab? *by Olivia Bellingham*
Two weeks ago, 18 scientists wrote a letter to the journal Biology *calling for a new investigation and describing both the animal-to-human theory and the lab-leak theory as "viable." The idea is made plausible...*

KRYSTAL WAGNER *commented*
C'mon folx, this was no lab leak, it spread from eating escargot.

RONNIE BARSTOW *shared a post*
April 28 at 10:33 AM

Sure enough, the tyrants at Chatspace took down the Tribune article about the lab leak and gave us a "community strike," whatever that means.

BRUCE P. MERRIMACK *commented*
Boy, that was fast.

RONNIE BARSTOW shared a post
May 3 at 5:18 AM

Taking a trip up to my buddy Chuck's cabin in Montana for a week or so, one of the last places in the country that hasn't turned into a government-run nanny state. There's even a big biker rally next week that sounds like a hell of a lot of fun. Internet's crappy up there, but I should be able to check in on my phone.

If someone wouldn't mind leaving some food out for CRAIG CLEMENTS, I'd appreciate it. I don't think he's been eating much, but he's still moving around in there, so hopefully he's on the road to recovery.

BRUCE P. MERRIMACK commented
Want some company, RONNIE BARSTOW? Can't say I'd mind some time away from the city, myself.

BRUCE P. MERRIMACK commented
RONNIE BARSTOW, I could drive us both up if you want. Got an extra fly rod, too, if you wanna do some fishing.

BRUCE P. MERRIMACK commented
You already leave, RONNIE BARSTOW?

RONNIE BARSTOW shared a post
May 12 at 6:10 PM

Hey fellow Freedom Fighters! Long time no chat! Been out deer hunting, horseback riding, and trout fishing with Chuck. It's like frickin summer camp! I'm on a library computer right now—yep, everything's still open up here—so I could check in.

Colleen isn't returning my phone calls, so maybe one of you *BRUCE P. MERRIMACK, SANDIE FRANK, KRYSTAL WAGNER, MARINA*

SCHULTZ could leave a note at my in-laws (I'll DM you the address) letting her know I'm okay and thinking about her?

RONNIE BARSTOW shared a post
May 25 at 3:44 PM

The meth heads have finally made their way up to Montana, some of them from that biker rally, based on all the leather. But instead of pissing their pants like the rest of the world, locals up here are just learning to live with it. Might stay another week or so just for the heck of it.

BRUCE P. MERRIMACK, SANDIE FRANK, KRYSTAL WAGNER, MARINA SCHULTZ Anyone drop off that note to Colleen yet?

RONNIE BARSTOW shared a post
June 4 at 1:27 PM

Running a bit low on supplies since the bikers looted the supermarkets. How are things back in the city? Library's closed now too, so I'm sending this from my phone. Can someone let me know if my posts are getting through?

RONNIE BARSTOW shared a post
June 6 at 9:11 AM

Chuck went out fishing yesterday and still hasn't come back. Gonna go look for him. And **BRUCE P. MERRIMACK** or anyone else, if you've got food—cans and dry goods, especially—I can get you directions to the cabin.

RONNIE BARSTOW shared a post
June 6 at 8:47 PM

Found Chuck wandering around the woods. Looks like the idiot ran into some bikers because he was all hopped up on meth. Dumbass was so high, he didn't even recognize me and started a fight. Even bit my fucking arm when I shoved him off. Not a bad wound, I cleaned it up just fine with some iodine.

I know it's Chuck's cabin and all, but I'm not letting that dipshit back inside until he stops taking that junk and cleans the fuck up.

RONNIE BARSTOW shared a post
June 7 at 4:12 AM
Looks like I got me a little case of the flu. Fever, chills, muscle aches, all that fun stuff. But to be on the safe side I chewed up a couple of the suppositories. Man, they taste like ass!

RONNIE BARSTOW shared a post
June 7 at 5:49 PM
Goddamn I feel like shit. Keep puking up the suppositories. But don't worry, I just need to get some shut eye and I'll up bright eyed and bushy tailed come tomorrow.

RONNIE BARSTOW shared a post
June 7 at 9:08 PM
cant sleep worst headache ever had feels like somene prying open skull with hndred chisels cant walk keep pising myself but dont even care love you colleen loveyousomuch

RONNIE BARSTOW shared a post
June 8 at 1:32 AM
hunbgryhmgryhugryhiungryungry

You are temporarily blocked
This is your second warning for violating Chatspace's Statement of Rights and Responsibilities. You are now blocked from posting content on Chatspace for 24 hours.

If you continue to abuse Chatspace's features, your account could be permanently disabled.

Which Is Witch?

Sore hip creaking, Elder Woodland was walking home for supper along the packed dirt of Restharrow's main way when shouting from the green made him turn his head and stop. Five villagers gathered around a man standing atop a small crate under the tall leafy oak.

Lean with a bit of paunch, skin that was always sunburned, and probably half Woodland's age, Master Keelson kept chickens for Farmer Saunters. Not knowing the man well and stomach grumbling with the thought of pea porridge, Woodland was about to continue on his way when a voice hailed him.

"Elder Woodland!" Yanking blue silk skirts above her ankles, a middle-aged matron hurried across the mown grass, frizzy blonde hair bouncing off a pair of sturdy shoulders. Goody Amaranth, Restharrow's best-known healer, grabbed the sleeve of Woodland's woolen cloak. "Come listen."

Despite Woodland's biting hunger, Amaranth was not one to be spurned, ensconced as she was with the village's wealthiest and unofficial advisor to the very Council he headed. So, he let the oft disagreeable woman lead him over to where Keelson, clad in coveralls, stood on his wooden crate yelling over and over, "No more will I stay silent!"

With the wave of a hand Amaranth quieted the young man, a single cluck beneath his muddy boots from a yellow beak sticking out between the slats. "Tell the Elder what happened."

Keelson nodded gravely and cleared his throat. "I have been seduced...by a witch!"

Woodland groaned quietly. Over the prior seven years, not a single accusation. And yet that year alone, with midsummer barely passed, this was already the third. One an aged potter with the habit of carving the evil eye into her dishware. The other, a mother who slandered the Council after it spurned her daughter for Queen of the May. The first had her home burned to the ground—sadly, with her inside—while the second had been exiled from Restharrow along with her family. Though neither had confessed, was it not better to burn a hundred false witches than to suffer a single one to live?

Ever a God-fearing man, still Woodland had always doubted the ubiquity of witchcraft—suspicions he, of course, kept to himself. For, as overseer of the Council, he was tasked with keeping the peace above all else, even if it sometimes made it hard to sleep at night. "And who might that be?"

"Some have whispered. I am pointing the finger," Keelson declared grandly. "It is none other than the Widow Caroches!"

A smile stole across Amaranth's wide face, which she quickly smoothed. This somewhat surprised Woodland, as both Amaranth and Caroches were members of the Guild of Healers. While Amaranth relied mostly on bloodletting and leeches, Caroches made tinctures, poultices, and salves from wild and cultivated herbs. Whereas Amaranth served only the wealthiest and high-status villagers, Caroches tended to its poor, even vagabonds and mendicants wandering in from the wilderness. Finally, while Amaranth lived in comfort with her merchant husband, Caroches had barely a shilling to her name—especially since the passing of her woodcutter husband years before. There was no reason whatsoever for Amaranth to envy Caroches—if anything, the opposite should've been true.

"Why do you believe her to be a witch?" Woodland asked Keelson, intending to get to the bottom of the matter right away, if only for the sake of his supper.

As Amaranth always attended to Woodland's infirmities, he'd only had a single pleasant, if brief, conversation with the Widow Caroches. And despite hair too long for a woman her age, donning the same few tattered hemp dresses along with perennially soiled fingernails, and never once setting foot within the village's humble church, she didn't strike him as a devotee to the dark arts. Which, naturally, meant little, he supposed, as were not the most powerful sorceresses adept at eluding notice?

Screwing up his face, Keelson stomped the crate, the chicken squawking in alarm. "I do not *believe*! I *know*!"

"My apologies." Woodland held up his palms, an errant breeze wafting the sharp reek of animal waste his way. Important as it was to avoid spilling innocent blood, it would do no good to be seen coddling witches. And Keelson, eyes wild, cheeks ruddy, lips flecked with spittle, did not seem a one easily cowed. "Please go on."

"As you may be aware," Keelson addressed his listeners, which had swelled to over a dozen, "I am now in the honey trade."

A few murmurs and nods from the villagers. Before the winter, Woodland had heard tell that Keelson was tending a swarm of bees he found in the forest, though most of them had died. Finally, it seemed, Keelson's hives had produced.

"Not long ago," Keelson said, "I was stung many times and in great pain."

"If only I had known." Amaranth frowned disingenuously, as Woodland was certain a poor farmer such as Keelson wouldn't have been able to afford her costly services.

"This occurred recently?" Woodland asked.

"October," Keelson said defiantly, locking eyes with the elder.

Though the sins of witchcraft did not fade with the seasons, Woodland was curious why Keelson had waited so long to tell his story. A passing snatch of Keelson's conversation overheard earlier that month at the tavern came to mind, something to the nature of, "It is always surprising when a woman has something remarkable to say." Clearly, this was not a man with much respect for the fairer sex.

Still, Woodland looked away, feigning interest in a puffy cloud drifting along the dimming sky.

Only then did Keelson continue with a mournful lift to his brows. "When I arrived, to my shock and dismay, Caroches was shamelessly clad in a skimpy gown which left little to the imagination."

Tsking loudly, Goody Amaranth shook her head.

"The widow bade me wait," Keelson said, "hastened to her garden, and returned with a fistful of flowers red as the devil's own arse." The villagers, grown to nearly a score, snickered. "With mortar and pestle, she ground the infernal petals into paste and asked to be shown my stings. When I said they were on my back, her eyes glowed with a fiendish light, and she demanded I remove my garment."

"The harlot!" None other than portly Mr. Linish, his broken-toothed mouth a wide-open O. While not an official member of the Council, for years he'd done menial tasks in hopes of someday being offered a seat. Having suffered through many of the man's bawdy tales, Woodland had a hard time believing his offense to be genuine.

"With the power she had over me as healer, and needing the balm urgently, how could I refuse?" Keelson asked of those gathered with a shrug. "After removing my shirt, Caroches applied the greasy unguent to my bare skin. As her fingers lingered overlong on my muscles, she whispered an evil chant so I could do naught but sit paralyzed, unable to break her spell."

The crowd had swelled to maybe thirty, nearly a third of Restharrow, everyone from mothers suckling infants to the doddering aged leaning on canes.

"What words did she say?" a quiet voice asked from the back of the crowd. Dark braids framing a lovely plump face, the young Miss Erica lived in the much smaller neighboring village of Deerhorn. Blunt, outspoken, and yet unmarried, she had on more than one occasion defended the reputation of those named as witches, to Woodland's grudging admiration.

"What would poor Master Keelson gain from fabricating such a tale?" Mr. Hallower, the lanky, hirsute proprietor of the village tavern, barked at the younger woman. "If anything, he risks his neck to inform us all. Selfless, courageous, and commendable!"

"Hurrah!" Linish bellowed. "Three cheers for our friend's extraordinary courage!"

Even Woodland felt compelled to join in on the applause, interrupted only by a squeal. The crowd parted, and Miss Erica had somehow fallen on her rump into a puddle. Mumbling swear words, she got up, skirts muddied, and stormed off without a look back. The ensuing laughter and jeers brought over even more folk, until half the village crowded in the green.

"It was only when I heard others speak of the widow's foul deeds," Keelson raised his voice so all eyes were upon him again, "I knew I could no longer stay silent."

Woodland perked up his ears. He hadn't heard enough of Keelson's story to say whether he trusted the man or not. But if there was more than one person making the same claims, it could all but prove their verity. "May we know their names?"

Brantle the gravedigger, grey-bearded and thick-muscled, glared redly at Woodland. "And risk the wrath of this witch?"

Annoyed and impatient at the delay, Woodland fired back, "How else can we know if what Keelson says is true?" Then regretted his haste soon as the words left his mouth.

"Would you question a slain lamb in the company of a bloodied wolf?" Hallower shouted, neck cording with fury.

As the elder searched the angry faces of the people of Restharrow, beads of sweat prickled his hairline. With a sinking feeling in his belly, he knew then that judgment had already been cast, and any words uttered in the widow's defense would fall on deaf ears. Setting his jaw, he toed a spot on the grass.

"And that is not the worst of it!" Keelson cried, tearing at his ginger locks. "The widow, in a most salacious manner, has been forcing her way into my dreams!"

A collective gasp from the townsfolk followed by a wave of scandalized whispers.

"That settles it!" Brantle thundered. "Are we to stand idly by as more of us fall under her spell?"

Woodland had to fight an impulse to race home. Whether Caroches was guilty or not—and without proof beyond one man's hearsay, it was far from clear—he wished nothing more than to wash his hands of it all. Yet perhaps he could still save a life.

As the sun sunk over distant hills like a stone cast into a pond, nearly thirty villagers gathered again on the green, each with lantern or farm tool— scythe, pitchfork, spade—in hand.

At a hastily called Council meeting, Woodland had convinced the other members to reluctantly agree that, while a visit to Caroches might be in order, she must be given a chance to defend her case before any actions were taken.

Short, slight, fair-haired, and carrying a lantern, black-clad Pastor Washerman—the Council's newest member—led the group, an unarmed Keelson by his side. Woodland, empty-handed, made up its rear. Cleaving the cool quiet darkness, they marched down the main way until the cottages became small, sparse, and ill-kept. Before long they veered onto a thin path through the hilly orchard, tree branches heavy with plump apples near ready for the plucking.

It was full dark by the time they reached the tall pinewoods on the outskirts of the village. And soon, the tiny cottage, a dim glow seeping through its few windows, bordered by a fragrant garden of sprouting herbs.

Without fanfare, Pastor Washerman strode up to the door and knocked.

Moments later it opened to a lone figure, nose and chin sharp in the light of the guttering candle she held. The Widow Caroches was tall for a woman, with long silver hair flowing down the shoulders of a tattered robe. Briefly, she scanned the mob but did not flinch, though she had to have been terrified. "How may I be of service?"

"We would like to have a word with you about a villager." Woodland stepped forward to stand beside Washerman. "A one Master Keelson."

"Keelson?" Caroches squinted, crow's feet creasing otherwise smooth skin. "Ah yes, the beekeeper. Has he gotten himself stung again?"

Woodland turned to the villagers. "Keelson, please step forward." The crowd milled about, but Keelson did not appear. And, oddly, upon closer inspection, was nowhere to be found.

"The man claims you—" Anxious phlegm collected in Woodland's throat, which he had to clear to continue, "—you tried to seduce him."

Caroches' thick eyebrows shot up. And then she laughed, a trilling lilt from high to low like a wood thrush. "What would an old maid like me want with a boy like him?"

"To bend him to your will at the Devil's bidding!" Brantle howled, several others joining in with yeas and harrumphs.

Caroches, to her credit—or revealing her guilt?—said not a word, perhaps knowing her only chance was to remain calm. Indeed, if her refutations were deemed credible by most, she might just emerge unscathed.

Woodland quieted the crowd, and, once all had fallen silent, said, "It is claimed you were dressed unbecomingly."

A smile broke out across Caroches' face, making her look ten years younger. Setting the candle down on the windowsill, she flung open her robe to reveal a loose nightgown over a lean and supple body. "Keelson arrived before the sun, banging on my door crying bloody murder. Deeming it an emergency, I did not have time to don my robe."

Shocking as it was to see so much bare flesh, Woodland had to admit it was an effective demonstration. And with Keelson absent, no one was there to naysay her. A few of the villagers rested the butts of their tools on the ground. Maybe the matter would be put to bed without much further to-do.

"What remedies did you administer for the stings?" Woodland asked.

"A bee balm salve." The widow drew her robe together, to the elder's relief.

"And you demanded he remove his shirt?"

She cocked her head like a quizzical dog. "I suggested he seek another to apply the salve, but he insisted that I be the one."

Once again, Keelson was not present to affirm or deny. Since there were no objections from the group, Woodland went on. "The claim is that you laid hands upon him in an illicit manner."

"I applied the salve to the stings, as requested," Caroches said with a shrug, picking up the candle again to light her angular face.

"Are we to believe one of Satan's tramps over an innocent child of God?!" Linish yelled, eliciting several grunts of approval and nods from his fellows.

While there was naught to keep any citizen of Restharrow from making false claims, Woodland hoped neither were truly lying, only Keelson simply misreading the situation. Unfortunately, the elder's line of inquiry thus far had yielded no ripe fruit. Yet there was one last question.

"What were the words you spoke as you applied the salve?" he asked.

Caroches' forehead creased. "Words?"

"Keelson claims you cast a spell upon him."

"I did no such thing." Her face was hard as quarry marble.

An impasse. The entire matter resting on what Caroches had said yet was denying. Keelson, of course, could negate the widow's words, but he had still not reappeared. Which meant that a relieved Woodland had no choice but to dismiss the entire affair.

But before he could speak, Amaranth shrieked, "Do not forget the dreams!" And she shoved her way to the front of the crowd.

"Dreams?" Caroches replied with a sneer, the bad blood between the healers on full display.

"You trouble him in his sleep!" Amaranth said.

A scoff from the widow. "Surely, I cannot be blamed for the wet dreams of a rutting buck."

Roars of outrage from a dozen throats, spades and picks thrust high. Woodland marveled at the sheer stupidity on display. Somehow, of everything revealed thus far, the unprovable dream is what upset them the most.

"Will no one speak in my defense?" Caroches seethed at the group. Then pointed a long-nailed finger at Mr. Linish. "After saving your daughter from snakebite, this is how you repay me?"

Linish opened his mouth to speak but then shut it, crossed his arms and looked away.

"And who threatened to burn down my home if I didn't administer to the poor young serving wench he impregnated?" she roared at Hallower, a charge which shook even Elder Woodland to the core.

271

A sob from the tavernkeeper's wife, a petite redhead in homespun dress, who slapped her blubbering husband across his bearded cheek and stalked off into the night. The lean man did not follow, only stood there rubbing his face.

Woodland was unnerved by Caroches' turning on the village, which could gain her no more favor than cornering a pack of wild beasts in a cave. It was time to bring things to a close before they got any further out of hand.

Woodland laid a hand on Caroches' shoulder, which gave off a faint scent of lavender. "However poor your judgment, no matter how many sins you may have committed, I do not believe you to be a witch," he whispered in her ear. "However, the good folk will not return home without their pound of flesh."

To Woodland's surprise, Caroches nodded somberly, clearly under no more illusions regarding her plight. "What would you have me do?"

"If you admit to, say, murmuring a few sweet nothings in young Keelson's ear, I shall dole out some light consequences so no other harm befalls you."

"None of this can end well for me." Her gaze was bleak.

"It is the only way."

A long pause, and Woodland feared the widow would flee. Or, even worse, curse them to a one, revealing herself as a loathsome enchantress after all.

But Caroches sighed. "I have been so lonely since my husband passed," her voice trembled ever so slightly, like a leaf in a morning breeze. "I meant nothing by it, just some playful words in hopes of feeling young again."

A weight lifted from Woodland, as if rocks had dropped from his pockets. At long last, the ordeal was at its end. And, within the hour, the elder could be home slurping soup in his armchair by the fire.

"There, there." Woodland patted the woman's forearm. "The worst is over." Then, turning to the villagers, he pronounced, "The evidence, as it stands, does not point to witchcraft."

As he'd expected, shouts and stomps of outrage from the mob. But Woodland held up his hands, and they settled down, his decades of service earning him that respect at least.

"Yet, due to her admission of improper remarks to Master Keelson, the widow Caroches has agreed to resign her seat on the Guild of Healers and shall not be in attendance at the Harvest Faire."

The widow hung her head, either in true shame or playacting for the crowd. To Woodland's satisfaction, the villagers did not revolt but stood there quietly whispering to one another. A few broke away and set off back towards town.

"You are free to go," Woodland said with a glad smile.

Nodding, Caroches slipped inside and softly shut the door behind her.

No outcry from those remaining. Just the clatter of a horse approaching, Keelson in its saddle. Woodland held his breath, certain the man would raise a hue and cry and rouse the mollified mob anew. But the chicken farmer, all eyes upon him, merely leapt from his mare and opened the two saddle bags. Curious, the villagers gathered around him as he took out several small ceramic jars.

One by one, Keelson passed a jar to each. Who, in turn, dug into their pockets to hand over a coin before walking off into the dark. When Keelson gave Woodland a jar along with a smirk, the elder unstoppered it and sniffed. Sweet and flowery, it was none other than the man's first batch of honey. Woodland, with no other choice, dug into his pocket and dropped a coin into Keelson's open palm.

Surely, this had not been Keelson's plan all along? To exaggerate Caroches' advances in order to win pity so as to sell his wares? Certainly, even Keelson could not stoop so low as to trade in a woman's reputation for a handful of silver? But if another conclusion was to be drawn, Woodland could not fathom it.

Indeed, Keelson greedily doled out jars until his saddlebag was empty and nearly all townsfolk had gone home. Except Amaranth, Hallower, Linish, and Pastor Washerman, who stood in a close circle talking. Brantle, meanwhile, crawled on hands and knees in the widow's garden, tearing up the plants.

Alarmed, Woodland rushed towards him. "What is the meaning of this?!"

Brantle paid the elder no more heed than a barking fox. Woodland reared back a boot and doled out a light kick to Brantle's ribs, which elicited no more than a laugh from the stout man.

Momentarily, Amaranth, Hallower, and Linish, too, wandered into the garden, where they stripped leaves, snapped flowers, and yanked up herbs by the roots, trampling the rest of the plants underfoot. Outraged, Woodland stood in their way, yet Linish grabbed the elder by the shoulders and tossed him to the ground like a sack of beans. As Woodland lay in the dirt, hip screaming in agony, Washerman reached into the pockets of his trousers to cast out handfuls of what looked like tiny seeds into the soil.

By the light of the pastor's lantern, Woodland, moaning in pain, crawled over to scoop a handful from the rows. There were white crystals in the moist soil. Not seeds at all but salt! Ruining the widow's crops...along with the medicine chest for Restharrow's poorest.

The elder's heart thumped so hard he set a palm against it. Already too much excitement for one night, what would keep the fanatics from setting Caroches' cottage ablaze in their frenzy? Even if he stood guard all night, he could do little to stop them. No, he had to warn the widow to hide away somewhere—a neighboring village, the forest, anywhere but home—until their blood cooled.

Woodland creakily got to his feet, hip flaring, to limp over to the cottage and knock on the door. No answer, so he rapped louder. Still no reply, he threw it open.

Caroches' swayed limply at the end of a rope tied to the overhead timbers, bare dirty feet brushing an overturned stool. Woodland let out a cry of anguish. Racing over, he grabbed hold of her scant form, choking on the stench of excrement. But alas, her body still, tongue fat and blue, she had already passed.

Sorrow's sharp blade gouged Woodland's guts. While the widow's expulsion from the Guild and her banishment from the Faire would've worsened her poverty, those misfortunes alone surely could not have pushed such a strong woman over the edge. Nay, she must have known how the merest charge of witchcraft—proven or not—meant a reputation forever sullied. That the most superstitious of Restharrow would ever be at her throat, and even those who knew her to be innocent would shun her. In a fit of temporary madness, she had chosen eternal damnation over social exile.

Briefly letting go of the corpse, Woodland righted the stool and with a kitchen knife cut the rope, grasping her body so it would not hit the ground.

A hot flame sparked in Woodland's heart. Anger towards the selfish Keelson, who would destroy another's livelihood solely to bolster his own. Towards Amaranth, Hallower, and Brantle, whose blind ignorance set a witch behind every tree. Towards false Linish, who would say anything to polish his dull image. Towards Pastor Washerman, all too eager to exploit the Council's might for his own naked ambition.

Woodland carried the corpse towards the door, staggering on his bad hip, though the body was light as a bundle of summer straw. While they would not show remorse, perhaps in time they might see what they had done to this blameless woman, to Restharrow, to themselves.

Yet when Woodland emerged into the night with the remains, they all cheered.

"And here is our proof!" Amaranth shrieked in glee.

"A witch, if there ever was one!" Brantle chimed in.

Linish danced a little jig, while Hallower clapped his hands as if at a puppet show.

Their faces contorted with toothy smiles, eyes flashing with bloodlust, Woodland, mouth dry and tasting of ash, finally saw them for what they were. Pitiful sinners who, since they could not find it in their hearts to do good, elevated themselves by casting down others. Dabbling in bigotry's dark arts, *these* were the true witches.

Then a poisonous thought which made the widow's body a hundred times heavy, so that Woodland fell to his knees and let her stiffening corpse roll to the ground.

Not just them.

For who was the one who may have nipped the entire hunt in the bud? Who escorted the very mob to her door? Who pronounced the widow guilty of something not even a crime?

True believers such as Amaranth, Hallower, and Brantle could see only through the smoked glass of their own righteousness. Parasites like Linish and Washerman had little to give beyond the compliance of a beaten dog. But Woodland had none of those excuses. He alone had the standing to protect the guiltless from the mob, the authority to speak facts without consequence.

No matter what he had told himself, had Woodland held his tongue to protect the village peace or to keep his own good standing? For which he had sacrificed his dignity, integrity, and goodness.

Kneeling in the dirt, eyes stinging and brain afire, Woodland knew that, if the others were witches, he was the one who had granted them their vile power. Making the Elder nothing less than the son of wickedness, the Dark One...the devil himself.

For which, maybe not that day, maybe not the next, but someday, he, too, would surely burn.

Master The Monster

He's not afraid of the dark of the night,
where the shadows are shown.
When the way turns twisted and broken,
he walks it alone.
He won't believe a word they're saying,
he knows it's all lies;
with his hands over his ears
he closes his eyes.

When he tries to tell the people
of the truth he has found,
they turn away, faces pale and puzzled,
and stare at the ground.

When the signs point to disaster,
there's a stench in the air.
Spring comes, turns into summer,
trees still leafless and bare.
He always says, "Beware not to wander

through the blank space on the map."
They nod and smile, but when he's not watching,
walk right into the trap.

When the breath of the beast is upon them,
with the teeth at their throat,
they call on him to master the monster
but never pay what he's owed.

What makes him different from all those
who walk on the Earth?
Did a dark star collapse in the cosmos
on the day of his birth?
Some say he's not a man
but something else in disguise;
if you can handle the answer
look straight into his eyes.

You'll find he's frightened as you are
of what lies past the veil.
He lets in a bit of the darkness
instead of just turning tail.

Other Books by Josh Schlossberg

Charwood, Aggadah Try It, 2023

After joining the Tenders—a band of backwoods activists claiming to solve climate change by burning trees for energy—Orna Tannenbaum falls in with Rowan, their odd yet charming leader.

But when Orna uncovers what the Tenders are really up to in the forest, she must apply the ancient wisdom of her culture to battle dark forces threatening to gain a foothold in our world.

Malinae, D&T Publishing, 2021

The absentmindedness. The nonsensical ramblings. The blank stares. Ward Ayers, physically disabled and confined to his Jersey Shore home, can only watch in dismay as his beloved wife Malina slips further and further into dementia.

But when Ward catches a glimpse of a strange appendage in place of Malina's tongue, he fears the woman he's loved for half a century isn't succumbing to Alzheimer's but transforming into something...not quite human. As he tries to make sense of his wife's disturbing changes, he starts wondering if he's the one losing his mind.

Until, finally, Ward uncovers the dark force behind Malina's decline and must plumb the depths of sacrifice and selfishness to reclaim his wife and preserve humanity's future.

Enter Josh's Worst Nightmare

Go to JoshsWorstNightmare.com or email
Josh@Joshsworstnightmare.com to subscribe to author Josh Schlossberg's
e-newsletter, where he surveys the dark landscape of biological and
ecological horror fiction.

You can also follow Josh's Worst Nightmare on Facebook, Twitter/X,
Instagram, and TikTok.